A PICTURE OF DEATH

Inspector Finch drew the photographs taken of the dead woman from their envelope. For a moment a sort of shock held both men silent. Lisa Harcourt had been blotted out—obliterated by someone made insensate by overwhelming emotion. Where her face should have been was only a mass of raw pulp. A lace scarf, matching her frock, was knotted about what remained of her neck.

Sergeant Archie Slater looked rather sick. "Now we've got to pin it on him," he muttered. "A fellow with a temper like that can't be allowed to run loose."

Finch nodded. "You know, Archie," he said slowly, "that woman begins to fascinate me. What can she have said or done to make anyone do that to her?"

Agatha Christie

DEATH ON THE NILE
A HOLIDAY FOR MURDER
THE MYSTERIOUS AFFAIR
    AT STYLES
POIROT INVESTIGATES
POSTERN OF FATE
THE SECRET ADVERSARY
THE SEVEN DIALS MYSTERY
SLEEPING MURDER

Carter Dickson

DEATH IN FIVE BOXES
THE SKELETON IN THE
    CLOCK
THE WHITE PRIORY
    MURDERS

Catherine Aird

HENRIETTA WHO?
HIS BURIAL TOO
A LATE PHOENIX
A MOST CONTAGIOUS GAME
PASSING STRANGE
THE RELIGIOUS BODY
SLIGHT MOURNING
SOME DIE ELOQUENT
THE STATELY HOME
    MURDER

Patricia Wentworth

THE FINGERPRINT
THE IVORY DAGGER
THE LISTENING EYE
POISON IN THE PEN
SHE CAME BACK
THROUGH THE WALL

Elizabeth Lemarchand

BURIED IN THE PAST
DEATH ON DOOMSDAY

Margaret Erskine

THE FAMILY AT
    TAMMERTON
NO. 9 BELMONT SQUARE
THE WOMAN AT
    BELGUARDO

Margaret Yorke

CAST FOR DEATH
DEAD IN THE MORNING
GRAVE MATTERS

Ruth Rendell

A DEMON IN MY VIEW
THE FALLEN CURTAIN
A SLEEPING LIFE

June Thomson

ALIBI IN TIME
CASE CLOSED
THE LONG REVENGE

E. X. Ferrars

ALIVE AND DEAD
EXPERIMENT WITH DEATH
FROG IN THE THROAT
LAST WILL AND TESTAMENT
MURDERS ANONYMOUS

THE
WOMAN
AT
BELGUARDO

Margaret Erskine

BANTAM BOOKS
TORONTO · NEW YORK · LONDON · SYDNEY

All of the characters in this book are fictitious,
and any resemblance to actual persons,
living or dead, is purely coincidental.

*This low-priced Bantam Book
has been completely reset in a type face
designed for easy reading, and was printed
from new plates. It contains the complete
text of the original hard-cover edition.*
NOT ONE WORD HAS BEEN OMITTED.

THE WOMAN AT BELGUARDO
*A Bantam Book / published by arrangement with
Doubleday and Company*

PRINTING HISTORY

Doubleday edition published November 1961
Bantam edition / December 1982

*Bantam Books are published by Bantam Books, Inc. Its trade-
mark, consisting of the words "Bantam Books" and the por-
trayal of a rooster, is Registered in U.S. Patent and Trademark
Office and in other countries. Marca Registrada. Bantam
Books, Inc., 666 Fifth Avenue, New York, New York 10103.*

PRINTED IN THE UNITED STATES OF AMERICA

O   0 9 8 7 6 5 4 3 2 1

Masters
of
Mystery

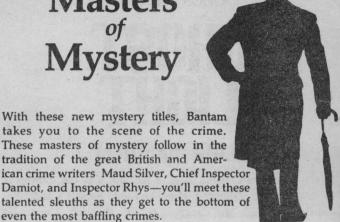

With these new mystery titles, Bantam takes you to the scene of the crime. These masters of mystery follow in the tradition of the great British and American crime writers. Maud Silver, Chief Inspector Damiot, and Inspector Rhys—you'll meet these talented sleuths as they get to the bottom of even the most baffling crimes.

☐	22702	MURDER GOES MUMMING A. Craig	$2.25
☐	22826	THE FAMILY AT TAMMERTON M. Erskine	$2.25
☐	22827	NO. 9 BELMONT M. Erskine	$2.25
☐	22828	CAST FOR DEATH M. Yorke	$2.25
☐	22858	DEAD IN THE MORNING M. Yorke	$2.25
☐	22829	DEATH ON DOOMSDAY E. Lemarchand	$2.25
☐	22830	BURIED IN THE PAST E. Lemarchand	$2.25
☐	20675	A MOST CONTAGIOUS GAME Catherine Aird	$2.25
☐	20567	EXPERIMENT WITH DEATH E. X. Ferrars	$2.25
☐	20040	FROG IN THE THROAT E. X. Ferrars	$1.95
☐	20304	HENRIETTA WHO Catherine Aird	$2.25
☐	14338	SOME DIE ELOQUENT Catherine Aird	$2.25
☐	14434	SHE CAME BACK Patricia Wentworth	$2.25

Buy them at your local bookstore or use this handy coupon for ordering:

The horrifying new novel by the author of
GHOST HOUSE

GHOST LIGHT

CLARE McNALLY

Pretty little five-year-old Bonnie Jackson was the darling of the stage world. Until the night she found herself wandering, terrified, through the darkness of the Winston Theatre—a night that would end with evil consuming the innocent girl in a horrible, fiery death. Now, fifty years later, Bonnie has returned. And she will command the spotlight once again. For pretty little Bonnie Jackson is about to perform her show-stopping act of revenge.

Read GHOST LIGHT, on sale November 15, 1982, wherever Bantam paperbacks are sold or use this handy coupon for ordering:

ABOUT THE AUTHOR

MARGARET ERSKINE has written over a dozen mystery novels in the classical tradition—carefully shaped and plotted and highly literate. The Erskines are a Lowland Scots family connected with the Stuarts by many intermarriages and from Bannockburn to Culloden, they fought on every battlefield of Scotland. Miss Erskine was educated by governesses and the vast resources of her father's library in South Devon. She now lives in London.

Ambrose," said Mark. "It was Lisa's coming that forced her hand."

"Some women are born to make trouble," said Finch sententiously.

"Just as some are born to make a man happy," declared Mark, smiling across at his wife.

Harriet grinned. "Don't you ever dare to go after another woman because I've learnt wisdom. I won't stand it. No, next time I'll make a great fuss. I'll scratch her face and pull out handfuls of her hair. She'll be glad to give you up—— And anyway, you won't want what's left of her."

Dr. Warry had to go off to see a patient, and it was left to Harriet to see Finch off.

He stood for a moment, staring about him, for it seemed to him that in a single night the whole aspect of the valley had changed.

Without the hot sunshine the yellowing trees on the green had a melancholy autumnal look. The dark firs towered black against a grey, weeping sky. And the two houses, with drawn curtains and empty gardens, appeared given over at last to such ghosts as cared to walk in them. To such an end had the story of Ambrose and Rachel Potter worked itself out.

He heard Harriet catch her breath on a sharp sigh, as if she too were oppressed in spirit.

He looked at her quickly. "You see, I was right," he said to divert her. "Lisa was only a symptom of your husband's illness. There was no need for you to worry."

"It was easy for you to be philosophical about it," said Harriet. "Mark wasn't your husband."

Finch stepped into his car, "Just as well perhaps," he said pensively, letting in the clutch. "Somehow I don't think we should have suited each other."

"Gessington rang up and told him that if he went into business, he'd do his best to ruin him," Harriet explained gleefully. "It would be funny to see Gessington trying to ruin a *bank*. Besides, one of these days he might want an overdraft, and then what fun David would have refusing him."

The talk drifted to the murders, as it was bound to do sooner or later. "Even though John's dead, I find it hard to forgive the Potters for being willing for David to take the blame," Harriet declared, shivering a little.

"Mrs. Potter did say he was so well placed as a murderer," Finch answered. "I suppose that counted with them."

"What I can't understand is why no one knew of that hiding place in the Swiss Cottage," said Mark.

"No one knew because Ambrose Potter took care that no one should know. After all, someone must have called occasionally at the Swiss Cottage. A servant with an important message. An estate worker seeking instruction. With one wife at Belguardo, Ambrose had to have somewhere he could hide the other."

Mark nodded. "I suppose that was the whole idea of the Swiss Cottage."

"Yes. There was only the one path by which one could reach the place. It was impossible to get to the verandah without making a great noise on the wooden staircase. Even so, I doubt if they'd have kept their secret if the affair had lasted much longer than it did. Let me see! Lisa was born in 1924. She was eighteen months old when she was supposed to have smashed the figure of Kuan Yin. Rachel herself died in 1927. How long did that give the pair of lovers? A year? Eighteen months? It could scarcely have been more."

"And then Ambrose Potter was left to live on for another thirty years," said Mark. "Wrong as was their behaviour, his fate arouses one's pity."

"And all those letters! I suppose they used the place as a post office when it was impossible to meet."

"I imagine that Rachel never meant to divorce

"Francis Harcourt will come back here, and Gurney will look after him simply because he won't have the energy to go away," said Finch, who had no trouble in following thoughts as slow and obvious as the Superintendent's. "And every year Harcourt will get more dried up, more aloof, and more erudite."

"And Mrs. Potter? What will she do after this?" Bannerman had asked sarcastically.

Finch shrugged. "Perhaps she'll tell us."

But Phoebe Potter had had only two remarks to make: the first to ask what was being done with her husband's body, then on its way by ambulance to the mortuary in Bramshot; the second to tell her visitors to get out. It was at this point that Battle, evidently an understanding dog, had rushed at Bannerman and bitten him in the leg.

Finch chuckled aloud at the recollection, turned the car down the hill, and so came again to Paradon. He stopped the car and dropped Slater. Then he drove on to Waltons.

Harriet and her husband came out of the house to welcome him, whilst the little maid beamed in the background. It was nice, Finch reflected, to see two people so obviously happy.

For a time they spoke of old times. Of London— without regret on Mark's part. He would go back, but not yet. Of Harriet's abortive career as a painter. She did not propose to take it up again, as she intended to have a large family. This brought Finch, rather tactlessly perhaps, to the subject of Paradon Belle, but this seemed now to be on the way to becoming one of those family jokes that never die.

They discussed David's future. A cousin, a banker, had written and offered him a post. It seemed likely that he would accept.

"He went back to London to finish his time at the motor showrooms." Mark smiled. "Bless the boy, having decided to wear it, he could hardly wait to don his hair shirt."

had poured down the hillside, at first in trickles and then in countless small rushing streams. In a few minutes the men had been soaked through, their clothes clinging tightly, their shoes giving out a soggy squelch at every step, as they lurched with one dead and one unconscious body through the woods.

Finch had taken off his coat. Slater and Peters had tried to hold it over John Potter like a canopy, stumbling along on either side of the improvised stretcher.

At the edge of the woods Finch had halted the little procession. One of the Bramshot men had taken his place at the foot of the stretcher. He had had a look at their prisoner and found him dead. The coat had been laid over him and the last stage of the journey had gone more easily.

It had seemed strange to step into the bright lights of the house, an incongruous bunch, wet, cold, dripping rain water upon the marble hall. Finch, lowering his end of the stretcher, thought how John Potter would have hated to be brought back to Belguardo, if he had been able to feel anything at all. But now only the ghosts peculiar to the place remained to be faced. And these, he had felt, had little chance against Sturgis's cheerful cynicism.

"Pity Potter died too late to make the first London editions," was all the newspaperman had had to say. He had, however, persuaded Gurney to make a great jug of coffee in readiness for their arrival.

The manservant himself had been up and fully dressed. He had made no enquiries, uttered no comments, just looked long and earnestly at the dead man and then had gone silently away.

"That's a mad fellow," Bannerman had grumbled, wringing the water from his close, curly hair, his sleeves, his trouser legs, as assiduously as a conjurer producing coin. The unspoken extension of his remark had been, Why couldn't he have been the murderer? The Superintendent was just beginning to realise the extent of the changes that must come to Paradon. Two estates broken up; for who would want to live at Belguardo? Which of the Potter boys would care to carry on the family name at the Hall?

affair. A man with such a strong Oedipus Complex as John Potter was certain to look for the mother figure in his wife—someone stronger and more possessive than himself, someone who'd give him, not only love, but support and counsel."

The Chief Constable looked at Finch mistrustfully. "Young fella, if you ask me, that's a damned unhealthy point of view. Have another sherry?" He smiled suddenly. "We ought to drink to Paradon Belle and her new progeny."

"Here, here!" said Bannerman, cheering up. "I'm told the doctor . . ." He plunged into details.

It was Finch's turn to stare. "Who—or what—is Paradon Belle?"

"It's old Winfold's prize cow. With Dr. Warry's help she was successfully delivered of her first calf last night."

"Then to Paradon Belle," said Finch. Adding, "And the county which bred her." He nearly burst out laughing at Slater's outraged expression.

The meeting broke up more amicably than at one time had seemed possible. The two Scotland Yard men left the police station on their way back to Paradon to collect their suitcases. At least, Slater was to collect them whilst Finch, who had already said goodbye to Peters, paid a farewell call on the Warrys.

"I wouldn't say that we'd been exactly a social success with the locals," Slater remarked.

Finch shook his head. "Certain lewd fellows of the baser sort, that's us. I should never have mentioned anything as indelicate as the Oedipus Complex."

"That's rich coming from someone who could describe a cow's beastly inside in such detail," said Slater indignantly. He added, "Well, at least the case has lasted out the heat wave. It'll be nice to be in London again."

The words took Finch back to the nightmare journey of the previous night. The storm had broken as they had been making their slow return to Belguardo. A few preliminary flashes of lightning, a rumble of thunder like an approaching train, and then rain, rain, and more rain. The ground, bare of grass and soft with the fallen leaves of past years, had been churned to the consistency of glue. Water

THE
WOMAN
AT
BELGUARDO

Chapter
1

Harriet Warry was drawn again and again to the window. Tomorrow, she thought, staring up to where the white house above her shimmered in a haze of heat. Tomorrow Lisa will be free. And she tried to imagine her married to David.

David, who had been gay and charming and inconstant and now was none of these things, who went through the days in a state of trance, seeming neither happy nor unhappy, elated nor cast down, drained of everything but his infatuation for Lisa Harcourt.

They had met, prosaically enough, at Matcham House school sports, where David had been a master. Even in its inception it had been a violent, blatant affair. Eyebrows had been raised, heads turned. David had been oblivious to criticism. Lisa had ignored it. She could afford to do so, for she was a rich woman.

Five weeks later Francis Harcourt had begun divorce proceedings, citing David as co-respondent. The case had not been defended, and tomorrow the decree nisi would be made absolute. Lisa would be free.

The morning passed slowly. Harriet's husband, Mark, came back to lunch. He was irritable and uneasy. Afraid, Harriet thought bitterly, that he might be wrong. Afraid Lisa might marry David after all.

After lunch it seemed hotter than ever. Harriet went upstairs. She lay on her bed and thought of her two children, who had gone, with their nurse, to stay by the

1

sea. Wondering, with a sense of almost physical loss, what they were doing and whether they were missing her.

Then, since this made her so unhappy, she closed her mind to them, only to be thrown back on the thought of Lisa, seeing her as she had been when she had come round to tell her, Harriet, of the divorce. Her eyes half closed and a little sly smile lingering round her lips, as if she were laughing inwardly.

I'm haunted, she thought. Ever since we came here I've been haunted by that woman. She did not see her as a ghost but as a sleek and sinuous white cat gnawing away at the foundations of her happiness until now there was nothing left.

What had gone wrong with her marriage? Even before Lisa had come into their lives there had been something. Mark had been a brilliant doctor with a large London practice. He had consistently overworked until a near breakdown had sent him into the country in search of health.

At first his rebellion and despair had seemed to draw them closer together. Then, almost overnight, he had changed. Become icily cold and polite, refusing with maddening consistency to admit that anything was amiss. Destroying her pleasure in the charming Georgian house which was now their home. Throwing her on the society of her babies: Giles, age four, and Theo, age two and a half.

In those first days at Paradon, Lisa had been away, staying in the South of France. Mark had met, and seemed to like, her husband, Francis Harcourt. A tall, elderly, erudite man, he had been to the house several times. When he had mentioned his wife it had been in a dry, paper-thin voice, so that they had had the impression of someone as old and aloof as himself.

Then Lisa had returned, lovely, lovely—and rapacious. She had annexed Mark as easily as later she had annexed Harriet's twin brother, David. She had become an unnamed third in all their conversations, so that gradually the rooms came to hold the echo of her voice as a shell holds the murmur of the sea.

Such a charming house, and so sensible of Harriet to play safe and keep it just period.

Babies may come trailing clouds of glory, but they are a bit stultifying.

The country suits Harriet, but a mangel-wurzel existence is not for you, my poor Mark.

The afternoon crept past. Outside, the garden lay shimmering and silent in the sun. Inside, with every door and window open, scarcely a breath of air stirred.

About half-past five the telephone rang in the drawing room. As Harriet picked up the receiver she stared with dissatisfaction at the anxious-looking reflection in the gilt looking-glass opposite. She saw a slight figure in white shorts and a turquoise-blue T shirt open at the neck. Long sunburnt legs, an oval unsmiling face, grey eyes, heavily fringed. Fair hair so fine and soft that it was never really tidy.

You're such a pale skinny thing, I declare it's really quite distingué.

"Hullo, ducky! Have you heard the news?" The slow, slightly husky voice could not fail to conjure up a mental picture of its owner to anyone who had met Phoebe Potter.

"News about what?"

There's something rather vulgar about Phoebe's looks, don't you think? She always reminds me of those plump pink goddesses you find painted on ceilings.

"News about my sweet sister-in-law."

Harriet's heart missed a beat. "Lisa? What's she done?"

"She's got herself engaged to marry a Mr. Gessington."

"Phoebe, no! Who told you, John?"

We're in love, David and I. We're going to be happy forever and ever.

"No, ducky. I've been a grass widow for the past week. John's been held up on business in London. He's been sleeping at his club and won't be home until late this evening."

"Yes—but what was the news about Lisa?"

"Oh, that was on the gossip page of the *Evening Echo*. A paragraph saying that it was understood that Mr.

George Gessington, the industrialist, will shortly be marrying Mrs. Lisa Harcourt of Belguardo, Paradon, near Bramshot, Kent."

"But she can't do that."

"She *has* done it, my pet," Phoebe retorted. Adding, with immense conviction, "The bitch!"

"Then what about David?" Realisation swept over his sister. "Phoebe, she hasn't even told him. At least, she hadn't last night, because he telephoned and he didn't say anything about it then."

We're in love, David and I. We're going to be happy . . .

"Now isn't that typical? Still, it was baby snatching on her part, wasn't it? How old is David? Twenty-six? Twenty-seven?"

"He's twenty-six."

"There you are, then. And Lisa is thirty-seven. Anyway, it's no use your worrying."

Harriet frowned impatiently. That, she thought, was practically Phoebe's theme song. Don't worry. Nothing really matters. Things will sort themselves out.

"I wonder when she's coming back from Italy."

"Harriet! D'you mean you haven't heard that either? You *are* behind the times. It's all over the village. Lisa *is* back."

"When did she arrive?"

"This morning." For a moment the husky voice sounded uncertain. "At least, she was in her garden this morning, but I saw that awful Budgen woman going round the house yesterday evening, so perhaps Lisa was home then."

The house was very quiet. Harriet had been conscious of the sound of the grandfather clock ticking in the hall. Now it was drowned by that of her own heart, beating high and fast. "I wish she'd stayed away forever!" she burst out.

From the other end of the line came an amused chuckle. "I bet you do," said Phoebe Potter. Then, as if convicted of an indiscretion, she hung up.

Slowly Harriet replaced the receiver, stood staring down, her expression stony, frozen. It is always a shock to find that what one had thought to be a secret was common knowledge. Although now that she considered it, she could see how ridiculous it had been to imagine that Mark's frequent visits to Belguardo would pass unnoticed.

I hope the divorce will make no difference to your friendship—yours and Mark's. And it hadn't—as far as Mark was concerned. He had gone right on seeing Lisa, had been delighted when he had heard that she was going abroad.

You see? She's bored with David. She'll never marry him.

When Mark came back for his six-o'clock surgery Harriet saw by his face that he had heard the news.

"So you were right," she said in a bright cold voice. "Lisa isn't going to marry David." Suddenly she felt sick with anger.

Mark came slowly into the room. He was a tall man of some charm and elegance. He had a long legal face, thin-drawn by ill health. Two deep lines ran down from his handsome jutting nose to the corners of the narrow, close-lipped mouth. His eyes were hazel. They were brilliant eyes, so deep-set that they seemed penetrating even when he was at his most casual.

He said quietly, "I'd give anything to have been wrong."

"I'm sure you would. As wives usually have to live where their husband's work takes them, you'll be losing Lisa." To give her trembling hands something to do, Harriet drew her workbasket towards her and took out a child's grey sock. "You'll lose her far more completely than if she had married David. This Mr. Gessington is hardly likely to be as easy to deceive."

Mark's face hardened. "What do you mean by that?"

Harriet laughed. All the hurt that she had endured was behind her words. "Oh, you needn't worry. It isn't as if Lisa had even been your patient."

There was a silence. Harriet stared at the washed-out sock in her hand. Her face wore the shocked, slightly incredulous look of one who has, without premeditation, said the one unforgivable thing.

Said Mark icily, "If you are insinuating that I have, at

any time, been Mrs. Harcourt's lover, you must be out of your mind."

"Mrs. Harcourt." The name seemed to goad Harriet on. "How formal we are all of a sudden. We've been here two years, and from the first it's been Harriet, Lisa, and Mark. Particularly Lisa and Mark."

Mark glanced deliberately at his wrist watch. "I thought that you were too sensible to be jealous," he said unfairly. "You should have told me." He picked up his bag and walked from the room.

Harriet sat and stared at the closed door. She sat very still. She could feel something hardening inside herself. It was as if her dislike of Lisa Harcourt had, at last, solidified into a black hatred.

The evening passed. The tall shadows stretched across the garden. The rooks cawed for a while and then fell silent. Tobacco plants and night-scented stock added their scent to the still air. It was stiflingly hot.

Harriet had been certain that David would get in touch with her as soon as he learned of Lisa's impending marriage. Several times she answered the telephone, but it was not David. Her anger against Lisa began to give place to anxiety for her twin brother. What was he doing? Thinking? Planning?

She pushed the workbasket from her. She telephoned to the house where he lodged, seeing it in her mind's eye—tall, grey, and dingy-looking—and he himself returning to it like a wounded animal to the solitariness of its lair. So strong was this mental image that it came as a shock to learn that he was not there.

She glanced at the clock. Twenty-three minutes past six. The motor showrooms where he now worked would be closed. For all that she tried the number and heard the telephone bell shrilling on and on among the rows of rich and elegant cars, no one answered it.

So now there was nothing to do but to wait. But wait for what? Anxiety tightened inside her like a fist.

"I shouldn't worry too much," said Mark, breaking a long silence. "David's probably drinking himself silly in some pub or other. After all, what else is there for him to do?"

"I don't know what he'll do," said Harriet slowly. "I just don't know," she said again, and felt her own helplessness wash over her like a cold tide.

It was very quiet now. A few birds stirred in the bushes. There was a vague hum of insects. Drowsy sounds that intensified the feeling of unreality that had seized on Harriet. The room, the house, the garden seemed to join her in a silent waiting.

At nine o'clock a small boy came with an urgent call for Dr. Warry.

"Mrs. O'Hara thinks she's dying again," Mark said, poking his head in at the door. "I'll have to go. The old lady's bound to be right sometime."

His house was in darkness when he returned at a quarter to eleven. As he opened the front door the telephone began to ring. For a moment he stood motionless on the threshold. No more, he thought, his eyes closed. No more. I can't stand it. He felt stripped, every nerve scraped bare.

The telephone went on ringing.

Dr. Warry straightened his weary back. He switched on the light and picked up the receiver. Odd, really, that Harriet had not remembered to switch it through to their bedroom.

"Yes?" he said. "Dr. Warry here."

At once there broke on his tired ears, like an explosion, a series of cries and sobs.

"Who's there?" he asked sharply.

"It's me, sir, Dimmick." Amy Dimmick, Lisa's personal maid.

"What's the matter, Dimmick? What's wrong?"

"It's the mistress. She—she's dead."

Mark felt as if a great hand had taken his stomach and squeezed it. He had to moisten his lips before he could speak. "Dead? Are you sure?" And then: "How did it happen?"

"Mr. Fray did it. He murdered her." Dimmick's voice rose higher and higher. "I saw him. I saw him. He——"

"Be quiet, woman!" Mark threw a quick, apprehensive glance over his shoulder in the direction of the stairs. He lowered his voice cautiously. "Listen to me. Don't touch anything. Don't do anything. I'll be with you within five minutes."

He put back the receiver. He took it up again and dialled the number of the Bramshot police force, hearing in his ears as he did so an echo of that earlier note of fear in his wife's voice.

Harriet twisted her hair into a chignon at the back of her head, peering at her reflection in the looking-glass.

One says something terrible is going to happen, but one doesn't really believe it, she thought; even when it has actually taken place, it is difficult to believe. I can say that Lisa is dead and that David is suspected of having killed her, but the words bring no sense of reality.

Perhaps that was why the reflection staring gravely back at her had changed so little. She had never had much colour, and she was wearing the same clothes as yesterday, for she was not going to let the village think that she was afraid.

Downstairs everything seemed heartbreakingly as usual. The grey-feathered wallpaper of which she had been so proud. The few good bits of walnut. A bowl of scarlet snapdragons. Gladys, their little maid from the village, was just disappearing into the dining room with a tray, laying the table for their eight-o'clock breakfast. Mark stood in a shaft of sunlight just inside the front door, reading the morning paper.

"How is David?" Harriet asked, hurrying forward. She thought impersonally that Mark looked ill and tired.

"Still dead to the world."

"Poor David! What a terrible awakening he will have."

"What a terrible head! Quite bad enough to keep his mind off other things," said Mark, an ironical twist to his lips.

Harriet nodded. "D'you mind having your breakfast alone? I want to find out what Uncle Charles means to do. I'll bring the car back before your surgery is over."

This was her mother's brother, Colonel Charles Roper, a retired Army man and Chief Constable for the district.

"It's a pity we didn't think of telephoning him last night," said Mark. "Then none of this would have happened."

Harriet's face whitened still further. "D'you suppose I haven't thought of that? Blamed myself over and over?"

"David has put him in a devilish awkward position," said Mark. He threw down the newspaper and stood jingling some coins in his pocket. He looked, Harriet thought in sudden panic, like a prosecuting counsel.

"I know." She spoke in a low voice. "And because he loves David he'll be the more determined not to show him any favouritism. I dare say," she added drearily, "he's just waiting for you to say the word to send out and arrest him."

"I don't see what else he can do," said Mark.

"He can give David a chance. He can call in Scotland Yard." Harriet was drawing a string pair of gloves nervously through her hands as she spoke. "I know just the man. A Detective Inspector." She seemed to see him as she spoke. A big man of quiet, drawling courtesy, immense strength, and complex mind. "I met him at——" She broke off. "Mark, why are you looking at me like that?"

"I was wondering whether you had gone stark, staring mad," said Mark harshly.

Harriet stared. "You speak as if you thought David did kill Lisa," she said wonderingly.

Mark shrugged. "He thought himself ill used and he was drunk."

"He *was* ill used. Everyone would sympathise with him over the way Lisa treated him," Harriet retorted hotly.

"Believe me, Harriet, there won't be much sympathy for the man who killed Lisa. You didn't see her dead. I did."

Harriet stared at him with a sort of fascinated horror, the colour gone even from her lips. "If—if Lisa died as you say, how can you believe David was responsible?"

"In one sense he wasn't responsible. When I found

him on our front doorstep he'd had so much to drink that he'd passed right out."

Harriet felt as if she were lost in a nightmare, in one of those dreams where nothing really is comprehended. She said in a low, trembling voice, "If *you* can believe him guilty, what chance has he? Far better call in a complete stranger, who will, at least, have an open mind." She took a step to pass him.

Mark moved swiftly. He barred her way. "Harriet, don't be silly. You're just wasting your time. This friend of yours will refuse to come."

"He won't know it was my suggestion."

"Your uncle will never agree to that."

"He's got to. It's David's whole future that's at stake."

Mark caught her by the arm. "You'll cry, I suppose," he said savagely.

"Will that be so surprising?"

"Oh, I don't doubt you'll twist him round your finger in the end, but I'm warning you to think what you're doing before it's too late. There's no telling what this chap from Scotland Yard will dig up, and once he begins, nothing is going to stop him." The words poured from Mark. His twitching face was only a few inches from her own. "You'll be thinking of him as a friend, but he won't be. However nice he may seem on the surface, in reality he'll be a spy, setting traps for you, turning every single item over and over in his mind until at last he unearths the truth."

"But I keep telling you—we're not afraid of the truth, David and I."

"Harriet, think back to last night. You were afraid then."

"I was afraid that David might kill himself. I never thought of him killing anyone else."

Mark threw her arm from him. "Great grief, Harriet! Can't you get this into your head?" He was almost shouting. "David was drunk—so drunk he was capable of anything. Anything at all."

Harriet said stonily, "I don't believe it."

Mark passed a hand over his face and tried again.

"You don't understand——" he began. He was shaking slightly. He looked a very sick man.

Harriet's face closed against him. "That's what you've always said. That I didn't understand. I didn't understand what it meant to have to give up your London practice. I didn't understand that Lisa was necessary to you. Well, you're right. I didn't understand any of that—and I don't understand now. But I can tell you this. Lisa may have come between you and me while she was alive. She's not going to come between David and me now she's dead."

Mark made one more attempt. "Harriet, believe me. Trust me just this once." His voice was hoarse and his face drained. "You don't know what Lisa was like. She could be damnably perverse and provoking. Enough to madden anyone——"

"Oh!" Harriet cried with a little gasp. "Oh!" The soft furious pink crept up to her forehead. "How—how dare you!" She struck away his restraining arm and rushed from the house.

As she got into the car she was aware that he had moved. His face, dark and grimly intent, was framed now in the hall window.

Chapter 2

Septimus Finch was aggrieved. He was a very large man, but his gently complaining voice was small and like that of a ruminating bee.

"I don't want to go into Kent," he was saying to his sergeant, Archie Slater, as they walked down one of the corridors of New Scotland Yard. "Sussex, yes. But Kent is a rude, rough county. My Aunt Lilian once had a cook who married a Kentish man—or a man of Kent, I'm not sure which. Everyone told her she'd regret it. And she did. She was back again in six months."

"Then the only one to suffer was her husband," Slater commented lightly.

Finch sighed deeply. "She never cooked another good meal," he said sadly. "My aunt had to pension her off."

"Bad luck, sir," said Slater. He added incautiously, "Still, we ought to enjoy getting out of London, this weather."

Finch was scandalised. "Enjoy going out of London just to arrest a miserable boy who happens to be the Chief Constable's nephew? Who was so drunk when he murdered his mistress that he's never going to remember a thing about it?"

"And jolly sensible too, sir, by the look of it," said Slater heartily.

"You can say that again." Finch paused at his own room to collect his hat and the murder bag that awaited him. "And why did this Chief Constable ask for me personally?" he continued, as a lift carried them to the ground floor. "I don't know him. Or his superintendent."

"Probably Colonel Roper remembers your name from seeing it in the newspapers."

Finch shook his head. "Not in Bramshot. It's a rural area. The only names that get remembered there are those of cows that have won milk-yield contests and men who have grown vegetable marrows of prodigious size."

"Cripes!" said Slater, appalled. "Just as well we're not going to be there long."

"Oh, it's not as bad as that. In fact I've had some notable encounters in the country." A faint, reminiscent grin flickered over Finch's face. "For one thing, it tends to individualism and freedom of thought. And there isn't much respect for an abstraction like Justice. A policeman coming into the place is a foreigner—in enemy territory." He was growing progressively more cheerful as he spoke. "A place like Paradon, now. The road through it leads only to a couple more villages, for I looked it up on the map. The only town anywhere near is Bramshot, eleven miles away. It's cut off. Self-sufficient. Probably hasn't changed much since Doomsday Book."

Slater nodded. "A close-knit community. Yes, I can see that."

There was silence for a moment. Then: "Not so much a community, perhaps, as a conspiracy," Finch corrected in his soft drawl.

They got into his car and set off on the forty-five miles into Kent.

Bramshot was a market town, asleep for five days out of seven. An ugly, old-fashioned-looking town. The police station was a new building, but as it had been modelled more or less on its predecessor it merely looked cleaner than its neighbours.

They were expected, and a police constable took them along to the room occupied by Superintendent Bannerman. There were two men in the room, two sad men sitting side by side in a melancholy silence.

One was the Chief Constable, Colonel Roper, long and thin with very clear blue eyes in a lined and whimsical-looking face, now set and oddly grey. The other, Superintendent Bannerman, was one of the largest men the C.I.D. detectives had ever seen—a monolithic slab of a man with a thick neck and square craggy head. His dark hair grew crisp and low on his forehead, and his shoulders were immense.

He bore, to Finch's fascinated gaze, a surprising resemblance to a black Galloway bull—even to the mean look in his eyes. A Galloway bull in an outsize, crumpled tussore suit.

Both men rose to their feet. Colonel Roper extended his hand. "So you are—Mr. Finch," he said in pleasant, rather clipped accents. "You're very welcome."

"Not quite half-past eleven. You've made good time." Bannerman smiled—and still managed to look ferocious. He lowered himself into his chair behind a massive desk. He looked less intimidating so—as an angry bull might when penned behind a stout, five-barred gate.

As Finch introduced his sergeant, his mind was busy. That odd little pause before his name. So you are—what? Or whom? He became aware that the Chief Constable was speaking again, inviting them to sit down. To have a cigarette, or something sent in from the canteen. He was very polite. Both men were smiling, but there was something uneasy and evasive behind their smiles.

"No doubt you were surprised, Mr. Finch, at being called in to investigate a case that seemed to hold so little of the element of mystery—but we were in a dilemma. The chief suspect—I might almost say the only suspect—is my nephew. An orphan, and perhaps doubly dear to me on that account."

Colonel Roper was seated again alongside his superintendent. His long legs were twined around each other like a corkscrew. He rested his elbows on the desk, fingertips together in a judicial attitude. But, Finch thought, there was no judgment in the man. Only a great grief and a heaviness of spirit held in check by an iron will.

"It seemed to me essential that I should avoid any appearance of favouritism. For this reason I was prepared to arrest and charge my nephew, David Fray, and then resign my position as Chief Constable. Superintendent Bannerman here, almost as fond of the boy as I am, favoured a different course of action, or rather, no action at all. He wished to do nothing, sit tight, and defy public opinion."

The Colonel made this remarkable statement with no change of expression, as if it had been the most natural thing in the world, whilst Slater gazed at Bannerman with a look of startled respect.

"Since we couldn't agree, we were forced to seek a third solution. I suggested calling in the Yard. Your name was put forward and the thing was done." Here Bannerman gave what Finch concluded was a grunt of dissent. "I can only add that there was never any idea of putting any pressure on you. Only of giving my nephew the benefit of your wide experience and—er—well-known qualities."

Finch had listened to this enraptured. So that was the explanation. That was how it had happened. And then he recalled that odd little pause before his name and realised that his coming had not been as simple as Colonel Roper had made it sound. There was some further factor, a third person, perhaps, who was, as yet, without a name.

"The case may look different when we get down to it," said he cautiously.

"Heavens man! *I'm* not expecting a miracle," said the Colonel sadly.

Then who is? Obviously not the Superintendent. Finch would have asked, but Bannerman spoke and the opportunity was lost.

"Now Mr. Finch knows where he stands, I'd better get on and give him the details," he said impatiently. In a deep, rumbling voice he recounted the circumstances of the divorce and what followed.

"Then, three months ago, on May fourth, Mrs. Harcourt decided to go to Italy for a change. She returned on Monday, August second—that is, the day before yesterday. She didn't tell anyone that she was returning and the news doesn't seem to have got out until next morning. At this time no one had any idea that she was contemplating marrying this man Gessington. That only became known when the five-o'clock bus to Paradon brought the evening papers. We know now that the impending happy event"— Bannerman's voice was heavy with irony—"was unknown to Mr. Fray also. He was shown the paragraph by one of his colleagues in the motor showrooms where he works..."

Finch raised an eyebrow. "He's no longer a schoolmaster? No, I suppose that was inevitable."

"That woman ruined him, body and soul," Bannerman declared heavily. He opened one of his vast hands as if releasing something, and his expression was sour. "I wish I'd killed her myself."

"Too late to think of that now," said the Colonel ironically. He had twisted his lean body and long legs into an even more tortuous position. A hand shielded his face from view.

Bannerman sighed gustily, and the papers on his desk rustled in a whispering way. "Mr. Fray left the showrooms shortly afterwards. His subsequent movements are obscure, but at approximately 7:40 P.M. (and most of the times given are approximate) he turned up in Paradon, driving his old sports car. He went into the White Hart and sat, uncommunicative and morose, drinking at one of the small tables. Fred Best, the licensee, says that he had been drinking before he reached there and, shortly before nine o'clock, refused to serve him any more. Whereupon Mr. Fray took a half-full whisky bottle from the pocket of his mackintosh."

"A mackintosh? in this weather?"

"It was his old Army issue. As to why he wore it"—Bannerman's voice, like his gaze, was unfriendly—"well, he usually did wear it to protect his clothes. His car was always breaking down, owing to its age. I can only suppose that he put it on from force of habit."

Finch could think of other, less innocent reasons, for the wearing of the coat, but he did not think it politic to mention them. The Chief Constable could think of them too. A sigh came from behind the shelter of his hand.

Bannerman glared defensively at both Finch and his superior. "Best," he went on loudly, "rather than provoke a row, and knowing the young man well, made no objection. At approximately 9:10 P.M. Mr. Fray left the White Hart. He made no attempt to get into his car but walked away in the direction of Belguardo. A young farmer, Nicholas Tice, saw him entering the drive some ten minutes later. Meanwhile Mrs. Harcourt had dinner as usual at eight o'clock. There were at that time in the house Mrs. Harcourt, her personal maid, Amy Dimmick, and the manservant, Gurney. This man waited on her at dinner and later, at about 8:30, took coffee out to her on the terrace at the back of the house. At 9:10 he went again to ask her if she required anything further. She was then lying on a chaise longue in what is known as the garden room, opening onto the terrace. She was smoking and reading a book. Gurney removed the coffee cup from the terrace and retired to his own quarters, a bungalow in the grounds at the back but out of sight of the house. He was, except for the murderer"—Bannerman's voice grated on the word—"the last person to see Mrs. Harcourt alive.

"At approximately 10:45 Amy Dimmick, going up to her bedroom, was startled to hear footsteps in the hall, going towards the front door. She went into her room to see who was leaving the house and heard a sound on the gravel outside. She looked out of the window and, by the light of the moon, saw someone whom she identified as Mr. Fray pick himself up from the ground and run from the house in the direction of the drive. She went downstairs to her mistress and found her dead body lying on the garden-room floor. She telephoned to Dr. Warry and he rang us up. He arrived at Belguardo at 10:56. Mrs. Harcourt, he says—and the police surgeon agrees—could not then have been dead for more than twenty minutes.

"There was no sign of a struggle. The book which she had been reading was lying open, face downwards on a table, within reach of her hand, as if she had placed it there when she was interrupted. There was a pile of ash in an ash tray, also the stubs of three cigarettes. They had been smoked quite evenly and corresponded to those in the dead woman's cigarette case and were all slightly stained with the same shade of lipstick as that on her lips. There was, in the ask tray, a cigarette which had burnt itself out. An inch and a half of ash. These stubs, and the ash, have all been sent to the forensic laboratory. Mrs. Harcourt's body was lying on the floor. The doctor says that she had been strangled with her own scarf."

"He thinks she must first have been knocked out by a blow of some sort, since she does not appear to have struggled," said the Colonel. His voice was strained, and a note of anguish had crept into it. "Then after she was dead a heavy stone urn was dropped on her face."

"Then the murderer was someone of exceptional strength?"

Colonel Roper bowed his head. "Not necessarily. The doctor says he was in a state of frenzy and so would have had a fictitious strength."

"Are there any bloodstains on David Fray's clothes?"

"Dr. Warry says not—but then, the murderer need not necessarily have bloodstains on him."

"Dr. Warry? What has he got to do with it?"

"When he got home last night he found his brother-in-law unconscious on the doorstep. He says that he was extremely dirty and looked as if he had fallen into every ditch between Belguardo and his own home, Waltons. It appears too that at some time during the evening he had been sick."

Finch raised an eyebrow. "And how is he this morning?"

"Feeling like hell, I should imagine."

"You haven't seen him since last night?"

"I haven't seen him at all."

"Nor I," said Colonel Roper from beneath his hand.

"There were no signs of robbery, I suppose?"

"None." Bannerman's tone was curt.

"Mrs. Harcourt had some valuable pieces in the safe in her room. They should have been in the bank, but she hadn't had time to put them there. We haven't had them listed officially yet, but the maid, Dimmick, says there's nothing missing."

"What fingerprints were there?"

"None at all on the urn. The manservant's were on the doorplate leading into the garden room. There are confused prints on the doorknob. The only ones which could be identified belong to Dr. Warry. These are on the inside knob. He had to close the door on the maid, Dimmick, who showed signs of becoming hysterical."

"Did he indeed?" Finch was interested in anyone who shut himself in with a corpse. "Was he alone in the room?"

Bannerman stared. "I believe he was." He was silent a moment, frowning to himself. Then he said, "Yes, he must have been alone because Peters, the local man, was with Amy Dimmick in the hall."

"Any other fingerprints?"

"Dr. Warry had left the prints of four fingertips on the table near to the chair on which the dead woman had been lying. He has a habit of leaning on them in moments of concentration."

Finch nodded again. So now they knew something else about Dr. Warry. He not only shut himself in with the corpse, but he concentrated. On what? There were infinite possibilities. And why had the maid, Dimmick, telephoned to the doctor in the first place? That, too, was an interesting question.

Bannerman was continuing with his report.

"Mrs. Harcourt's prints were in several places: on the glass doors leading into the garden, which she had folded back, on the head of the long cane chair, on the book—in fact, just where you'd expect."

"And no unidentified prints?"

"None."

"About this Amy Dimmick—didn't she call the manservant, Gurney?"

"She did not. I didn't ask why, but I suspect it was because there's no way of communicating with the bungalow except by going there. And, since the path is through overhanging trees and shrubs, she probably felt afraid to go."

"Fair enough." Finch cracked his finger joints in an abstracted way. "Perhaps you know why Mrs. Harcourt didn't tell anyone that she was returning? Was she afraid of Mr. Fray?"

Bannerman gave him a sour look. "I should imagine that she had never feared anyone in her whole life."

Finch raised an eyebrow. "And now she's dead. Well, well!"

The Chief Constable emerged from the shelter of his hand. "I've been thinking about that, and I believe the answer to lie in heredity," he said. "The Potters—she was a Miss Potter before her marriage—have always been noted more for their egotism than for any decent human feelings. Her father, Ambrose Potter, was a case in point. His rows with his wife shocked the whole countryside. Finally he did something that left him ostracised for the rest of his life. And you know the saying, 'Like father, like child.'"

"What's the story?"

"Well, he was a queer chap. He'd lived most of his life out East, where his family had big business interests. He was a middle-aged man when his father died, and he inherited the family property and came to live with his wife and their one son, John, at the Hall, a big gloomy Elizabethan mansion on the south side of the valley.

"When the boy was fourteen and Mr. Potter himself about fifty, a beautiful young woman, Diane Priestley, came to the village. She was a student at an agricultural college and was camping out with some girl friends. The story goes that she was hunting for fossils in a disused quarry near the Hall when he came upon her. Five days later he walked out on his wife and son and set to work to build another house for himself and this young woman on the *north* side of the valley. This is the house known as Belguardo. And there"—the Chief Constable's voice dragged a little—"their only child was murdered late yesterday evening."

"Did Ambrose Potter marry her mother?"

"Not at once. Naturally enough, he wanted a divorce. And, equally naturally, his wife was determined not to give him one. She was a high-spirited woman, and for a time there existed a state little short of war. He cut off supplies. She retaliated by holding a sale at the Hall of his personal wardrobe. Then she had all the county calling to commiserate with her. So he bought four great mastiffs who roamed the valley, terrorising the villagers and effectually preventing anyone leaving or entering the Hall. How it would have finished I don't know, but abruptly the whole affair came to an end. The young woman was found to be pregnant.

"Mrs. Potter, who had a great love for children, at once began divorce proceedings. Mr. Potter, in gratitude, made a settlement on her and her son which included the Hall and all the land on their side of the valley. The divorce was expedited and Mr. Potter married just in time for Lisa to be born in wedlock."

"That's quite a story," said Finch slowly. He wondered just how much light it threw on the murdered woman's character. It was a fascinating speculation. "Are any of them still alive?"

"None of that generation. Rachel Potter died in—let me see—1928 or thereabouts. The second Mrs. Potter died in the early days of the war. Ambrose himself lived to be over eighty and broke his neck falling down some steps. His son, John, still lives at the Hall."

"What effect did his father's behaviour have on him?"

"John never spoke to his father again, which was a pity, but then, he idolised his mother. Keeps the anniversary of her death. Bedroom as it was. Flowers on the grave. All that sort of thing. He was determined to give her everything she'd lost materially by Ambrose's desertion—but she didn't live long enough to see him do it. He bought a partnership in a small firm making a breakfast cereal and built it up into a really big concern. He's a very sound fella—well thought of, too."

"And the feud?"

"Died out after Ambrose Potter's death, though I believe that John Potter and his half-sister were speaking to each other before that."

Superintendent Bannerman had been showing every sign of restiveness. Now he said, "Since we've given Mr. Finch the details of the affair, perhaps I can get on now with something else."

"No, no, Bannerman, you stay." Colonel Roper waved

him down. He turned to Finch. "Not done with us yet, eh?"

"Not quite, sir." As Finch spoke, he was aware of the Superintendent's immense outline sinking slowly behind his desk, like a torpedoed battle ship, crippled but still full of fight. "How about Lisa Harcourt's ex-husband? What sort of man is he?"

"He's a great deal older than his wife and was a friend of her father. He collects Chinese porcelain and is, I understand, a great authority on it. He's even been known to have been consulted on behalf of the British Museum."

"Where is he now?"

"When he left his wife's house he moved across the valley to the Hall. He has been there ever since."

"Did that cause any friction between Mrs. Harcourt and her half-brother?"

"I never heard that it did." The Chief Constable added, with the first sign of bitterness he had shown, "With Lisa Harcourt it seems that what was past was of no further interest."

"I understand that she was a rich woman?"

"Yes indeed. Her father left her a large fortune. He bought an adjacent property whilst Lisa was small, and he already owned Paradon and the greater part of Bramshot."

"And who gets it now?"

"I have no idea."

"I see. One more question. What sort of man is Dr. Warry?"

Colonel Roper glanced at Finch quickly. "You know that he married my niece, David's sister? Yes! Apart from that, he is a very brilliant doctor. Quite wasted down here. But he had a breakdown from overwork and had to give up his London practice. He's a bit temperamental and moody perhaps, but I suppose that's not to be wondered at."

Finch noticed a certain undertone of stiffness in the Colonel's voice. Did he too find Dr. Warry's behaviour suspect? Or had he some private reason for disapproval? he wondered. "Was he a personal friend of Mrs. Harcourt's?"

"I believe so," said the Colonel briefly.

So that was it. "Thank you. Is there anyone else I should know about?"

The Colonel sighed. The shadow of tragedy was back on his face. "I think not—unless you unearth a suspect for yourself. Mrs. Harcourt had a large circle of friends—mostly men. She was a very beautiful and attractive woman."

"I'll bear that in mind," Finch promised.

"Now, about your lodgings." The Chief Constable unwound himself. He looked more relaxed. "We're in a bit of a quandary there. Paradon's eleven miles from here— eleven miles from anywhere, to be truthful—and it's small. There're only two places where you can stay. One of them is the White Hart, which has obvious drawbacks."

"Mr. Finch being such a well-known gentleman, it won't be long before the place is full of newspaper report- ers," said Bannerman with a hostile stare. The fact that they were now committed to employing this man from Scotland Yard seemed to bear more and more heavily on him.

"What's the second choice?" Privately Finch consid- ered the solution of the case too obvious to interest Fleet Street. Besides, there was a London murder that was attracting all their attention.

"The second choice is the local police station." Colo- nel Roper's voice was apologetic. "It's modern enough. Too modern for Paradon. It's square and bright red. My predecessor had it built ten years ago and the local gentry haven't stopped complaining yet. Then, Peters himself is a widower. I don't know how he manages. It may be pretty rough."

"I'll stay at the police station," said Finch decidedly. "If there's no Mrs. Peters there'll be no one to gossip. And with three able-bodied men in the place it'll be strange if we can't make ourselves comfortable."

The Chief Constable gave a sigh of relief. "That's settled, then. The Superintendent here will get on to Peters and tell him to expect you."

"We had some food on the way down," said Finch. "I'd rather he met us at Belguardo." He rose to his feet.

He asked for the typed report of the proceedings of the night before.

"There're the photographs too." Colonel Roper turned to Bannerman. For a moment an odd little silence fell. In it the heat seemed suddenly to become palpable. Sounds were magnified. A bluebottle threw itself endlessly against a windowpane and the sound of a police car starting up outside was loud in the room.

Bannerman gave a sudden grunt, an angry sound. He groped in one of the drawers, extracted a long envelope, and threw it down on the desk.

The Chief Constable picked it up. He had become very pale. "You'll need these," he said quietly. He passed the envelope to Finch, shook hands with the two C.I.D. men. "You'll let me know how you get on, won't you?"

Bannerman had sunk into a state of profound gloom from which he did not trouble to rouse himself.

A young constable at the outer door gave them directions to get to Paradon. Neither Finch nor his sergeant spoke until they were out of sight of the police station.

"Superintendent Bannerman—his idea of policemanship," Finch murmured. "And yet you know, Archie, I have a feeling there's a third party involved somewhere along the line. Someone who tipped the scales against the Superintendent."

"Nothing would surprise me now, sir," Slater declared, grinning. "All I say is, roll on Paradon." He added a few moments later, "*You* think David Fray is guilty, don't you?"

"It certainly looks that way. The only point in his favour is the time factor. What on earth was he doing for an hour and twenty minutes?"

"Talking, perhaps. He and Lisa Harcourt hadn't met for ten weeks. *And* in the interval she'd fallen for someone else."

"Talking? In his state?" Finch added, "You know, Archie, if it wasn't for this time lag I'd be inclined to suspect that David Fray was no more drunk than you are. That he came down with the express intention of killing a faithless mistress."

"In that case an alibi would have been a damned sight more useful than a plea of amnesia," Slater retorted.

"Under the last Homicide Act drunkenness *is* a sort of alibi. Leads to diminished responsibility. David Fray may be sharp enough to have thought of that. But that again would bring us back to the time lag. He was defeating his own ends by letting her be such an unconscionable time a-dying."

"Well, sir, he was sharp enough to have worn gloves or to have wiped off his fingerprints."

"Perhaps," said Finch dryly, "his brother-in-law was kind enough to wipe them off. By his own admission Dr. Warry was in the garden room alone and with the door closed for some time."

The car was now outside the town. Finch drew up in the shade cast by a clump of chestnut trees, a small oasis in a hot, staring landscape. He drew the photographs taken of the dead woman from their envelope. For a moment a sort of shock held both men silent. Lisa Harcourt had been blotted out—obliterated by someone made insensate by overwhelming emotion. Her light dinner dress, hideously stained, had been half torn from her body—a lovely body, lithe and firm and high-breasted. One arm lay at a curious angle, as if wrenched from its socket. Where her face should have been was only a mass of raw pulp. A lace scarf, matching her frock, was knotted about what remained of her neck.

Slater looked rather sick. "Now we've got to pin it on him," he muttered. "A fellow with a temper like that can't be allowed to run loose."

Finch nodded. There was an oddly speculative look in his eyes. "You know, Archie," he said slowly, "that woman begins to fascinate me. What can she have said or done to make anyone do that to her? And it's not a case of the 'female of the species.' Old man Potter was just as deadly."

Chapter
3

Police Constable Peters was a phlegmatic man, comfortably rotund in figure. He was surprised when Bannerman telephoned to say that he must take in the two London detectives—surprised, but not alarmed. His house had all the modern conveniences, which was more than could be said for some in the village. He saw nothing wrong in its honest red bricks.

Thinking the matter over in his slow way, even his surprise died. Paradon being a small place, and the gentry being all related to the dead lady, his house was the obvious choice, the White Hart, no doubt, being considered too public.

Not that this had been Fred Best's opinion. His voice had been raised in angry protest when Peters had called in to borrow some extra bed linen.

What was there private about it? he had demanded. Hadn't Gladys Paisley overheard Mrs. Warry telling the doctor that she meant to get the Scotland Yard Inspector down? There was no secret about it. Everyone knew it. Leastways, everyone but the London Inspector himself.

This aspect of the affair struck Best suddenly as extremely amusing. He had had to laugh, a rumbling laugh that had made his great paunch shake, and P. C. Peters had so far forgotten his official dignity as to emit a series of hearty chuckles. It was, he reflected afterwards, the only amusement they were likely to get from the whole sorry business.

"An old friend of the lady's, so I heard tell," Best had added with a sly look. "That was real smart of her. An admirer—like myself."

Peters shook his head doubtfully. "The Inspector's coming because he's one of Scotland Yard's best men. And how that can benefit Mr. Fray, I don't know," he said glumly.

He went home and made up the two extra beds. Then he looked into the front parlour, where the table had been laid by Mrs. Walsh, the woman who came in to do his housework.

He mounted his bicycle and rode away in the direction of Belguardo, where he was to meet the C.I.D. men.

Finch and Slater made good time from Bramshot along a road which ran through rich, parklike land. A haze of heat shimmered in the near distance. Cows and horses stood motionless under the trees. Here and there, through a gap in the thick summer hedge, they saw a cottage or a solitary farmhouse standing in a fold of the hills. But for the most part they saw only hedges and trees, great oaks and chestnuts, and the white dusty road turning so often that it too gave a suggestion of isolation and secrecy.

Gradually the land became more heavily wooded. The road, running high along the hills, afforded an occasional view of a long, narrow valley lying below them. The car skirted a deep, disused quarry, its stony face sprinkled with reluctant vegetation, and drove into Paradon down a road roofed by trees.

The village was small and built around a green. The light was soft and vague, full of a faint, whispering rustle where a breath of wind, blowing along the valley, stirred the leaves. There seemed no other sound. No one was about. Cottage doors were closed and windows draped with lace curtains and blocked with potted plants.

"Enemy territory!" said Slater in disgust. "They couldn't care less."

Finch was amused. "It's easy to see you're a Londoner. Why, behind every curtain there's someone watching us. And for those that haven't the felicity of seeing us, there'll go a description that would delight the heart of your superiors."

"If you say so, sir," said Slater, unconvinced.

The car skirted the village green, went past the White Hart, a picturesque building in rosy brick, past a Georgian house standing in a pleasant garden, with an orchard at the back. This was Waltons, home of the Warrys but called after their predecessor, old Dr. Walton, who had fallen in love with the house and had settled there in preference to living in the bigger, adjacent village of Durrington.

The car went up the hill on the far side, between bushes white with dust. It turned in between handsome black and gilt iron double gates. The drive beyond was straight, wide, and beautifully kept. It was also steep. Rhododendrons lined it on either side and were massed on the lower slopes. At the end where the ground had been levelled, framed in green, stood the house known as Belguardo. Behind it the hills rose again, steep and heavily wooded, with tall fir trees, incongruously dark and forbidding in that setting.

It was somewhat baroque in character, with walls which were dazzlingly white and with a great deal of ornamentation. Urns decorated the flat roof, and there was a surprising and frivolous-looking dome. The long double row of windows sparkled with reflected light. Six narrow steps led to a door of carved Italian walnut. There were clipped bay trees in tubs. Beds were filled with sprawling petunias, phlox, and summer daisies. The sunlight poured down, sweet as run honey. There was a vague sound of insects moving drowsily in the heat. The whole scene had a curious and touching beauty. A strange creation for a hard case like Ambrose Potter to have dreamed up, Finch reflected. It was as if all the imagination, tenderness, and poetry of which he had been capable had been concentrated in this one act of homage.

The local constable came out of the house, a stout, homely figure, perspiring in a heavy uniform and regulation helmet.

"Peters, is it?" Finch asked in a voice that struck the

constable as surprisingly small for so large a gentleman. "I understand you're going to put us up. It's very good of you."

"It's an honour, sir," said Peters. His rather bovine stare missed little of this friend of Mrs. Warry. A real gentleman, he thought, as was only to be expected. And artful as a dog fox, for he decided rightly that no Scotland Yard detective could be as innocent and sleepy as Detective Inspector Finch appeared to be.

Finch returned to his contemplation of the house. "What was the second Mrs. Potter like?"

"She was beautiful, sir, and kind of retiring." Peters spoke vaguely. He added apologetically, "There don't seem to be much to say about her, if you get my meaning."

Finch nodded. It was ironical, he reflected, that in this place which had been designed for no other purpose than to enshrine the second Mrs. Potter, she was, of the whole family, the least remembered. For all that, the thought of her lingered at the back of his mind.

He turned from the house and looked across the valley.

To his surprise the sense of privacy was destroyed entirely by a large grey mansion standing directly opposite on the other hill. It was old, bleak, and gaunt-looking, and was already in shadow. Woods surrounded it on three sides and spread away across the hill. Only in front the trees had been cleared, almost as though the two houses had been intended to face each other—"Window to window, as long as they both shall stand," Finch murmured aloud.

Peters gave a slight cough.

Finch turned his mild gaze on him. "Yes, Peters?"

"Mrs. Potter—the first Mrs. Potter—gave the order for the trees to be felled. That was on the day she heard that the house was to be called Belguardo. Mr. Potter was away at the time and she reckoned she'd give the place a fine look he hadn't expected."

"That was before she agreed to give him a divorce?"

"Yes, sir."

"Did they ever become more friendly?"

"No, sir. She never forgave him for leaving her as he did. And, what with everyone siding with her, Mr. Potter and his new wife found themselves quite cut off up here. I reckon Miss Lisa, as she was then, must have been terribly lonely. She lived like a little princess, but she never had no friends of her own age."

"Didn't she go away to school?"

"No, sir. Mr. Potter couldn't bear her out of his sight. I reckon that was hard on her too."

Finch nodded. And both children, no doubt, made to participate in their parents' quarrel, filled with the poison of their anger and retrospective wrongs. And of the two, Lisa must surely have suffered most.

Finch rang the bell.

There were a couple of Bramshot constables on guard inside the house. One of them, a fresh-faced boy called Reeves, opened the front door, trying not to look excited.

Finch stepped over the threshold and the tenuous shade of the second Mrs. Potter vanished, a featureless phantom, infinitely remote from the hard modernism of her daughter.

The hall was large and square. It looked as if it had only just emerged from the hands of an expensive interior decorator. Black and white marble squared the floor, part of the original scheme. The walls were white, hung with pale and ghostly-looking ferns framed as pictures. The elaborate iron staircase was white with a black carpet. The tables were of some black plastic substance and the chairs were of white hide. There were masses of cut flowers, white roses, heavily scented freesias, and phlox. A white china figure of a leering satyr stood in a niche, holding up a lamp.

It struck cool after the heat outside. Cool and very, very quiet.

The main rooms opened from the hall. The drawing room was on one side. On the other were the dining and morning rooms. Between these last two rooms were the back stairs and a lobby leading to the kitchen premises and the laundry. Directly opposite the front door were three wide steps leading to the garden room, where the unfortunate owner of all this luxury had died.

This was L-shaped, the two parts divided by a small archway. Very little of the inner room could be seen from the door. There was a bar built into one corner, with a fine array of bottles and glasses. One wall, opening onto a flagged terrace, was formed entirely of glass panels, which could be folded back out of sight. The ceiling and walls were of white and the floor of light cork tiles.

There were shell-shaped cane' chairs and serpentine long chairs piled with cushions. There were iron tables with glass tops, and everywhere—in stands, tubs, and on shelves—were strange green plants. One of these had covered one wall entirely and now seemed to be advancing inexorably across the ceiling.

It all looked, like the hall, new, up-to-date, and very, very expensive.

It was easy to pick out the chair on which Lisa Harcourt had been used to lie. It was larger and more elaborate than any of the others. It had so much the suggestion of a throne that the picture of the lonely little girl was overlaid by that of the woman, spoilt and arrogant.

Beyond the glass wall was a paved terrace. A long stone pergola was hung with roses. Musk and white alyssum grew in the cracks between the sun-baked flags. A small fountain raised three pale pink marble bowls, diminishing in size, one above the other.

Nothing could have looked more peaceful.

Nor, as Bannerman had said, was there any sign of a struggle inside the room. Yet the chalk outline on the floor and the stains on the cork flooring bore witness to the brutality of the crime that had been committed.

A stone urn lay overturned close by, earth and a trailing plant of green ivy spilling from it. Its flat base, some two feet square, was hideously stained and spattered on the underside.

Finch looked at it in silence a moment. "He had the strength of ten—but not because his heart was pure," he murmured. "And I can very well do without that urn. It can go to the forensic laboratory, along with the clothes worn last night by David Fray." He added a moment later, "One thing's obvious. The dead woman wasn't afraid of her visitor. Look at the chair on which she was lying. Its head is not five feet from the glass wall, which, I imagine, would have been open at least in part on such a hot night."

He glanced inquiringly at Peters, who said, "Yes, sir. When I got here the whole of the glass wall was folded away."

"There you are, then. Lisa Harcourt had two ways of escape open to her, had she cared to take them. One, onto the terrace. The other, into the hall. Instead, she put down her cigarette, intending to resume smoking it later; for that must have been the meaning of the inch and a half of ash which was found unbroken in the ash tray. She walked up to her murderer—why? To taunt him, argue, or merely because he invited her to do so? We don't know. We only know that whilst she was standing there facing him he must have struck her, strangled her with her own scarf, and then dropped that urn, complete with potted plant, smack on her head."

"What gets me," said Slater with a wry look, "is the fact that he doesn't seem to have been able to leave her alone."

Finch said soberly, "At that moment he must have hated her beyond anyone else on earth." He added, "Even so, she must have had time to scream at least once. It was a still night. Why wasn't she heard?"

Peters gave his respectful cough.

Finch turned his mild eye on him. "Yes, Peters?"

"It was the fountain, sir. It was going when I got here last night. The Superintendent had it turned off because of the noise. Said it got on his nerves. Swore at it something awful, he did."

Finch nodded. "Yes. If the fountain were going, that would explain it. But we're still left with another mystery. How did David Fray manage to exist for an hour and twenty minutes without a drink? True, he may still have had his own bottle with him, but he'd hardly have drunk from that in the presence of his hostess."

"There wasn't any sign that he'd had a drink, sir,"

Peters answered him. "The Superintendent had a special search made for glasses. It didn't look as if anyone had been at the bottles neither."

"Then did the murderer have time to wash the glasses and put them back? Did someone else do it?" Finch was thinking of David Fray's brother-in-law, Dr. Warry. "Or was the unexpected visitor not offered anything?"

"Since Mrs. Harcourt was used to men, she probably knew better than to offer that young man a drink," Slater suggested. "In the state he was in he might have passed out on *her.*"

"As he did later on Dr. Warry's doorstep? Perhaps you're right and that is the answer."

A meerschaum pipe with a gold band lay on a small table. Finch picked it up and smelt it. "Wonder where that came from? It hasn't been smoked in years."

Peters gave his respectful cough.

"Yes, Peters?"

"It belonged to the late Mr. Potter, sir. One of a set. The workmen found it when they were doing some repairs to what's known as the Swiss Cottage."

Finch replaced the pipe. He fell silent. He was still wearing his hat. Now he pushed it to the back of his head. The room had seemed a cool oasis from the sun, but the contrast with the outside was wearing off. The heat had moved in again. So had the quiet.

"Tell me about last night," he said to Peters.

The constable drew himself up. "On the night of Tuesday, August third——" he began in an official tone of voice.

Finch waved a dissenting hand. "In your own words, Peters. I can read all that sort of stuff in the report given me by Superintendent Bannerman."

Peters visibly relaxed. "Well, sir. It was at 10:55 when I was rung up from Bramshot. And what with having to dress and push my bike up the hill it was 11:14 when I got here. Dr. Warry opened the door. He looked terrible. So did the lady——"

"The——" Finch glanced at the chalk outline. "Oh, yes. I see."

"Miss Dimmick was in the hall, carrying on some- thing dreadful. I came in here——" Peters broke off, glancing rather anxiously at Finch.

"What did you do?"

"That's it, sir," said Peters embarrassed. "I didn't know what to do. There was no one about. Only Mrs. Harcourt lying there dead and past all help, a red rose tucked into her bodice like a pool of blood. And that there great stone pot lying close to her hand, spattered with brains and blood. There wasn't a sound——" He broke off to add conscientiously, "Leastways, there was Miss Dim- mick creating in the hall and all them moths throwing themselves against the ceiling, so——"

"What lights were on?"

"The ceiling lights"—these were three inverted yel- low cut-glass bowls—"and the lamp on the table by Mrs. Harcourt's chair. The room fair blazed with light. That's what must have attracted the moths. I heard Miss Dimmick tell the Superintendent it was like that when she came down."

"What? All the lights on? That's very curious." Finch stood a moment, staring unseeingly before him, knowing suddenly, with a sharpening of all his faculties, that this was not going to be the simple case that he had expected.

That David Fray had come and gone without trace might very well be due to the machinations of his brother- in-law, Dr. Warry. But why the lights? Had the young man dropped something incriminating and turned them on to facilitate his search? If so, he must have been pretending to be drunk. But if he had been pretending he would surely have remembered to turn the lights off again before he left. Even so—— Finch shook his head, visualising the scene.

The lights streaming out into the night, shining on the plume of water thrown up by the fountains and on the dark woods beyond, lighting up both victim and assailant as if they had been surgeon and patient in an operating theatre.

It didn't make sense.

"What did you do then?"

"I closed the glass panels so no one could get in that way, and went back to the hall. The doctor said, 'You must stay with Dimmick whilst I complete my examination of the body.' Then he came in here and closed the door behind him. I don't know whether it was hearing her mistress called 'the body' that upset her, but Miss Dimmick went off screaming and crying again. Kept saying that Mr. Fray should be served the same way. Then when I did get her quieted down the Superintendent arrived."

Peters' lugubrious tones indicated that this had not improved matters. He added reflectively, "They came from the other side of Bramshot, the Bannermans—farmers. A large family, all wonderful big and strong."

Finch considered the mental picture evoked. He suppressed a shudder. "What happened then?"

"The Superintendent said I'd better get off home, as there was nothing more I could do. As I was leaving, Colonel Roper arrived. 'My God, Bannerman,' he says, 'this is ghastly.' And the Superintendent said, 'It's what you make it, sir'—though what he meant I couldn't tell."

"Did you see anyone as you went home?"

"No, sir." Peters looked at him shrewdly. "I kept my eyes skinned too. About twenty minutes later I saw the doctor's car pass, going very fast. It turned in at the drive at Waltons and that's all I did see. I went to bed after that."

"Was Dr. Warry Mrs. Harcourt's doctor?"

"I don't think so, sir. But, truth to tell, I can't ever remember her needing a doctor."

"Yet I understand he visited her fairly frequently."

"Yes, sir. In a social manner, as you might say. He saw a lot of her when he first came here two years ago."

"And she dropped him, I suppose, when she took up with David Fray?"

Peters frowned consideringly, breathing heavily the while. "I don't think so, sir," he said cautiously at last. "Not actually *dropped*."

Finch wondered exactly what degree of friendship this indicated. Slater's long, lantern-jawed face wore a cynical look.

"Is Dr. Warry liked in the village?"

"He wasn't at first. Too sharp-like and scolding, but it was only his way. He's a real good doctor, and he doesn't mind how often he comes to see you. Not, that is, if you really need him."

"And his wife?" Finch looked at Peters curiously, wondering why he suddenly looked so wooden-faced.

"She came from these parts. The Frays owned a big place over Durrington way, but the land was sold off long ago and the house and home farm went after Major Fray was killed in the Normandy landings."

"And David Fray?"

Peters looked at Finch, a queer mixture of sorrow and bewilderment on his face. "I've known him all his life, sir. When I saw what he'd done I could hardly credit it." He added earnestly, "But it was the drink what did it, not him. Mrs. Harcourt treated him awful bad, and he was no saint."

Finch nodded. He looked pensive. "Not even a plastered one, perhaps." He added, "About the Potters. What does the family consist of?"

"There's the squire, his wife, and their children, all married and living away from home." Peters grinned widely. He was relieved to have got away from the sad subject of David Fray and the delicate one of Mrs. Warry. "The squire's a very pleasant gentleman. Takes a great interest in the village. Always ready to help anyone in trouble."

"The villagers went to him in preference to Mrs. Harcourt, did they?"

"Lor', sir, no one ever went to her!" Peters seemed flabbergasted at the idea. "She wasn't interested in anyone but herself—and clothes. Seems she needed them to visit friends in Paris. Always popping over to Paris, she was. Leastways she was until she met Mr. Fray."

"Well, that was natural enough," said Finch.

He gave orders for the fountain to be turned on and the glass wall to be folded back. He stepped out onto the terrace and paused for a moment, halted by the pure heat that rose to greet him. He saw that the wide flagged path extended to right and left, stone pergola, seats, roses, and still more roses. This seemed to be all the garden there was.

Beyond the right-hand walk and rising from a clearing in the woods was the roof of a wooden building.

"What is that?" Finch asked. "Some sort of summer-house?"

"That's the Swiss Cottage, sir, although some folk still call it Fray's Folly. It was built about sixty years ago."

"*Fray's* Folly?"

"Yes, sir. The land adjoining this used to belong to the Frays. Mr. Potter bought it off them, long ago. He used to use the Swiss Cottage a lot."

"The Swiss Cottage looks a very private sort of place," Finch commented.

"Yes, sir." Peters added, rather awkwardly, "They do say that Mr. Potter didn't get on with his second wife. Fair turned against her, he did, and had the Swiss Cottage done up so that he could get away from her."

"Did Mrs. Harcourt use it?"

"Not as yet, sir. It's been closed since Mr. Potter died five years ago. But just before Mrs. Harcourt went abroad she gave orders for it to be put in proper repair. A London firm did it, and a nice job they've made of it, so I've heard tell. Had it wired for electricity and all. They only finished there the other day."

"I see. And where is the manservant's bungalow?"

Peters pointed. "It's in the woods, sir. In that direction. There's a path runs to it from the kitchen, crossing the terrace farther down and leading to the village."

"Sounds a more sensible way of leaving the scene of a murder than by the front door," Finch commented.

"That it does, sir." Peters was turning crimson in the heat. He took off his helmet and wiped his forehead with his handkerchief.

"Men who bash their lady friends and allow themselves to be seen getting away afterwards can't be said to be particularly sensible," said Slater. He still felt that their quarry was not worthy of the chase.

By now the fountain had filled the three marble bowls. It threw a graceful plume of water into the air. The water ran from one basin to the next like lace and the quiet was broken by the sound of its busy splashing.

"Archie, you go into the garden room and scream. Wait three minutes, then begin again."

Finch walked a little way away from the house. He listened. After a moment he heard a series of falsetto cries, faint and so mingled with the sound of falling water as to be robbed of all urgency.

He walked along the pergola in the opposite direction to the Swiss Cottage until he came to an opening into the woods. He went down the path and came in sight of a neat small bungalow. He rapped on the door, but no one answered. He stood there waiting in the thick shade.

The woods about him were very quiet. He could hear the water of the fountain faintly splashing into the basin. He heard a lark singing in the open country. Far away a farm dog barked. No sound came to him from the house.

He retraced his steps.

Slater, seated comfortably in one of the shell chairs, one leg crossed over the other, his ankle clasped in his hand, was uttering cries expressive of the utmost torment and terror.

Peters, who had a simple taste in humour, was purple in the face with suppressed merriment.

"I can hear you now," said Finch, entering, "but I didn't hear a sound once I'd left the terrace."

Slater looked aggrieved. "It brought the local man in at the double. He thought I was a sex maniac."

"Turn the fountain off again, Peters, will you?" Finch said, eyeing him with mild amusement. "Then we'll interview Amy Dimmick—in the room from which she saw David Fray."

Peters went out onto the terrace. A moment later the plume of water faltered and failed. The room became secret and silent again, shut away at the rear of the house.

Amy Dimmick had a room only three doors down from that of her mistress. It was a pleasant, well-furnished room. The maid's personal possessions, of which there were many, were of good quality and in quiet good taste. Obviously she had made herself very comfortable.

She herself was in the middle fifties, a thin, sharp-featured woman with a sallow complexion and eyes swollen with crying, too disintegrated by grief and horror to indicate any distinct character. At Finch's entrance she rose shakily from her chair.

"I'm sorry to have to disturb you at such a time," said Finch in his soft voice, "but there are questions that I must have answered. My sergeant here will take down what you say and afterwards you can sign the statement. Then we shan't have to go over it more than once."

"I understand, sir. I'll do my best, but I—I'm not in a fit state——" A spasm of emotion twisted her face. She sank, trembling, into her seat. "It—it's like a horrible dream. I can't believe it's true."

"You never thought that Mr. Fray might be dangerous."

She wiped her eyes. "Never, sir, not for a moment."

"Yet when you saw him leaving the house you went straight down to your mistress?"

"I wanted to know what she'd told him and how he'd taken it. I felt glad he knew at last. I never thought of his killing her."

"Did Mrs. Harcourt know that the announcement of her impending marriage to Mr. Gessington was coming out that day?"

"Yes, sir."

"Did she tell Mr. Fray beforehand?"

"No, sir," Dimmick hesitated. "She didn't know how to do it."

"So she just left it? I see. Didn't either of you think that he might come down here and make a scene?"

"We didn't tell him that we were coming home. The mistress was so happy, she dreaded anything happening to spoil her return."

"Then if you didn't let him know that you were coming back, how d'you think he knew?"

Dimmick hesitated—less, it seemed, to consider the question than because it had not occurred to her before. "I—I couldn't say, sir."

"What brought Mrs. Harcourt home at this particular time?"

"Mr. Gessington had to come back. Something to do with his business. The mistress decided to travel back with him."

Finch nodded. He had not sat down. Now he moved to the window and looked out. The bedroom, he saw, was to the right of the hall, above the drawing room. "I understand that you heard David Fray in the hall. Tell me about it."

"Well, sir," began Dimmick obediently, "I'd spent the evening in the laundry, washing and ironing the things we'd brought back dirty from Italy. I finished about twenty to eleven and went up the back stairs and along the passage towards my room. It was very quiet and still everywhere. That's how I came to hear him—Mr. Fray, I mean. First I heard the door of the garden room open and close. I thought that it was the mistress coming upstairs to bed, but it wasn't. It was a man's footsteps. They crossed the hall towards the front door." Horror born of later knowledge took the words from her mouth. For a moment there was silence, each one of them hearing those footfalls sounding from the darkened hall, aware now that behind them had been black hatred and murder. "I hurried into my bedroom to see who was leaving. As I did so, I heard a sort of—scrambling sound, as if someone had slipped on the gravel outside. I looked out of the window and there was Mr. Fray running from the house towards the drive. Mr. Fray——" She shuddered and was still.

"Would you come to the window, please, and point out his exact position when you saw him?"

Dimmick followed him slowly, reluctantly. She pointed. "It was there."

"I see. Between the drawing room and the hall window?"

"Yes, sir."

Finch frowned a little. "Odd he should have come out of the front door and gone in that direction, away from the village."

Dimmick looked down her long thin nose. "He was drunk, sir."

"But even a drunk behaves with a certain amount of reason."

Dimmick lowered her eyelids. "Indeed, sir?"

"You are quite certain that the man you saw was Mr. Fray?"

"Oh, yes. There was a bright moon and I could see quite plainly." Dimmick added, as if to substantiate her story, "He had no hat and he was wearing a dark suit. I thought that he must have come straight from his place of business."

Finch looked at her quickly. "Wasn't he wearing his old Army mackintosh?"

"That nasty old thing? No, sir. He was not."

Finch's eyebrows rose. "He was, you know, when he left the White Hart. I wonder where it's got to. You haven't noticed it anywhere in the house?"

"No, sir. But that doesn't mean that it isn't here. I've scarcely been out of this room."

Finch frowned thoughtfully. So David Fray had discarded both the mackintosh and the bottle of whisky. Why? Because there was blood on the one and water in the other? "I suppose he *was* wearing the mackintosh when he was seen coming up the drive." He opened his dispatch case. He took out the report Bannerman had given him and flicked over the pages. "Yes, here it is. *'I knew Mr. Fray well. Besides, no one could mistake that awful old mac.'*"

"Does it mention the whisky bottle, sir?" Slater asked.

Finch read on. "No, but that might easily have been overlooked. It's one thing to recognise a man you know under those conditions, quite another to see anything as small as a bottle. Archie, send Peters on his bicycle to the White Hart. Tell him to find out what happened to the whisky bottle and what brand it was. And whether Mr. Fray took it away with him. Then tell the two Bramshot men to begin a search for the mackintosh. Tell them the ground floor first. It shouldn't be far away." He added, "Then telephone Bannerman about the urn and the clothes David Fray was wearing at the time of the murder."

As Slater left the room he turned back to the maid.

"Just between ourselves, what would have been Mrs. Harcourt's reaction to Mr. Fray's turning up drunk?"

"She'd never have put up with it. Ordered him off, as like as not." Dimmick was rocking her skinny body to and fro in anguish.

"Even though his condition was her fault?"

"She wouldn't have thought of it like that." Dimmick added spitefully, "Gentlemen should be able to hold their liquor—particularly in the presence of ladies."

"Then what do you think happened in that hour and twenty minutes?"

"Hour and——" Dimmick looked blank.

Finch looked at her curiously. "So you didn't know that Mr. Fray was here all that time?"

"No, sir."

"And now that you do?"

Dimmick looked uncertain. "Maybe he slept it off somewhere in the house without the mistress's knowing."

"And then woke up and killed her? What could have made him suddenly decide to do that?"

Dimmick looked past Finch and at something beyond his left shoulder. "He was still in love with her!" she cried out as if it were an insult.

"Would you have known if there had been anything else? Were you in Mrs. Harcourt's confidence?"

Dimmick looked at him. "Completely, sir." She spoke with emphasis. "I came here when Mrs. Harcourt was only eighteen. And right from the first we were like sisters. She'd been longing for another woman to talk to—about clothes and Mr. Right, when he came along; for no one but men ever came to Belguardo. Several of the families living round would have been willing to bury the hatchet and ask her out, for she was a lovely young thing and an heiress, but she wouldn't have it. If her father wasn't good enough for them, she'd say, then neither was she." Dimmick's eyes filled with tears. "Oh, she was the sweetest, gayest thing. And so beautiful it was a pleasure to dress her!" She brushed away her tears. A vengeful look came over her face. "How could Mr. Fray have done it? How could he?"

Slater came back. "Reeves and Dickenson are searching the ground floor for the mackintosh. Peters has gone on his bike to see Fred Best at the White Hart, and they're sending out from Bramshot to collect the urn and the clothes."

"Right! Now, let's get on." Finch turned back to the maid. "Miss Dimmick, since your mistress obviously was dead, why did you telephone for a doctor?"

"I didn't think of Dr. Warry as a doctor. He was a friend of the mistress's, and—well, he's the sort of gentleman one would think of in an emergency."

"So he was a friend of Mrs. Harcourt's? Even after she had fallen in love with Mr. Fray?"

"Oh, yes, sir. He used to laugh and tell her she'd never marry him. Not a young cub like that, he'd say. Sometimes he'd get quite angry about it."

"And what did you think of the possibility that Mrs. Harcourt would marry Mr. Fray?"

Dimmick smirked. "I always felt that Mr. Right would come along."

"David Fray not being Mr. Right?" Finch fancied that whatever doubts had grown up in Lisa Harcourt's mind, this woman had helped to plant them there.

"Oh, no, sir. He's a nice enough young gentleman, and well connected. But he'd no money and no position."

"And Mr. Gessington?"

"He was everything a lady like my mistress could ask for. A big handsome man, the sort anyone could feel proud to go out with. And so rich—and generous. There wasn't anything he couldn't buy."

Dimmick's prim voice glowed with satisfaction untinged with regret. For the moment she had forgotten that the marriage between her mistress and this elegible suitor could never now take place.

"What d'you think your mistress saw in Mr. Fray?"

Again Dimmick's eyes strayed past him to the far wall. "She was depressed. Always saying that life was passing her by. It was in one of her black spells she met Mr. Fray. He was gay and young and handsome. It was an infatuation on her part."

"And it wore off?"

"Yes, sir. Long before she'd met Mr. Gessington. She was sorry for Mr. Fray, of course, but he made her feel trapped. For all that, I suppose she would have married him if she hadn't met the other gentleman."

"You met Mr. Gessington abroad, I think?"

"He came to stay in the same hotel. The Ritz-Imperial in Rome. We'd been there about three weeks then, and the mistress was talking of moving on, on account of the heat, when he arrived."

Finch nodded. "I suppose it's not difficult for a man to get acquainted with a beautiful woman—even in an hotel as large as the Ritz-Imperial." He was curious about this meeting.

Dimmick looked prim. "It wasn't like that. The mistress had met him once or twice in London and hadn't noticed him much. It was being thrown together in a foreign place that did it."

"Where is Mr. Gessington now?"

"In London, sir. He phoned about half-past eight this morning—as soon as he'd seen the news in the newspapers. I suppose I ought to have let him know last night, but what with the shock and one thing and another"— Dimmick's voice shook—"I never gave him a thought."

"What did he say?"

"Not very much. He—he seemed sort of stunned. He kept saying over and over that he just couldn't believe it." Dimmick added rather querulously, "I did think he'd have been down before now. I don't know what can be holding him up, I'm sure."

"He said he was coming here, to Paradon?"

"Yes, sir. 'I'll motor down,' he said. 'I want to be certain that everything's being done that ought to be done.'"

Finch glanced at his wrist watch. The time was twenty minutes past three. If Mr. Gessington meant to come down, it was odd that he hadn't arrived before this. "One last question, Miss Dimmick. When you went downstairs to the garden room, did you hear or see anything to suggest that anyone but Mr. Fray was about?"

Dimmick frowned. She hesitated, looking away, past

Finch's shoulder. He was getting used to this habit of hers. Then she said slowly, "I wouldn't like to say for certain, but I did think for a moment that I saw something moving on the terrace outside. A sort of tall shadow behind the fountain. That was before—before I found the mistress. But it was all so vague. I shouldn't like to give you the wrong impression——" She folded her thin lips and fell silent.

"Just tell me what you *think* you saw. Something may turn up later to substantiate your story. If not, there's no harm done."

"For a moment I thought that it was that Gurney snooping about. It wouldn't have been the first time I'd caught him at it."

"Does Gurney snoop about?"

Dimmick looked more thin-lipped than ever. "He does, sir. He puts his nose into everything." She added venomously, "If you ask me it's because he hasn't enough to do. It's daily women for this and daily women for that. And all because my lord can make a few foreign dishes and probably poison us at the same time. And so I often tell the mistress."

The words brought fresh realisation of what had happened. Dimmick's face crumpled. She put her long bony hands up to her face. Her shoulders shook. "She was so good and kind. I don't feel I shall ever forget..." Her voice trailed off, smothered by her emotion.

"Try not to give way," Finch said gently. "I may need your help. There isn't anyone else who knew Mrs. Harcourt as you did."

Dimmick dried her eyes. "That there isn't, the poor sweet lamb." A flicker of animation passed over her face. "And don't you go believing anything that Gurney tells you. He's a liar and a mischief-maker."

Slater closed the bedroom door behind himself and his superior.

"There you are," said Finch. "All sweetness and light."

"What—Miss Dimmick?" Slater was incredulous.

"No, no! The dear departed. We're only going to see her at second hand. A little distorted, like amateur snapshots. There'll be others—but that's the first. Sweetness and light." Finch's gentle murmuring voice ran on. "Miss Dimmick—she's still with us, and pretty obvious at that. She's a snob. She suffers from jealousy. She's acquisitive and a born intrigante. If this business opens out we're liable to have trouble with that one."

Chapter
4

The kitchen was a very cheerful room. The floor was squared in two shades of blue. The walls were of a paler shade of the same colour. Yellow Formica covered the table. High stools and two bucket chairs were upholstered in yellow plastic to match. A large electric fan fixed high on the wall sent out a current of cool air.

Its two windows, romantically wreathed in roses, looked out on a peaceful scene. Some cows on the brow of the hill. A glimpse of the village shimmering in a haze of heat, so that it looked as if it were under water. Tall trees circled by wheeling pigeons, and, nearer, the glossy dark green of rhododendrons.

A man sat at the central table, facing the door—an incongruous figure with a great wasted frame, enormous bony hands, and a large face which should have been fat but was merely flabby, like a balloon from which much of the air has escaped.

Spoons and forks were piled in an untidy heap in front of him as if he had pushed them away from him with an impatient movement. A leather for polishing silver was crumpled in one great hand.

His face was a mask from which all expression had been withdrawn. For all that, there was something in his features and in the way he sat hunched over the table that suggested suppressed violence.

When he saw the two C.I.D. men his expression changed, became good-humored and faintly satirical. Life came back to his eyes, which looked now both acute and knowledgeable. He was, Finch thought, an unusual type to find in such a backwater. His rightful place would surely have been in a West End restaurant as a waiter, or behind the bar in a night club.

"Pleased to see you, sir—at least, as pleased as one can be in the circumstances." He spoke with a Cockney accent. He would have brought forward a chair, but Finch waved it away. Instead the Inspector hooked his foot in the rungs of a stool and drew it towards him.

"Yes, it's a bad business," he agreed in his languid, slightly drawling voice. He seated himself, picked up a spoon, and looked absently at his own reflection in its bowl. "You go ahead with what you're doing. I only want to ask you some questions—the answers to which my sergeant will take down in his own inimitable way, thus saving us all a lot of trouble in the future."

"Anything you say," Gurney responded affably. He sat down again. "Actually I only began cleaning this lot for something to do. It leaves you feeling a bit out on a limb when your job suddenly folds up on you."

"Been here long?"

"Seven years. I came here with my wife, but she died shortly afterwards. Mrs. Harcourt suggested that I stay on and she'd get extra help from the village."

"Don't you find it a bit quiet?"

Gurney grinned. There was not much humour in it. It was more a drawing back of his lips from his teeth. "At first I thought I'd go balmy. The stillness and then the way some sound would break in. An owl—or a cow that had lost its calf. And that perishing view. The village and some old man plodding through it at two miles an hour. Or the mad excitement of seeing the bus crawling up the opposite hill four times a day like a red caterpillar on wheels."

"Then why d'you stay? Or, for that matter, why did you come? You're a Londoner, aren't you?"

"That's right. A Cockney, born and bred. As for why I came, it was my health. I'm a chef by trade. My misfortune was that I was a territorial as well. I was called up when World War II broke out. I was wounded and taken prisoner. I stayed in the prison camp just long enough for the Boche to do what he could for this foot of mine—and that wasn't saying much. Then I and another chap made a dash for it. We got clear away, then he was killed in an air raid. Killed by one of our own chaps. That was a laugh, wasn't it? I reached home, but what with sleeping out in wet clothes, drinking from ditches, and the like, I've never been the same since. I went back to my old job—I'd been second chef in a restaurant in the Strand—but six months later I developed t.b. The doctors cured me, but there were no more bright lights for me."

Gurney had been polishing the silver as he spoke. Now he picked up a spoon, as Finch had done. He too looked at his reflection. He laughed briefly, as if what he saw afforded him a bitter amusement.

"I broke out once. Went back to London to my old job, plus a bit of the fun I'd been missing. I was back in the sanatorium in no time. I knew then that I was trapped for good."

The choice of words startled Finch. Had Gurney meant trapped by ill health? Or could it be that that prototype of sweetness and light, Lisa Harcourt, had included him among her slaves?

Finch's face showed nothing of his speculations. It remained as bland as a poker player's. He said aloud, "T.b. is not to be trifled with." He felt for his cigarette case. "I see you still smoke."

Gurney glanced at his yellow-stained fingers. "At times I smoke like a chimney," he admitted, taking one.

Finch lit it and his own. He tipped back his stool until it balanced on two legs. He blew a series of smoke rings and watched them drift away, to be caught up in the current of air set going by the electric fan. He was thinking that there was some other quality behind Gurney's flabby good nature. He fancied that it might easily turn to malevolence.

"Let's get back to business. About Mrs. Harcourt's return. Were you expecting her?"

"I knew she'd be coming back shortly, because she'd written to say so, but I didn't know the actual day. She turned up on Monday afternoon, round about five, and that was that."

"How did she seem?"

"On top of the world. Laughing and singing. Turning on the fountain. Filling the house with flowers. She was a great one for flowers."

Finch raised an eyebrow. "And now she'll have lilies," he drawled.

Gurney met his eye with a hard blank stare. "That's right," he said slowly. "So she will."

"What sort of woman was she? Easy to please?"

"Yes and no. If she was down, then nothing was right."

"Did she tell you that she wanted the news of her return kept secret?"

"Yes, sir. But she ought to have known you can't keep anything secret in a place like this."

"What reason did she give for wanting secrecy?"

"She said she didn't want to be bothered with visitors— meaning the Potters. Very friendly, the Potters."

"For what reason?"

Gurney shrugged. "Don't ask me. Unless they thought they'd got the best of things and wanted to rub it in."

"You don't think they might have been genuinely friendly?"

"Might have been—only things weren't usually as simple as that for Mrs. Harcourt."

"A woman who complicated life, was she? Well, let's get on to last night. I understand that you took in her coffee and that later you spoke to her again in the garden room. Did she say or do anything to suggest either that she expected a visitor or that she was in any way nervous or apprehensive?"

"No, sir."

"And the whole evening you neither saw nor heard anything unusual or suspicious?"

"Nothing."

"Then let's go farther back—to the divorce. What made Mrs. Harcourt fall for a man so much younger than herself?"

Gurney shrugged. "He was young and good-looking." Adding with an odd inflection, "She was a lady who loved beauty."

"Miss Dimmick," said Finch experimentally, "says it was because she felt that life was passing her by."

Gurney made a grimace. "Oh, her! What does an old maid like her know of a lady like Mrs. Harcourt? I tell you, she was a strange one. No one did things as she did them. Nothing turned out as you'd expect. She was——" Again he hesitated, searching for words. He gave it up. Began again. "Take that affair with young Mr. Fray. It was too hectic by half. She was like fireworks going off. And it didn't have to be that way, Mr. Harcourt not being one to interfere. But there she was, burning him up and herself too. But dissatisfied all the time—as if she had the feeling that there must be more to love than what she was getting."

The words came slowly now, almost tentatively. The dark, brooding look was back on the ugly face. Before, he had been speaking for effect. Now he had forgotten his audience. It was almost as if he had entered some secret, unknown country and was trying to find his way about in it.

"Many a time after Mr. Fray had left the house I've gone in to see if she wanted anything, and there she'd be, sitting huddled up in one of the big chairs in the drawing room, looking dead to the world and staring, staring... It'd fair give me the creeps to see her. What did she really want?" Gurney looked at Finch without seeing him, aware only of his own bewilderment. "A man can't do more than tear out his heart. But it wasn't enough. It was never enough. And the queer thing was that the next day she'd be way up in the sky again, all sparkle and fun."

"How long did this go on?"

"Until after Mr. Harcourt got his divorce. Then she seemed just to fold up. Very quiet, she was then. In herself, I mean. All the life seemed to go out of her. The parties and the dashing about stopped. She just stayed home, seeing no one, moping and brooding."

"And Mr. Fray?"

"He liked it." Gurney laughed harshly. "Poor boob, he liked it. He seemed to think that everything was all right because he didn't have to share her with anyone else. There was only the two of them at last. Her sitting mute and staring in one chair and him sitting watching her in another. He didn't seem to see that she wasn't really there. That she wasn't there for him any more."

"Then what happened?"

"All of a sudden she picked up again. In May, that was. Why it happened I never knew—unless it was that she'd decided not to marry Mr. Fray after all. For a couple of days she was running about the house, upstairs and down, singing and laughing. Planning new clothes with that maid of hers. And him following her about, pleading and protesting. Shouting at her. Sometimes he'd break down and cry like a baby. I reckon he knew well enough then that he'd lost her."

The picture conjured up by Gurney's words made an unpleasant impression on Finch. It was Ambrose Potter over again. There was the same egotistical disregard for the feeling of others, the same seeming inability to see any point of view but one's own.

"What happened after that?"

The manservant seemed to emerge as from a dream. He looked startled, even a little alarmed at himself. Finch knew then that from now on he would hear only facts.

Gurney spoke flippantly. "She just packed up and went off to Italy. To look for the sun, she said, though as I remember it, it was sunny enough here at the time."

"When did you hear of her engagement to Mr. Gessington?"

"That first evening. Not that I wouldn't have known. She was wearing a ring with a diamond the size of a shilling."

"She doesn't seem to have told Mr. Fray?"

"No, sir."

"You don't sound surprised."

Gurney shrugged. "She was like that. What was past was past."

"I see. Now let's get back to the Potters a moment.

You said that they behaved in a very friendly manner towards Mrs. Harcourt. What were her reactions to Mr. Potter, for instance?"

"He irritated her. Many a time she'd try to take the mickey out of him, but he'd just laugh. 'You're an unhappy woman, Lisa,' he'd say. 'That's what's the matter with you.' She'd swear at him then. 'Bloody prig' was the least of what she called him. But it wasn't any good. She couldn't rile him. He was the one man who didn't want anything she'd got."

Again, Gurney's choice of words caught at Finch's attention. "Mr. Potter is that rare thing, eh? A happy man?"

Gurney smiled rather sourly. "That's right, sir. He's got enough money, two fine children, and a wife he dotes on. Yes, he's happy, right enough."

"How about Dr. Warry? Is he a happy man?"

"He was properly soured, sir—like me. The country nearly sent *him* balmy too. Never heard him say a good word for it, not that he often mentioned it. He was a great one for talking, but it was usually plays, books, night clubs. Stories of this and that celebrity. Listening to him, I could see how quickly things changed. Only three years and most of it was new to me."

"*Three* years?"

Gurney's eyes dropped. He fiddled with the silver. "Three years since I came out of the sanatorium."

Finch looked at him curiously. "So it was from here you broke out?"

"That's right, sir." He sounded surly.

"And you came back?"

The man raised his eyes to meet Finch's. Again the detective became aware of the violence that lurked just below the surface. It peered out at him from eyes narrowed between creases of fat. "Yes," he said shortly. "Yes, I came back."

Finch ground out the stub of his cigarette. He threw it into the sink bucket. "Tell me, what were the relations between Mrs. Harcourt and her husband before David Fray came on the scene?"

"I don't think there were any, as you might say. They kept themselves to themselves. He had his part of the house. She had hers. I never heard them quarrel. He was polite to her. Sort of formal—as if this was a hotel and they were two strangers who happened to be living here."

"Then *he* didn't want anything from her either?"

Gurney grinned maliciously. "I wouldn't say that, sir. There's some china and jade in a cabinet in the drawing room. I've heard her say he only married her because of it."

"She said it to her husband?"

"No, sir. To the guests at the dinner table. Sort of posing as a woman who'd been deceived but laughing all the time too."

"Didn't Mr. Harcourt attend her dinner parties?"

"No, sir. Mostly he had meals in his own room. I'd take them up and he'd sit there at the table, eating and reading some book."

"I see." Finch spoke slowly. "How d'you think he felt about the divorce?"

Gurney shook his head. "That's a question I've often asked myself. Mr. Harcourt was one of the old sort. Very proud and stiff. Not one for washing his dirty linen in public. He must have felt it." After a pause Gurney repeated, "Yes, he must have felt it quite a lot."

Chapter 5

Neither David Fray's old Army mackintosh nor the whisky bottle were to be found. They were not in the house, nor in the garden surrounding it. The Bramshot men were certain of that.

They had searched the rooms, the roof, and the space under the roof. They had searched the boilerhouse, the terrace outside the garden room, the toolshed, and the flower beds and bushes round about.

They reported their failure to Finch. It suggested a hitherto unconsidered possibility: that David Fray had spent some time in the grounds before coming to the house. He sent one of the men to fetch Gurney.

He heard the manservant approaching before he actually came in sight. Step, pause, drag. Step, pause, drag. The sound had, he reflected, like the man who made it, a faintly sinister flavour.

Gurney entered the hall, moving crab-wise, swinging the leg with the built-up boot in a wide circle, dragging it a little before he put it down. He paused, his eyes flickering across the faces of the watching men. "Enter a war hero." He smiled mockingly, resting his weight on the back of a chair.

"Too bad," said Finch in his soft voice, thinking how incongruously this potentially violent man fitted in with the chill, sterile beauty of the black and white room.

"I wanted to ask if you'd seen Mr. Fray's mackintosh.

It seems that he was wearing it when he arrived but not when he left."

Gurney stared. "I haven't seen it, sir." He spoke slowly, as if considering what he had just heard. "It must be about somewhere."

"So one would imagine," Finch agreed dryly. "Then there's another point I want cleared up. When you left the house last night, what lights were on?"

"None, sir—except the one in the garden room. I turned the kitchen light off before I left."

"The *one* in the garden room?"

"The lamp on the table near where Mrs. Harcourt was lying. She hated what she called a glare."

"The ceiling lights were on when Miss Dimmick went down."

Again Gurney gave the impression of a man silently resolving what had been said to him. "I've never known her to have them on," he said slowly at last. "Not those lights. I remember her once coming in when I was on the steps, washing the leaves of that plant on the ceiling. 'See, Gurney,' she said, looking up at me, 'those lights make unbecoming shadows on my face. I'm quite hideous like this, aren't I?' But she wasn't hideous. Nothing like it." His grip on the chair back had tightened. His voice trembled a little, as if he were reliving a scene that had been shut up inside him too long. And for a moment it seemed hotter and closer than ever, as if the words oppressed the air with a sense of outrage.

Dimmick came down the stairs. She had bathed her eyes and tidied her hair, but she still looked disoriented and lost.

Finch went to meet her. "Just the person I need," he greeted her. "Tell me, what lights were on in the house when you came downstairs last night after seeing Mr. Fray from the window?"

"None, sir. The mistress didn't want them shining out and perhaps attracting visitors. 'If the house is in darkness,' she said, 'they'll think we've gone to bed early and don't want to be disturbed.'"

Finch noted that where Gurney had said a straight-

forward "the Potters" Dimmick alluded to "visitors." It
confirmed his impression of her as a secretive woman.
"Was the front door locked?"

"Yes, sir, but Mr. Fray had a key."

"Did anyone else have one? Dr. Warry or Mr. Potter,
for instance?"

"Oh, no, sir."

"If anyone had rung the front doorbell, who would
have answered it?"

"Gurney, sir. Or if he was off, I'd have done it."

"Did Mrs. Harcourt ever answer it?"

Dimmick smiled pityingly. "The mistress? Never, sir.
Not, that is, unless she happened to be in the hall and saw
someone she knew coming to the house."

"Would you have heard the bell in the laundry?"

"Oh, yes, sir. But no one rang it last night." Dimmick
became aware of Gurney's presence. Her expression became sour and waspish. "Idling again, Gurney? Haven't
you any work to get on with?"

Gurney shifted the balance of his ungainly body from
one foot to the other. "With the mistress dead, it's argu-
able whether I have any work. Or, indeed, whether I'm
employed here at all." Adding with immense satisfaction,
"And that goes for you too, Miss Dimmick, I fancy."

The woman stared at him silently a moment. All sorts
of expressions passed across her face. Blank incomprehen-
sion, incredulity, and then the shock of complete understanding.

She, Amy Dimmick, was without work or home.

To Finch it seemed that she was holding her breath,
that behind that sour façade all was confusion, a cumpling
and falling into ruin. She put her hands suddenly to her
face. She turned, stumbling, up the stairs, weeping as she
went.

"Some people," said Gurney to no one in particular,
"don't ever seem to know what's going on around them."

Finch sent Slater to telephone to Bramshot. "Tell
them that I want enough men to comb the grounds here.
Then join me in the drawing room."

The drawing room was a big room, running the width

of the house. It had two windows looking out onto the front. Three more faced the woods and the rhododendron clumps. It was a beautiful room—too beautiful, perhaps, for Lisa to have wanted to change, with its biscuit-coloured walls, flower-strewn carpet, rich French furniture, and exquisite brocade curtains, its paintings by the French Impressionists hanging on the walls.

Among all this beauty two things caught at Finch's attention: a display cabinet containing jade and Chinese porcelain and a large photograph of the dead woman which stood, palely reflected, on the polished surface of a magnificent grand piano.

He examined the photograph first.

So this was Lisa. Lisa of the dark eyes and magnificent figure. The long curving neck and small proud head. The masses of hair piled high in what he thought of to himself as a snail's shell. The finely boned wrists and ankles.

He reflected that, with every interview, he was coming to know her a little better, that sooner or later he would arrive at the one thing she had done which would betray her essential self. Then he would know for certain just why she had been murdered.

He noticed suddenly that where his breath had fallen on the silver frame it had brought out some fingerprints. "Gurney for a ducat," he murmured aloud. He was finding the case full of interest.

He crossed the room to look in the cabinet. He knew enough about such things to recognise the value of its contents. Dark green jade and light, yellow and light brown, lavender and blue. And a thick yellowish-white which he had a vague idea was known as mutton-fat, though looking at its wonderful lustre, he could not help deciding that in this he must be wrong.

There were plates and bowls and vases, equally lovely. And pottery horses richly saddled, with arched necks and flowing manes. Finch did not doubt that Francis Harcourt, that expert and ardent collector, had indeed coveted these.

Slater came into the room. "The Superintendent wasn't

at the police station, but they're arranging to send some men over at once." He was attracted, as Finch had been, by the photograph of Lisa Harcourt.

"How alive she looks," he said after a moment, under his breath. "And as if she knew all the answers."

"In which case her spirit is somewhere still around, suffering from a feeling of acute astonishment and annoyance," Finch murmured, prowling about. "And this must be Mamma and Papa on the mantelpiece." He was enchanted to make their acquaintance, for he was a man of almost insatiable curiosity. "He's like a Viking, big and bold and fair. An open-air type. Just the sort to buy mastiffs and range the hills with them."

"And his second wife—wow! She's even better-looking than her daughter. And yet there's a sort of emptiness in her face. I can see how old man Potter came to get tired of her."

Finch nodded. "Looks by Mamma. Character by Papa." He added thoughtfully, "It was certainly some combination. Lisa was a lovely feline creature. Trouble is, she didn't walk alone. Within the past twelve months there've been David Fray and George Gessington. And it seems reasonable to suppose that there have been others."

"Mr. Harcourt not being one to interfere," said Slater, mimicking the manservant's Cockney voice. "Even so, I can't imagine that she ever fancied Gurney."

"No—and yet what combustible material was there. That ugly devil was obsessed by her. Deliberately tormented by her." Finch was thinking of the picture that Gurney himself had conjured up. The lovely flawless face raised, like a pale flower, to the hungry gaze of the misshapen man above it. The man who had hoped for nothing. Expected nothing. For whom time had passed as empty of meaning as footsteps down a long corridor.

"He was forced to stand by and watch other men triumph where he had no hope of succeeding. And now she was planning to marry one of them. Perhaps in her new life there was to be no room for Gurney. She may even have dismissed him last night. Perhaps he found that he couldn't face life without her. Perhaps his iron self-control broke at last and he struck her down."

"If David Fray wasn't the murderer, Gurney would certainly be my choice."

"Yes. Beware of Passion that's both meek and wild."

"Keats," said Slater promptly.

Finch looked at him. "Archie, I wish you wouldn't do that," he complained.

"Oh, I dunno, sir," said Slater airily, glancing at him out of the corners of his eyes.

Finch wagged his head dolefully. "You're an irreverent young man," he said. "I can see no future in front of you. Only a——"

But the gloomy prognostications of Slater's superior were doomed to remain unuttered. From outside there came the sound of a car's engine. A magnificent black Aston-Martin sports car came tearing up the drive.

"Dramatic arrival of the tardy lover," said Slater, grinning. He seemed to be enjoying himself.

Finch was already moving towards the door.

Reeves, the young police constable, was in the hall and announced the newcomer's arrival. Although he tried to keep secret his awareness of this man's connection with the case, his face was pinker than ever from suppressed excitement.

George Gessington was a big, handsome man, big and important-looking. He was blond, with slate-grey eyes, decided brows, and a thrustful jaw. It was essentially a bold, even a ruthless face, the face of one who ordinarily knew what he wanted and saw that he got it.

This made the more impressive the sickly complexion, the air of utter exhaustion and misery that hung over him. His character, his whole personality, seemed to have received a blow that had, for the moment, left him defenceless and at a loss.

He was wearing an expensive lightweight grey suit. His tie was loose. This seemed to bother him, for he made several ineffectual attempts to flatten it to his chest, rather as one might slap at a buzzing mosquito.

Finch went to meet him. "Mr. Gessington? I expected you earlier."

"Earlier? I've been on the road since first thing this morning." Gessington spoke in a jerky, rather staccato manner. "And there aren't many cars that can overtake mine."

Finch raised an eyebrow. "I was given to understand that you were coming from London." He was trying to see this man in relation to the dead woman. Not a womaniser or a philanderer, Gessington's approach, he judged, would have been a straightforward one, man to woman.

"London? I was in Newcastle." Gessington spoke absently. He was staring round the hall in a haunted way. It reminded Finch that the industrialist was seeing Lisa Harcourt's house for the first time. It was inevitable that he should be moved by it.

Finch introduced himself and his sergeant. He suggested that they should go into the drawing room and continue the interview there.

Gessington nodded briefly. "So you're from Scotland Yard?" he remarked, following the detective. "Then there is some doubt as to David Fray's guilt?"

"You think him innocent?"

Gessington made a weary gesture with one hand, a square, very strong-looking hand, well kept and the back covered with fine fair hair. "I don't know what to think. If he did do it, then he isn't the boy Lisa told me about. And we talked about him a lot." Adding, "As a matter of fact, Lisa had him on her conscience. She had tired, but he hadn't."

Gessington was again throwing those haunted, sur-reptitious glances to right and left. It was as if he could not bear to take in the whole lovely room in one all-embracing stare.

"She talked of him, and—well, the adjectives she used weren't any you could apply to me. Gentle, consid-erate, chivalrous, and—what's that silly expression women use?" He clicked his fingers in the air. "A sweetie-pie. That was it. She alluded to David as a sweetie-pie." His voice died, suddenly struck down by these echoes from the irrecoverable past.

"Mrs. Harcourt and Mr. Fray don't seem to have been very well matched," said Finch dryly.

Gessington frowned wearily. He rubbed his pink-rimmed eyes. "I know. But Lisa's circle down here was, of necessity, restricted. She was married to a man old enough to have been her father, who, in all respects, might as well have been her father. She was getting on in the thirties—and she was bored."

His eyes fell on the photograph on the piano. He put his hands up to his face, a man beleaguered past endurance. It was a shocking thing in one so self-assured, so cushioned by material circumstances against outrageous fate. His action seemed to shock Gessington himself, for when he dropped his hands, he seemed to have come to some terms with himself. He looked calmer. His voice when he spoke was firmer. It was, Finch thought, characteristic of him that he made no apology for his sudden loss of control.

"I can't understand why David didn't accept the fact that Lisa had ceased to love him. It's an ordinary enough situation. And he's a sportsman—supposed to be."

"Perhaps he might have accepted it if Mrs. Harcourt had explained."

Gessington's face hardened slightly. He braced himself as if against a blow. "Explained what?" he asked harshly.

"That she intended to marry another man."

"But she did explain. We talked it over. I offered to do it myself, but Lisa said that it would come better from her."

"The first David Fray knew of it was when one of the men he works with showed him that paragraph in the evening newspaper."

Gessington's mouth closed for a moment in a trap-shut line. "The stupidity of it! Why didn't she tell him?"

Finch chose deliberately to take his words as a question to be answered. "Her maid says it was because she didn't want anything to disturb her happiness. The manservant says she was like that. And that what was past was past. You can take your choice."

Gessington gave a sour smile. "I admit that she often managed to surprise me."

"In what way?"

"She could show a complete, an almost terrifying indifference to everything but what she wanted at that moment." He paused—not so much, Finch thought, from indecision, as to calculate the effect of his words. This deliberation on his part gave to them an added importance. "From childhood she had been accustomed to have her slightest whim indulged. It had become inconceivable to her that she should not have what she wanted. If life would not give it to her, then she took it for herself. Not telling anyone. Not consulting anyone. She could hurt one most damnably and seem quite unable to appreciate what she had done."

Finch looked at him curiously. "And so——" What was the man getting at?

Gessington didn't answer at once. Instead he gave Finch a long, thoughtful stare. When he did speak, it was to say simply, "I wondered whether she might not have hurt someone else besides this boy, David."

"Can you suggest anyone?"

Gessington shrugged. "That surely is your province."

"But you must have drawn your own conclusions?"

"My only conclusion was that David did not do it."

"And if he did do it?"

Gessington's face became suffused. The veins stood out like cords on his neck. His eyes gleamed red. "Then damn him!" he cried. "Damn him to hell!"

The furious words shattered the silence of the soft footed room, ricochetted off the pale walls, and went booming out into the hall, startling the two Bramshot men by their sheer animal fury.

Gessington's face paled. He looked shamefaced and, at the same time, desperate. "From Dimmick's description— Lisa seems to have been——" His mumbling voice faltered to a stop.

Finch understood what he was trying to ask. "Mrs.

Harcourt felt nothing beyond the first blow. And that took her by surprise. She had no time to be frightened, even," he said quietly. He added, intentionally brisk, "Did Mrs. Harcourt speak of her ex-husband?"

"Not very often. From what she did say I gathered that he was utterly wrapped up in his collection. Everything was subordinated to that. She was married at twenty, and, as you probably know, he was twenty-six years older than she was. A stiff, proud man with this one overwhelming interest in life. It was no wonder that their marriage came to grief. I'm only surprised that it lasted as long as it did."

So Gessington did not know that Mr. Harcourt had not been one to interfere! Or did he? Finch had been aware of a curious conviction growing in his mind in connection with George Gessington.

It was that, shocked and broken as he undoubtedly was by his loss, he yet had come to Paradon with some quite definite plan in mind, a plan so desperately important to its author that at times it superseded both grief and mourning, so that he gave an uneven performance, veering between the natural outraged man and the man whom he would wish to be. It made him very interesting. Very interesting indeed.

"Have you any idea how Mrs. Harcourt left her money?"

"None at all." Gessington spoke curtly. He had himself well in hand again.

"Then let's go back a bit." Finch seated himself on a corner of a massive Regency table, one long leg dangling. "When did you reach Rome?"

"The twenty-seventh of May."

"What took you there?"

"My father had died recently and I had planned to visit each of our foreign representatives in turn—Paris, Rome, New York. As you probably know, I met Lisa in Rome. After that my business interest didn't seem so very important." His face twisted sourly, as if a whole trip of his life had suddenly gone dead behind him.

"And the announcement of your impending marriage?"

"I wanted to take Lisa to New York with me. It didn't leave us much time."

"I understand that you travelled back to London with her and her maid?"

"I did. We parted at Victoria. I went straight to my office. There was a lot to catch up with."

"Where were you yesterday evening? Say, between ten and eleven o'clock."

The question brought Gessington up with a jerk. He seemed to find it outrageous. "You ask *me* that?"

"I have to ask everyone even remotely connected with the case," Finch answered.

"Remotely connected?" Gessington spoke harshly. "I was hardly that." Then common sense reasserted itself. "I was in Newcastle—staying at the Royal. I'd motored up the night before."

"Thank you. How pleasant it is to hear an alibi like that," said Finch blandly. He asked with real interest, "What are you thinking of doing now?"

"I shall stay at the local pub for a few days." Gessington smiled faintly. "I hope you won't take it amiss, Inspector, but I have a wish to do a little detective work on my own. I shan't get in your way, I promise you."

Finch smiled with pleasure. How satisfactory to know that he was going to have the equivocal and bereaved Mr. Gessington right there under his eye. "As long as you pass on any information you may pick up——"

"Of course." Gessington smiled a rather formal smile. "I still can't believe that it was David."

"You may be right. And if anything turns up bearing on that, I'll know where to get in touch with you—the White Hart."

They went into the hall together.

Finch, opening the front door, saw at the end of the green tunnel of shrubs a sentinel figure. Tall, stiff, shrouded in black, her shadow a jackknife outline, thin and sharp on the dusty road.

Amy Dimmick, as if she had been looking out for Gessington, appeared at the top of the stairs. For a moment the two stood looking at each other. Gessington silent, jaw set, a rock of a man. The woman, her face pale, her eyes holding a hard, dry glitter.

"Oh, Mr. Gessington, sir! My poor lady!" Dimmick stumbled down the stairs towards him.

"I know! I know!" Gessington spoke harshly. "But you must pull yourself together. Tears won't bring her back. She shall return no more to her house, neither shall her place know her any more."

It was odd to Finch to hear this worldly-looking man paraphrasing from the Bible. It made him wonder about Gessington's daily environment. Odd, too, to see how Dimmick had revived. Become herself again—a thin-lipped, sharp-eyed, and competent self.

"I know, sir. It—it all happened so suddenly. There were you seeing us off. And the house safe and peaceful. So much to look forward to——"

"That'll do, Dimmick. This is neither the time nor the place." Gessington's face was ghastly. "I shall be at the White Hart for a few days. Come and see me there."

"Very good, sir." Amy Dimmick obediently fell back.

Gessington got into his car. He went streaking off down the drive at breathtaking pace, as if he thought that his own personal pain could be left behind.

The car turned into the road and so out of sight. The hot silence returned. And in that silence and heat, on the same spot on the road, a figure in black stood again, motionless, staring towards the house.

Dimmick gave an exclamation. "Oh, poor Miss Budgen! And in all that mourning too," she cried, tut-tutting.

Finch turned to look at Dimmick. "Who's Miss Budgen, and why should she be in mourning?"

"She's Admiral Budgen's daughter, sir. She's a bit weak in the head, but there's no harm in her. She was fond of the mistress. Forever bringing her little presents. Flowers or eggs from her hens. She'd recite poetry to her or even sing. Gregory chants, I think the mistress used to call them. Sometimes it'd get on her nerves, but she wouldn't have her shut out."

Finch was surprised at this new picture of the late Mrs. Harcourt. He reflected that between David Fray's love-making, Dr. Warry's jealousy, Gurney's hungry surveillance, and Miss Budgen's chanting she must have led a pretty full life.

"Where does Miss Budgen live? The Admiral, I imagine, is dead?"

"Oh, yes, sir. Miss Budgen's quite alone in the world, and lives in an old Army hut in the woods. She has a tiny income, but it isn't enough. The mistress used to give her money and clothes. I don't know how she'll manage now, and that's a fact."

"It's a moot point how any of you will manage," said Finch rather absently. He had noticed that the spot occupied by the figure in black was suddenly empty, peculiarly empty. Miss Budgen's tall thin figure seemed to have a significance out of all relation to its actual importance. "Have you any idea who gets Mrs. Harcourt's money?"

Dimmick seemed to think the question in very poor taste. "No, sir," she said distantly, "I'm afraid I have no idea." And she folded her lips even more thinly.

Finch and Slater returned to the drawing room. They began a search of drawers and cupboards.

Lisa Harcourt had been a woman without a system. Drawers, cupboards, even ornamental boxes and vases yielded their quota of letters—some from David Fray—string, receipts, bills, and used envelopes.

"She seems to have stopped in London on her way to Italy and shopped in a big way," Slater remarked. "There're literally dozens of bills and receipts."

"Same here," said Finch. Adding with excusable exaggeration, "And every third one for a hat."

He fell silent, a handful of miscellaneous papers piled on the table in front of him. He was conscious of a vague feeling of disquiet lying at the back of his mind. He cracked the joints of his long fingers like pistol shots and sighed audibly. "What's that fellow Gessington playing at?" he murmured disconsolately. "Something—but what? I wish I knew."

Chapter
6

The search went on. Outside, the sun was sinking behind the hills. The house and the plateau on which it stood were in shadow. It was still intensely hot. Inside, the house seemed to give off an intense quietness. An air of uneasiness prevailed, as if in echo of Gessington's wild passion.

Finch and Slater worked methodically through the downstairs rooms. As they did so, Finch's eyes strayed again and again towards the windows, until he realised that he was looking for Miss Budgen's return, expecting to see her at the end of the drive—tall, thin, shrouded in black, mourning for a dead woman.

The search followed the same pattern as it had in the drawing room. There were bills, receipts, invitations, used envelopes, occasional love letters from David Fray.

There was a fat telephone pad with pages of past messages. A surprising number of them began, "Mr. Potter telephoned——"

At the top of the back stairs the two men came on a suite of rooms. This, Finch decided, must have been Francis Harcourt's. It was entirely cut off from the rest of the house. Sitting room, bedroom, bathroom, they were completely empty; the walls were marked as if some sort of fittings had been removed from them—panelling, perhaps.

"So Harcourt remains Mr. X., the unknown quantity," Finch remarked, when the two men had satisfied themselves that nothing of its late occupant remained.

"You think he's important?"

Finch looked up from poking between two loose boards. "Everyone we've come across in the case so far has reacted to Lisa Harcourt pretty strongly. It'd be queer if the man most closely related to her should not do so."

"Gurney seemed to think that he was neutral."

"Yes but what sort of neutrality? Armed or indifferent? They'd been married seventeen years." He straightened his back. The floorboards had yielded nothing more important than a little pile of dust and the top of a collar stud. He added, "Harcourt appears to have taken his furniture and effects with him when he left. And that looks more as if he struck a bargain with his wife than that he walked out on her in a fury—which in itself suggests a certain degree of indifference."

A sound from outside attracted his attention. A police car was turning in at the drive. It was followed by another and another.

Finch glanced at his wrist watch. "A quarter past four," he said. He went downstairs, followed by Slater. They met Peters coming in search of them. "The men have arrived from Bramshot, sir," he said.

There were a dozen of them in charge of a sergeant. He was a brisk man in his early forties. He stepped forward when he saw Finch and saluted. "Sergeant Pickering, sir, in charge of the search."

"Glad to meet you, Sergeant. You know what you have to do?"

"Find the Army mackintosh Mr. Fray was wearing. Also a whisky bottle bearing a 'Highland Burn' label."

"That's it. And, from the medical evidence, David Fray can't have had more than five minutes at the outside in which to dispose of them. On the other hand, he may just have wandered away before the murder and lost them." Finch added, "Have you arranged any means of communication?"

"We each have our whistles, sir. One short blast repeated at intervals means that the mac has been found; two, that it's the bottle. In either case, everyone to stay where they are unless recalled by one long blast from me."

"Good! That seems a very sensible arrangement. I'll

leave you to get on with it." He raised two fingers to the brim of his hat in salute. Then went back into the house.

Slater and he went upstairs again—to Lisa Harcourt's bedroom. It was beautiful and luxurious. The carpet was thick and soft to the feet, the air delicately scented. The bed appeared soft as a cloud and large as a billiard table.

There were some photographs of men, sentimentally inscribed—and more of Lisa herself.

Slater was drawn to these last. He regretted her death. It seemed such a waste. "She looks so gay," he commented. "Seductive too."

"I suppose if one were a realist one would have at least one sad photograph taken." Finch was opening the drawers of the dressing table as he spoke. They were so tidy that he concluded that Dimmick and not Lisa had had charge of them.

Slater turned, staring. "A sad one? Why?"

"In case one met with misfortune. But then one would want degrees of sadness." Finch was watching Dimmick going down the drive, a prim, decorous figure, neatly dressed, with hat and gloves, carrying a large black plastic shopping bag fastened with a zip. "You know, Archie," he added, turning from the window, "I believe I've got something there. A photograph to match every mood. The maid might change them when she brought up the early-morning tea."

Slater grinned. "Influenced by the post perhaps. Or her mistress's expression."

"Or her own feelings." Finch spoke slowly, held by the idea. He dropped his voice. "Madam, today you're going to die. Have you a photograph sufficiently despairing?" His mind dwelt momentarily on the manservant, Gurney.

"Wouldn't be many murders if the victim were warned beforehand," Slater remarked prosaically.

"Too true." Finch was searching among the photographs. "No photograph of David. And, stranger still, none of George Gessington."

"Perhaps he was waiting to get home to have some taken."

"Perhaps—yet it still remains odd. A woman in love usually insists on a photograph of the beloved to console her solitary hours."

A search of the room revealed what was to Finch an even stranger state of affairs. The room had yielded up the usual crop of letters, bills, receipts, and love letters from David Fray, but nothing at all from Gessington.

Finch was aware of a feeling of uneasiness creeping over his thoughts. It was bound up, he found, with a picture of Dimmick walking away from the house, carrying a large black bag.

"That's it!" he exclaimed. "That's what Gessington told Dimmick when he telephoned. To remove his letters and photographs."

Slater made for the door. "If Dimmick has them——"

Finch shook his head. "Dimmick *had* them," he corrected sadly. "It's my bet they're now back where they originated—with Mr. Gessington. I saw her leave the house about fifteen minutes ago."

"Blast!" said Slater, halting in his tracks. And then: "But why did he do it? Even if they were red-hot——" He broke off, listening.

Quite loudly and not far from the house one of the police whistles was sounding. It was a single short note, over and over.

The missing mackintosh had been found.

It was hanging in a clump of rhododendrons at the top of the drive. A branch had gone through it from hem to collar, first impaling its wearer and then taking it off his back. It hung some four feet up, giving a grotesque suggestion of being still occupied by a dwarf or a crouching figure.

"There's a path runs through the rhododendrons from the corner of the house to peter out in the woods," Sergeant Pickering explained. "It looks as if Mr. Fray got off the path, tripped over the broken azalea you see there, was thrown forward into the shrubs, and, what with the dark and his condition, had difficulty in finding his way out again."

Finch congratulated the sergeant, remarked that the

sun would soon be sinking behind the hill opposite, and left him to get on with the search.

"We'd better see if Gurney can rustle up some sandwiches for us," Finch remarked as they reached the house.

"Not yet you won't, sir," said Slater. "Look who's come." Superintendent Bannerman was stepping nimbly from a police car.

"I know. I've seen it too," Finch murmured. "Ferdinand the Bull. Never mind. If we keep quiet, perhaps it will go away again."

The Superintendent walked purposefully towards the front door.

"No luck," said Finch sadly. "I'd better go out and meet him."

They met on the doorstep. "I want to speak to you," said Bannerman, without any form of greeting. He looked loweringly about him.

"The drawing room, I think," said Finch.

The door shut and Bannerman, in the centre of the room, said accusingly, "What's all this about searching the garden and woods? It seems to me, Mr. Finch, that all you're going to do is to explain how the boy spent the missing hour. He could easily have let himself into the house and murdered Mrs. Harcourt on his way back from the woods."

"That's true. On the other hand, the situation here was a good deal more explosive than anyone imagined. For instance, Gurney was in love with the dead woman. Had been for years."

Bannerman stared. "Gurney? The manservant?"

"Why not? An oyster may be crossed in love." Here Slater would have murmured "Sheridan," had he not caught his superior's eye—a surprisingly chill and forbidding eye. He contented himself with a replica of Peters' polite little cough when that worthy had some information to impart.

Finch withdrew his gaze. "Gurney may have disliked the idea of Mrs. Harcourt's remarrying even more than did David Fray. He had motive, opportunity, and the right psychological setup for the crime." Finch had an almost passionate interest in human nature. Now as he mentally contemplated his suspects his face wore a look of innocent pleasure. "Then there's her half-brother, John Potter, and all those telephone calls."

"What kind of telephone calls?"

"Quite innocuous. That's what makes them so interesting. Two, three, or even four times a week he rang up Lisa Harcourt. To ask her out, to tell her some bit of local news, or just to pass the time of day. It was almost as if he were trying to convince himself that he liked her. Even, perhaps, that he didn't hate her."

"Theories, Mr. Finch." Bannerman slammed a great fist in the palm of his other hand. "Give me facts."

"You know that we found the mackintosh? No?" Finch explained, adding, "Well, here is a fact. If David Fray had stumbled in the direction of the house when he emerged from those shrubs last night, he would just about have reached the place where the maid, Dimmick, saw him last night."

Bannerman stared. "How d'you know where he came out?"

"We can tell by the number of branches he broke. We could, if necessary, plot his whole course inside the hollow shell of those rhododendrons by the white stumps of broken wood."

Bannerman's mind worked slowly. "But the maid says she heard him crossing the hall."

"She heard a man's footsteps."

"Two men? Perhaps she was lying. Otherwise it would be too much of a coincidence to be credible."

"It'd be a bit of a coincidence for David Fray to have gone into the house, murdered Mrs. Harcourt, and returned to fall at the same spot where he had been before."

Bannerman tugged at his lower lip. "I know which coincidence I'd like to believe."

"And really," Finch continued, ignoring this, "there's always the chance that the murderer was someone whom we haven't yet suspected. Someone who saw David Fray entering the gates of Belguardo. Someone who had long had murder in mind and required the perfect opportunity, the ideal scapegoat."

"But that would have been a premeditated murder. Not, as this one was, the sudden violence of someone provoked beyond bearing."

Finch looked at him in mild surprise. "But naturally he'd commit the murder as he'd imagine a drunken, jealous man might commit it. And it wouldn't have been so difficult. To have had the wish to murder he must have had hatred too." He added thoughtfully, "And then there's Lisa Harcourt's fortune. Who gets that? Obviously, someone who wouldn't have inherited if she'd lived to remarry."

Bannerman was a persistent if slow thinker. "So Mr. Fray may not have murdered Mrs. Harcourt after all?"

"If we discover that Lisa Harcourt said or did something so outrageous that David Fray might have been expected to have been turned into a madman, then we must believe the second of the two coincidences. The fact that she had fallen in love with someone else was hardly motive enough for what was done to her."

The search continued. Stumbling and swearing, the police pushed their way in and out of the ever-spreading rhododendrons, becoming more and more certain that their quest was hopeless. How could they expect to find one small object in all this gloomy, sprawling thicket?

Gradually they were reinforced by some of the villagers home from work. These included Fred Best from the White Hart. Spread out like beaters at a shoot, they advanced very slowly, and the voice of Superintendent Bannerman goaded them on.

Finch and Slater had a hurried meal of sandwiches and tea. They had scarcely finished when a police constable appeared. Mr. Fray, he said, looking embarrassed, was at the front door.

The young man had not entered the house. He was standing quietly outside in the hot sunshine. He was of medium build, and had a look of race and breeding. His eyes were grey and heavily fringed. In spite of delicately cut features, there was a good deal of character in his face.

His lips closed firmly and his chin was square and determined.

It struck Finch with a sense of surprise that, in all the long hours of the day, he had given scarcely a thought to him as a human being, had not tried to picture him or his way of life. Now he was conscious of a feeling of familiarity. It was almost as if they had met before. But there was no recognition in the young man's level, if bloodshot, gaze.

"You're the police, aren't you?" he asked abruptly. "I'm David Fray." He paused, as if for a moment he had been struck by the new and sinister connotation that name now bore. "I thought that if I came up here and went into the house I might remember what happened last night."

"How much do you remember?"

"Of what happened after I got here? Nothing. I remember Ted Dudley showing me the paragraph in the *Evening Echo*. He said——But you won't want to hear all that."

"Indeed, yes. It will help to recreate the day in your mind."

David nodded acceptance. "Ted said, 'I say, old chap, isn't this your lady friend?' I remember feeling just as if someone had kicked me in the stomach. I didn't answer. At least, I don't think I did. I just walked out of the place and back to my room. I had a bottle of whisky there. I drank some neat in my tooth glass." He smiled faintly and without humour. "After a bit I felt awfully sad and rather romantic. I remember experiencing what might be described as a great desire to be alone. It was all rather gloomy and romantic, and I decided to get out the car and come down here. A sort of farewell party all to myself."

"Did you know that Mrs. Harcourt was back?"

"Hadn't an idea of it."

"Then who told you?"

"No one. At least, I don't think so. That's the awful part of it." David was frowning painfully. "I must just have met her by accident." He shook his head as if to clear it. There was a sick look on his face.

"D'you remember going into the White Hart?" They were walking slowly towards the house as they spoke.

"Yes—and that's the last thing I *do* remember. It's after that that it's a blank."

"And when your brother-in-law told you?"

Said David in a low voice, "I couldn't believe it."

Finch paused outside the open front door. "Well," he said mildly, "suppose we get on with the experiment. We'll go into the house. Then you come in by whatever way was customary."

David nodded. He ran his tongue over his lips as if they had gone dry and wiped the palms of his hands on his trouser legs.

Finch and Slater went into the house. They took up their position in the black and white hall. Already it was growing shadowy. The stillness seemed intensified by the project in hand.

David Fray paused in the doorway, staring in. The light shining down on his fair head deepened the shadows on his face. He no longer seemed conscious of the presence of the two C.I.D. men.

His eyes—they were, Finch reflected, the second pair of haunted eyes which had looked on the scene that day—passed over the hall. "I must have come in this way," he muttered to himself. "I always did. Lisa didn't like anyone to go round by the terrace. There'd have been flowers and that silly white china satyr holding up a light. Lisa wouldn't have heard me coming. The fountain would have drowned any sound. She wouldn't have known that anyone was there until I'd actually reached the inner room."

He had crossed the hall as he spoke. There was about him an air of grim purpose and determination. Enter a murderer, Finch thought. He wondered whether the young man's allusion to the light had been deliberately misleading.

"I came in. She was lying on that chair. Reading the latest best seller perhaps. And smoking. She smoked a lot. She'd look up and see me. And she'd say . . ." His voice trailed away. His face in the shadows looked white and strained. "I can't remember," he said in a flat voice.

He took up his part again with the same hurried muttering, like that of a feverish patient. The light was going from the garden room, and his face was ghastly in the greenish reflection from the plants. "Perhaps she didn't speak. Perhaps seeing her there and knowing that she was going to marry someone else..."

He paused—a long pause, as if he were attentive to something in that room, as if he sought desperately to join himself with the events of the previous night. "We used to make a joke about that wretched plant. 'How is the *Philodendron scandens?*' I'd say. And she——" He broke off. A nerve twitched at the side of his mouth. Beads of sweat sprang out on his forehead.

"What would she say to that?" Finch asked in a voice so soft that it scarcely disturbed the timeless quiet.

"She'd say, 'As you see, it hasn't strangled me yet.' That's what she'd say. And I——" A harsh gasping breath that was half a sob broke from him. "But she wouldn't have said that last night. Or did she?"

He walked slowly forward into the room. His eye fell on the chalk outline. For a moment he stared down in horror, struck dumb as its full implication sank in.

For the first time he looked directly at Finch. "But why did I do it?" he asked him in a low shaken voice. "I knew that she'd finished with me. I knew it when she went to Italy. She never wrote to me once the whole time. I wrote every day for a bit and then I stopped. I tried to pretend that everything would be all right once she got back, but I didn't really believe it."

"I suppose you noticed a change in her even before she decided to go abroad?" Finch asked, testing him in the light of what Gurney had said.

David shook his neat blond head. "Her decision took me completely by surprise." He smiled thinly. "It—it just seemed incredible at the time."

"And when she had gone? How did you feel then?"

David shrugged. "What is a drug addict like when his supply is suddenly cut off?" he asked drearily.

"As bad as that, was it? Well, let's get 'on. Mrs.

Harcourt is lying propped up on all those cushions. You've walked round to where you now stand."

"Mark says I caught the ends of her scarf and strangled her." He was staring blankly into space. "She was fond of scarves. She had such a lovely neck." He looked at Finch with sick eyes. His face was paler than ever. "But why didn't she run? I suppose she thought it inconceivable that I should attack her." His voice rose. "Damme! It *is* inconceivable. What devil's words did she say to me to make me do it?" He stood a moment. Then he struck his forehead with a clenched fist. "I can't remember! I can't remember anything."

"D'you remember having a drink in here?"

David's eyes went automatically to the bar. "No."

"D'you remember what the room looked like when you came in? All the lights burning?"

David smiled his thin, smile. "There you *have* got it wrong. Lisa would never have turned on more than the one."

"*You* turned them on. Remember?"

The young man made no attempt to deny it. "Did I? But why? Why should I have done it? To look at her, perhaps? To see her for the last time?" He was trembling slightly.

This was a possibility that had not occurred to Finch. Yet it might well have occurred to a man mad with jealousy. To look on the face of a false love. To see every lineament, every fleeting expression. And then to strike it down. Obliterate it forever. It would explain the violent, otherwise senseless dropping of the stone urn on the dead face.

It was not often, he reflected grimly, that a suspect suggested a plausible motive for his own crime. In fact he couldn't remember its happening before. But David was in a special category. *The man who couldn't remember.* He might well have made the suggestion because, subconsciously, he did remember. And that that was the way it had been.

The three men went back to the hall.

Peters was there. "Evening, Mr. Fray, sir." His honest

red face managed to look anxious, fond, and encouraging all at one and the same time.

"Evening, Peters. This is a nice mess I've got myself into this time," David said with a ghastly assumption of ease. He smiled, and again the sense of familiarity seized on Finch.

"Haven't we met before somewhere?"

"I don't think so."

Unthinkingly Peters gave his respectful cough.

Finch turned. "Yes, Peters?"

The constable looked unhappy. "I wasn't going to say anything, sir."

Finch walked towards him. "I think you were."

Peters looked more unhappy than ever. "No, sir. Just a cough, sir. Caught me all of a sudden."

David was smiling faintly, puzzled, a little amused. "I'm quite certain we haven't met before," he said. "After all, I can still remember everything that happened to me before last night."

They went outside. The voice of the Superintendent was raised suddenly. It rose harshly from the woods like the cry of a pheasant.

A pale smile flitted across David's face. "Bannerman," he said. And then: "What's he doing?"

"He's directing the search for the whisky bottle you had with you when you left the White Hart. I suppose you don't remember what you did with it?"

"Threw it away, I suppose—but hardly down in the woods."

"Your old Army mackintosh was found hanging in the centre of a clump of rhododendrons."

"Was I wearing that? I must have been soused." He smiled briefly, turned away, and vanished down a path through the rhododendrons, going towards the village.

The light under the trees began to go. The sweating beaters gave up the search whilst Bannerman and the two C.I.D. men held a hurried consultation in the hall.

"No good going on any longer," said Bannerman gloomily. "It's not quite nine o'clock, but already the light's tricky under those trees. And that bottle won't be easy to find even by daylight."

"Of course, it may not be there at all," said Finch. "It may be lying somewhere between here and the White Hart."

"If it were, someone would have found it by now," said Bannerman. "The village is behind this search to a man. It's only the darkness that's against us. The hills, and all those damn trees——" He stared morosely out of the window, gnawing his lower lip.

There was a knock on the door. Amy Dimmick came in, a pale smile on her face.

"Excuse me, sir," she said to Finch. "But I've been thinking about Mr. Fray, and I did wonder whether perhaps he went to where he and the mistress used to picnic last summer."

Bannerman whirled on her. "Where's that?" he barked.

Dimmick looked affronted at his rough manner. "It's an open space right under the hedge which shuts the farm up above from the woods," she said distantly. "It's before you get to the Swiss Cottage. If you follow the hedge you can't miss it."

"Thank you very much, Miss Dimmick," said Finch in his pleasant voice. "We should just have time to look there before the light fails."

"I'm sure I wish you success," said Dimmick primly. She left the room.

Slater stared after her. "It seems she's behind this search too. This morning she was all for revenge."

"And this evening she's acting for our Mr. Gessington. I told you she was acquisitive. I admit such a complete change is a bit surprising——"

"Oh, come on!" cried Bannerman impatiently. "While you stand talking it's getting darker."

The three men made their way diagonally towards the boundary hedge. It was shadowy under the trees and very close and hot. They came to the hedge and saw beyond it a sunken lane, fringed with cob nuts, and beyond that a field of stubble with some sheep in it.

They walked along under the hedge. It was rough

going, with bramble bushes, rabbit holes, and the roots of trees to trip them up. But suddenly they came on an open space. It was covered with rough grass and bracken, enclosed by trees and yet open to the sun and sky. The daylight still lingered here, and the roof of the Swiss Cottage was not far away.

It was at once obvious that someone had been lying there, breaking the bracken and flattening the grass. Some-one who had been sick too. The whisky bottle was there, containing, to Bannerman's obvious relief, dregs of whisky but also something else.

A small bunch of keys on a ring.

"And from their rather disgusting condition," said Slater, "neither they nor the whisky bottle can have been planted there."

"David's keys?" said Bannerman. He took them from Finch. "Then he couldn't have opened the front door." He stared, bewildered, from them to the C.I.D. Inspector. "Then who was it that woman heard crossing the hall last night?"

Chapter
7

The Bramshot Police drove away. They took Reeves and Dickenson with them. Peters was to stay on duty until another man came out from the town to relieve him.

Before he left, Superintendent Bannerman made a point of thanking Dimmick for her suggestion. He took her into the drawing room and explained. "So you see it is possible that it was not Mr. Fray whom you heard in the house," he ended.

Finch, listening in silence, saw the woman's eyes open wide, burlesquing pleasure at the news. But deep down in them was a sudden stark astonishment.

Finch decided that he would call it a day. He told Peters. It seemed to outrage the P.C.'s sense of hospitality.

"It don't seem right, sir, me not being there. But what must be, must. I'll give you a key, and if you wouldn't mind helping yourself to anything you see..." He was acompanying Finch and Slater to their car. He added confidentially, "There's a dozen bottles of beer in a bucket down the well, if so be you have a mind for it."

"Beer! That loveliest of words! Peters, I can see you're a man after my own heart." Finch paused behind the steering wheel. "By the way, I meant to ask you, what other messes has Mr. Fray got himself into?"

"Other messes? None as I know of—barring the divorce." Peters face cleared. "Oh, you was thinking of what he said. He meant when he was a nipper. Very high-spirited he was—like his sister."

"Mrs. Warry?" Finch noticed with interest the same blank look come over the constable's ruddy face. He wondered what was wrong with the doctor's wife. Some ghastly facial disfigurement, perhaps? Or was she mentally deranged? He drove slowly away, turning the possibilities over in his lively and inventive mind.

As the car turned into the highway Finch switched on the headlights. They illuminated the figure of a man walking up the road towards them. He was short and squat and wore a gay tartan cotton shirt outside a pair of threadbare corduroy trousers. He had a round red face, blunt features, and prominent greenish eyes. Steel-rimmed spectacles balanced low down on his short broad nose. This was Owen Sturgis of the *Daily Record*. He recognised Finch's car and sprang into the centre of the road, waving wildly.

Finch slammed on his brakes. "Hullo, Owen! You tired of life?"

Sturgis grinned. "I knew our police were wonderful." He came up to the car and rested arms, hairy as coconuts, on the door.

"I'm surprised to see you here," Finch remarked. "Does it mean that the mystery of the body in the furnace has been solved?"

"It means that I'd rather be down here with the boy murderer and you."

"I'm touched," said Finch. "You the only one?"

Sturgis nodded. "The others labour under the delusion that the solution of this crime is obvious and foolproof, even when you get to work on it," adding tolerantly, "But they'll learn."

"I don't know that I altogether like that remark. You know me. I just like things to be ordinary. When they're not, I get nervous."

Sturgis grinned. "Of course I know you. If I didn't, I wouldn't be here. How's it going?"

"It has its points."

Sturgis looked at him, a gleam in his shrewd green eyes. "Such as the great Mr. Gessington?"

"Impressive, isn't he?"

"Not as impressive as his old man. I come from the same North Country town, so I know. He looked like a retired bruiser and had the heart of a maiden aunt. He was a pillar of the Non-Conformist Church"—which, Finch reflected, must account for his son's familiarity with the Bible—"and a great anti-man. He was anti pretty near everything that makes life enjoyable."

"And George Gessington?"

"He and his old man agreed to differ. He's a social animal. Fond of society, women, the theatre—he's even been known to turn up at a race meeting, though I doubt if Pop ever knew that. He'd probably have cut him off with a shilling if he had."

Finch nodded. "How's he getting on at the White Hart?"

"When I got there he was in the public bar, treating the locals. He was drinking whisky and looking, as you said, impressive—very impressive—and just oozing money and power. He was saying that he didn't believe that that young chap, David Fray, was the murderer. What's more, he seemed prepared to back his belief with money."

Finch's brows shot up. "What?"

"It's a fact. At least he'd be grateful for any evidence to prove his contention. And money's the form gratitude usually takes in a man like that."

"Did he say why he was prepared to give young Fray the benefit of the doubt?"

Sturgis pulled down the corners of his long, froglike mouth. "He said it'd have been what his old man would have done in the same circumstances."

"And would he?"

"Oh, sure, sure! Only his old man never did have his prospective bride flattened by a stone urn."

Finch nodded. "It's certainly big-hearted of George," he murmured. Adding pensively, "But not altogether convincing." He told Sturgis about the absence of letters or photographs and his suspicions concerning them. "I expect he's burnt them by now—a photograph being a bit stiff to go down the lav."

"Want me to look in his bedroom grate?"

"If you wouldn't mind."

"Of course not. Murder, theft, arson. Just mention it, and I'm your man."

"Thanks. Archie can move up, and we'll give you a lift back to the village. We're going to have something to eat at the local police station where we're staying. You can ring me up there."

As the car moved on, Finch told Sturgis what had happened up to date. "Of course," he ended, "the finding of the keys proves nothing except that David Fray couldn't have let himself into the house by the front door. But Mrs. Harcourt might have let him in. He might have gone round and in by the terrace—but somehow I don't feel he did."

Sturgis chuckled, a single diabolical chuckle. "I bet you don't. That's what I'm counting on."

Finch put him down out of sight of the White Hart. He was glad that he had taken this precaution, for when he drove past, he saw Fred Best's large pale face at the bar window.

They had no difficulty in finding the police station. In a village that was all indefinite contours and soft colours it was angular, ugly, and vividly red.

As the two C.I.D. men walked up the neat cement path they were thinking of Peters' beer from the well, ice-cold and beaded with moisture. They felt that they had deserved it, but they were destined to be disappointed. They had only had time to carry their suitcases upstairs when the telephone began to ring.

Owen Sturgis was at the other end. "I thought you'd like to know that as I passed Fred Best's private room I heard him telling someone over the telephone that the coast was clear. He didn't say which coast, but I can guess."

"Thanks. I'll get back there by what's known as devious routes," Finch assured him. "What about the letters and the photographs?"

"Something was burnt in the grate in George Gessington's room. I couldn't tell what it was because the ashes had been ground into powder. Most efficient job—but then, he's probably a most efficient chap."

As Finch hung up, his mind was busy. To whom had the message been sent? Not to the man of money, George Gessington, for he was on the spot. Nor was there any reason to believe that it had been to John Potter or Francis Harcourt, for they would surely have first met and tried to assess the potentialities of the detective in charge of the case. There remained, then, David Fray and the unknown, the puller of strings——

"Yes, but if there's something going on at Belguardo, what is Peters doing about it?" asked Slater.

"That," said Finch in his soft voice, "is one of the things I mean to find out."

He remembered the farm track which ran along the crest of the hills above the house. He decided that they would leave the car there and make their way down on foot.

Dusk was falling as they went through the village, past the gates of the Hall, past the quarry where Ambrose Potter had met the young woman who was to become his second wife. They turned off the Bramshot road and went bumping and jolting over the uneven surface of the sunken lane.

They stopped the car and got out. It was very quiet. In spite of being so high up, scarcely a breath of air stirred. The trees towered above them, dark and silent, their long shadows stretching across their path to the stubble field beyond.

They entered the woods, and darkness engulfed them. They went slipping and stumbling down the hill, added by the pinpoint light from their torches. They emerged close to the bungalow.

There was a light in one window. Finch peered in and saw Gurney sitting immobile at a table. There was a cup of coffee cooling in front of him, but he was not drinking it. He was alone, staring straight in front of him with the light shining down, carving the lines deeper on his ugly face.

They came out onto the terrace. The white house gleamed palely in the dusk, like a pearl, and the utter silence of a country night fell about them.

They peered cautiously into the garden room. It was

dark and seemingly empty. They walked round the house, their rubber-soled shoes making no sound. They looked in at the drawing-room windows. There was no one there. They reached the corner of the house and halted, caught by the sound of voices. They looked at each other in surprise, for it was a woman's voice, youthful, and, to Finch, vaguely familiar.

Peering round the corner they could see the shadowy outline of the stout constable and, facing him, a female figure, slight, boyish, with long slender legs.

"But, Peters, you could come with me. I wouldn't touch anything."

"It can't be done, ma'am. You must see that. It's my duty to see that no one enters the house without the Inspector says so." Peters sounded desperate, goaded, as if he knew himself to be no match for his companion.

Finch stepped into view. The result was unexpected. The woman threw a startled look over her shoulder. Then she took to her heels. Across the gravel sweep, between the rhododendrons, and away.

Slater was outraged. He set off in pursuit, his long legs gaining on the fleeing girl.

"Run, Miss Harry!" Peters called. "Run!"

Why, the old so-and-so, Finch thought. And in the middle of the thought his mind clicked and he had it in his grasp: that tantalising half memory that had eluded him earlier when he had been with David Fray.

Harriet! Harriet Warry—née Fray. He had forgotten her surname, but he remembered her well enough. A nice kid, a nice happy kid. Clever too.

For all Slater's superior speed, Harriet might have eluded him among the shadowy shrubs had she not caught her foot in a root and fallen.

Slater was standing over her in a minute. "Allow me to give you a hand up," he said sarcastically.

"You just try it," said Harriet furiously. She rose to her feet, brushing the twigs from her shorts and pushing the fair hair out of her eyes. She was looking rather uneasily over her shoulder at Finch's dark, advancing outline.

"What made you think we wouldn't be about?" Slater asked.

"I have my spies," she answered haughtily.

"Pretty inefficient ones."

The slow pink spread over Harriet's face. "Oh, I see it now. Someone heard Fred talking to me over the telephone and warned you about it. What a mean, sneaking thing to do."

"Well, I'll be——" Slater bit back the words.

"Now I begin to see daylight," said Finch, advancing on her. "My old chum, Harriet. You always were a bossy little thing."

"Septimus, I wasn't." Harriet shifted, storklike, from one long leg to the other. She looked very small and defenceless between the two tall men, but this, as Finch knew and Slater suspected, was misleading. "I was so desperate, though. And," she added beguilingly, "I remembered how clever you were."

"Now, young Harriet, soft words butter no parsnips." He looked at her more closely. "And there was I, thinking that young Mrs. Warry must have been hideously disfigured in some accident. Or even that she was out of her mind."

Harriet stared. "Why on earth should you have thought that?"

"Because whenever your name came up, Peters looked so unhappy."

Harriet's soft pink mouth widened uncontrollably into a smile, and her eyes twinkled.

"It's nothing to laugh at. Suborning the police is a pretty serious offence."

"I haven't suborned the police. I haven't suborned anyone."

"Didn't I hear Peters shout to you to run—and he must have known I wanted to speak to you."

"Oh, Peters! That wasn't suborning. That—that was just natural. I've known him all my life and he's always been on my side." She added quickly, "Until tonight. You must have heard him refusing to let me into the house."

"Yes, I heard him." Finch's tone was dry. "Very strong-minded of him too."

A dimple appeared in Harriet's cheek. Hurriedly she suppressed it. "I thought you'd knocked off for the night."

"I'm sorry to have disappointed you."

"It's not me as much as Uncle Charles," said Harriet candidly. "I promised him I'd keep out of your way."

"Uncle Charles!" Finch echoed pensively. "I must admit I'm surprised at your Uncle Charles."

"He would never have listened to me if he and the Superintendent could have agreed," she hastened to assure him. "But they were having such a terrible row and neither would give in. Of course, Uncle Charles could have overridden Bannerman, but it wouldn't have been very pleasant for him. Besides, they've known each other all their lives."

Finch nodded. "How nice that is. Everyone knows everyone." He added, "And I suppose they all know that you were responsible for getting me down here."

"Oh, no, Septimus. I didn't tell anyone but Mark—my husband. I can't really understand how Peters knew."

From out of the shadows cast by the house came the smallest and most deprecating of coughs. Harriet heard it and interpreted it correctly.

"Oh, dear! I remember now!" She was conscience-stricken. "I was in the hall when I told Mark. Gladys Paisley must have overheard me."

"Your maid? I see." Finch added gloomily. "By rights I ought to ring up the Yard and ask to be replaced."

"If you do, Uncle Charles will arrest David and then the real murderer will never be caught."

Finch was silent a moment. "I can see your point. Only you must see mine. If I stay I'll go on to the end—whatever that end may be."

Harriet nodded. "Of course you must do that."

"I have a horrid feeling you'll be sorry."

Her face whitened a little. "No," she said obstinately. "No."

"All right! We'll leave things as they are." Finch spoke briskly. "Peters, you stay on guard. Harriet, you and I will go and sit on one of the seats on the terrace and talk. Archie can see we're not overheard."

"Yes, Septimus," said Harriet meekly.

It was wonderfully peaceful. The air was warm. The flowers glimmered palely and their scent hung heavily about them. There was a faint glow behind the hill where the moon was about to rise. The only sound came from an occasional night beetle droning past.

"Why did you come here tonight, Harriet?"

"It was because of David. He had a—a sort of half memory of something he saw in the hall last night. Something unusual, I mean. Only he can't remember what it was. So I thought that if I could have a look round I might spot something that was different."

"You shall have a look presently." Finch felt for his cigarette case. So David Fray remembers being in the hall, he thought. He felt disappointed. When they were both smoking he said, "Who do *you* think killed Mrs. Harcourt?"

Harriet looked at him, startled. "I—I hadn't thought. I never got past thinking that it wasn't David. Nothing," she added firmly, "will ever persuade me that he did it."

"In that case, suppose you give your mind to the question now. And I mean now while I'm with you. I don't want you getting any bright ideas and testing them out when you're alone. This is murder. And if your brother is innocent, then the murderer is still loose and on the prowl."

Harriet shivered in spite of the warm air. "How horrible that sounds." She looked at him gravely with eyes as grey and level as her brother's—and a great deal less bloodshot. "I suppose Gurney might have done it. He's a violent man. He once nearly strangled a man in the White Hart who had spoken disrespectfully of Lisa. Then there's John Potter. She was always trying to annoy him." Gravely she considered and then dismissed him. "He never did lose his temper, so I don't see why he should now.

"There's Phoebe. Lisa was always needling her. About her clothes, her housekeeping, her—oh, just about everything she did or didn't do. And Phoebe's awfully matter-of-fact. I can imagine her deciding that Lisa ought to be put down and making a thorough job of it. Only she's so lazy. I just can't imagine her walking all the way here to do it.

Introducing the first and only complete hardcover collection of Agatha Christie's mysteries

Now you can enjoy the
greatest mysteries ever written
in a magnificent
Home Library Edition.

Discover Agatha Christie's world of mystery, adventure and intrigue

Agatha Christie's timeless tales of mystery and suspense offer something for every reader—mystery fan or not—young and old alike. And now, you can build a complete hardcover library of her world-famous mysteries by subscribing to <u>The Agatha Christie Mystery Collection.</u>

This exciting Collection is your passport to a world where mystery reigns supreme. Volume after volume, you and your family will enjoy mystery reading at its very best.

You'll meet Agatha Christie's world-famous detectives like Hercule Poirot, Jane Marple, and the likeable Tommy and Tuppence Beresford.

In your readings, you'll visit Egypt, Paris, England and other exciting destinations where murder is always on the itinerary. And wherever you travel, you'll become deeply involved in some of the most ingenious and diabolical plots ever invented ... "cliff-hangers" that only Dame Agatha could create!

It all adds up to mystery reading that's so good ... it's almost criminal. And it's yours every month with <u>The Agatha Christie Mystery Collection.</u>

Solve the greatest mysteries of all time. The Collection contains all of Agatha Christie's classic works including *Murder on the Orient Express, Death on the Nile, And Then There Were None, The ABC Murders* and her ever-popular whodunit, *The Murder of Roger Ackroyd.*

Each handsome hardcover volume is Smythe sewn and printed on high quality acid-free paper so it can withstand even the most murderous treatment. Bound in Sussex-blue simulated leather with gold titling, <u>The Agatha Christie Mystery Collection</u> will make a tasteful addition to your living room, or den.

Ride the Orient Express for 10 days without obligation. To introduce you to the Collection, we're inviting you to examine the classic mystery, *Murder on the Orient Express*, without risk or obligation. If you're not completely satisfied, just return it within 10 days and owe nothing.

However, if you're like the millions of other readers who love Agatha Christie's thrilling tales of mystery and suspense, keep *Murder on the Orient Express* and pay just $7.95 plus postage and handling.

You will then automatically receive future volumes once a month as they are published on a fully returnable, 10-day free-examination basis. No minimum purchase is required, and you may cancel your subscription at any time.

This unique collection is not sold in stores. It's available only through this special offer. So don't miss out, begin your subscription now. Just mail this card today.

☐ Yes! Please send me *Murder on the Orient Express* for a 10-day free-examination and enter my subscription to <u>The Agatha Christie Mystery Collection</u>. If I keep *Murder on the Orient Express*, I will pay just $7.95 plus postage and handling and receive one additional volume each month on a fully returnable 10-day free-examination basis. There is no minimum number of volumes to buy, and I may cancel my subscription at any time.   07013

☐ I prefer the deluxe edition bound in genuine leather for $24.95 per volume plus shipping and handling, with the same 10-day free-examination.   97054

Name_____

Address_____

City_____ State_____ Zip_____

X
**Send No Money...
But Act Today!**

BUSINESS REPLY CARD

FIRST CLASS   PERMIT NO. 2154   HICKSVILLE, N.Y.

Postage will be paid by addressee:

The Agatha Christie
Mystery Collection
Bantam Books
P.O. Box 956
Hicksville, N.Y. 11802

Then there's old Miss Budgen. Lisa was often most horribly rude to her. I don't know why she went on seeing her, except that, in some horrible way, they were two of a kind. But she couldn't have done the murder because one of her arms was stiff. The muscles had shrunk or something."

"So out goes the Admiral's daughter as a suspect. And, let me tell you, I've been assured by Dimmick that Miss Budgen loved Mrs. Harcourt dearly."

"She couldn't have loved her," Harriet retorted. "She was just out for what she could get. She was Lisa's spy. Always collecting bits of news for her in the village. John—John Potter thinks Lisa paid her for it, but I don't think anyone would do that."

"True bits of news?"

"Yes, she had a mad sort of flair for finding things out. John called them—Lisa, Dimmick, and Miss Budgen—the three assassins, because they were always killing something. A reputation or—or happiness," Harriet added in a small voice, "Lisa never saw anyone happy without wanting to destroy their happiness."

"Being rejected by her fellows in her childhood probably had something to do with that," said Finch prosaically. He was thinking, not of the dead woman, but of his own instinctive feeling that Miss Budgen was important. He blamed himself for not having followed it up. It was an omission that must be remedied. He added, "Miss Budgen's been hanging round the drive gates off and on all day."

"I expect she wanted to see what was going on."

"There may be more in it than that," said Finch thoughtfully. "A woman of that sort was bound to be one of the first to learn that Lisa Harcourt was home. In which case she'd have been certain to have come round to see her. There would have been the news of the village to retail, her own pickings——" He paused for a moment. Then he said, "Yes, she must certainly have seen Lisa before her death."

Harriet shivered. "You make everything sound so—sinister."

"Important—not sinister." He smiled at her, adding briskly, "How about Mr. Harcourt as a murderer?"

Harriet frowned thoughtfully. "I can imagine him murdering Lisa—but not like that. He—he's proud and—and rather melancholy, like a Spanish grandee. If he had decided to kill her he'd have gone about it in some awfully subtle way with a great deal of planning behind it. I can imagine him handing her a cup of cold poison and being frightfully polite about the whole thing, but not losing his temper and—and strangling her."

Finch looked at her sideways through the dusk, without turning his head. "And your brother?"

Harriet's face clouded over. "David has a quick temper. He—oh, I can't imagine him committing a murder, but if he did, it would be just like this one. Done on the spur of the moment and with no finesse." She added sadly, "I think he believes he did do it."

Finch nodded. "I think so too."

"I haven't told him yet about your finding the keys."

"Who told you that, Fred Best?"

"Yes. You know what villages are like."

"Yes, I know," said Finch comfortably. "How did your brother come to meet Lisa Harcourt in the first place?"

"It was at the school sports. David was a schoolmaster and Lisa was one of the guests that day. It was just bad luck, because that sort of thing wasn't in her line."

"Malignant fate, eh?" They were silent a moment; then he said, "Let's talk about something more cheerful than murder. Your marriage, for instance."

Said Harriet in a low voice, "That's hardly more cheerful—and not much more alive."

"I see. I'm sorry. Was it—Mrs. Harcourt?"

"Not altogether. It began before that." Harriet explained about the move, her own delight in the return to the scenes of her childhood, and her husband's changed attitude towards her.

A little pause followed. Then Finch said, "I suppose it never occurred to you that in your husband's state of health he may have bitterly resented your pleasure in what probably seemed to him little short of a living death?"

Harriet was shocked. "Oh, no! Mark isn't like that. He'd never be so petty."

"You'd be surprised how petty a sick man can be," said Finch dryly.

Harriet shook her head. "It wasn't that. I'm sure of it." She sighed unhappily. "Oh, Septimus, he isn't the man I married."

"Any idea who he is?"

"There's no need to laugh."

Finch laid his hand over hers. "I'm not laughing, Harriet. Whatever else I may be doing, I'm not laughing."

An added chill crept over the girl's spirits. "Septimus, who *did* kill Lisa?" she asked, whispering. And a faint breath of wind carried her words to her companion, giving to them an unreal and slightly clandestine air.

He looked at her gravely. "I wish I knew, Harriet."

They strolled slowly back to the house, Harriet's arm through his. He was just as she had remembered him. Such a *comfortable* person in time of trouble, she thought.

"Do they go to bed early at the Hall?"

"What a queer question! No, not before eleven at the earliest."

"Good! Then I think I'll go up there tonight. You've whetted my appetite."

She pressed his arm. "Don't say that, Septimus. As if you were hunting them. I've known them all my life."

"But I *am* hunting someone. Someone I must catch, because once a man has murdered, he's liable to do it again. Once he's realised how easy it is to take life, it seems to him the perfect answer to any problem. Besides, killing arouses a great and wicked pride, and that's a dangerous thing in itself."

Peters had not turned on the lights in the hall. He sat rather sadly in the dark and wished that his affection for "Miss Harry" had not betrayed him.

He rose heavily to his feet when he saw the two men from the Yard and Mrs. Warry. He would have switched on the lights, but Finch gripped his arm to stop him. It was a reassuring grip, and Peters' heart lightened.

"The lights weren't on when your brother was here last night," Finch told Harriet.

"Not on?" She was dismayed. "But then David couldn't have seen anything in here."

"Nothing static, no. But if he saw something moving——"

Harriet caught her breath, spoke softly, since the house seemed held in an intense quietness. "Something— or someone? The real murderer perhaps. On the stairs— or going through a doorway. A shadow that moved——" Her voice died as the full implication of what she had said sunk in.

Somone David knew. A familiar outline that he may have recognised at the time. Someone, then, that she knew too. Someone willing to hide behind David, leaving him to take the blame——

The telephone shrilled suddenly, an unbearable reverberation on her quivering brain.

Slater answered it. He handed the receiver to his superior. "Superintendent Bannerman on the line, sir."

"That you, Mr. Finch? I've been trying to get hold of you for some time." Bannerman's voice boomed through the silent room. "This is a nice thing. Dr. Warry was at Belguardo last night. A Mr. Sowerby saw him. Reliable chap. A bank manager. Saw his car going in at the drive at about ten o'clock or thereabouts. Saw the doctor, too, in the light from his headlamps."

Finch had had a moment of prescience when Bannerman had begun to speak, but it had come too late. The damage had been done. "Thanks," he said awkwardly. "That's very interesting." He replaced the receiver, cut off the Superintendent in mid-boom.

It seemed very quiet again now. No one attempted to switch on the light. It was as if only darkness made the situation bearable.

Harriet stood rigid, staring at the telephone with a sort of fascinated horror. Slowly she withdrew her gaze. She stared at Finch bleakly. There seemed no way out of the situation in which they found themselves.

"So you were right," said Harriet at last. "Quite right.

I shouldn't have sent for you." Her voice broke. She turned on her heel and ran from the house.

"This," said Finch sadly, "is one hell of a case."

Harriet fled through the rhododendrons like a lost soul, her mind in utter confusion, whilst darker and darker thoughts followed each other until, at last, she seemed caught up in a nightmare more horrible than anything she had imagined possible.

Her own home loomed up, square and comfortably proportioned. Only it wasn't a home any longer. Indeed, she did not see how she was going to go on living with Mark. For the first time she was thankful that, since coming to Paradon, they had occupied separate bedrooms.

Mark came into the hall. He might have been waiting for her. He looked a man of desperate decision. "Harriet, I've something to tell you."

She paused, her face a white, defensive mask. "You're too late," she told him. "I know already. You were at Belguardo last night." She moved towards the staircase.

"That's what I wanted to explain——"

She paused on the stairs, looking back at him. "Keep your explanations for the police. I don't need them." She was conscious suddenly of her own utter weariness, of great banks of fatigue settling over her. She heard her voice clear and distinct, and yet as if it spoke from a long way off. "Now I understand," it said, and with every word it diminished, until at last it was less than a whisper, "how important it was to you that matters were left as they were—that everyone should go on believing David was guilty."

Chapter
8

To Finch it seemed that the flavour had gone out of the investigation. "There's a saying, 'Never do business with friends.' It ought to be amended to, 'Never go detecting for friends,'" he grumbled to his sergeant.

The two of them were on their way to the Hall, but merely in preference to going to Waltons to interview Harriet's craven husband. Finch expected nothing of the household. Curiosity, he told himself, had died. Phoebe Potter might be a one-eyed albino and he wouldn't even pause to wonder what John Potter had seen in her.

The moon was up and the Hall, bathed in its chilly light and seen close at hand, appeared as gloomy and forbidding as it had done by day when viewed across the valley.

Finch rang the bell. As he heard it jangling somewhere inside he was conscious of a faint stir of curiosity. Harriet or no Harriet, he could not help speculating. After a little while the door was opened by Phoebe Potter, a very stout dachshund at her heels.

Her appearance did nothing to lessen Finch's interest. Here was no one-eyed albino but a ripe and opulent beauty—a big, deep-bosomed woman with a pale skin set off by a black chiffon, ankle-length dinner frock. She had corn-coloured hair and round baby-blue eyes. She moved slowly and lazily. Her voice when she spoke was sweet and indolent.

For all that, Finch thought that Harriet had underestimated Phoebe Potter. She had the rather terrifying tenacity of the single-minded. He could imagine that, had she felt it expedient, this white and gold goddess would have found the necessary energy to take her to Belguardo— or anywhere else.

He introduced himself and his sergeant. "I'm afraid this is a very late call. If you'd like us to come back tomorrow, please say so."

"Oh, no! Do come in. My husband has been restless all day, wondering whether he should go over and see you. Your visit will set his mind at rest."

"And Mr. Harcourt? I'd like to see him."

"Francis?" The blue eyes opened wide. "Of course! How silly of me. But he's always so immersed in his books that I've given up thinking of him as taking an interest in anything else."

She led the way into a great panelled hall. It was pleasantly untidy and smelt faintly of furniture polish. Obviously it was much used—at least, in a summer such as this.

A man's voice came from the depths of one of the comfortably sagging leather armchairs. "Who was that, Phoebe?"

"The police, dear. Not the locals. The others."

"Scotland Yard?" John Potter rose up, pipe in hand. He shook hands with the two detectives, a firm, friendly clasp. "This is a terrible business," he said. "My poor sister—or rather, I should say, half-sister. But make yourself at home, Inspector. You too, Sergeant. What can I offer you? Coffee? Cigarettes? A drink?"

He was much the same build as George Gessington— a big man, but genial, easygoing, and softly cushioned in flesh, a man who looked tolerantly, through horn-rimmed spectacles, on the world around him.

When they were settled Finch asked, "You didn't see Mrs. Harcourt after her return home?"

"No, I'd been away for a few days. I only reached home late last night—by the 8:10 from London. My wife told me that Lisa was back, but I could see that the house was in darkness. I'd had a pretty strenuous day and was

tired so I decided not to go up. I wish now I had done so.
I might have prevented this ghastly tragedy." He hesitat-
ed, frowning. "Quite frankly, I have difficulty taking it in.
That Lisa should have died—like that. It seems incredible."

"Oh no, John," said Phoebe. She was nursing the
dachshund in her lap, gently pulling its long, shining ears.
"It was just the way it would have happened. Suddenly!
With a whoosh and a bang! By someone who couldn't bear
her another minute." She added meditatively, "And, of
course, Lisa should never have had all those creepy crawly
green plants. So sort of primeval. Like the beginning of
the world."

"Really, Phoebe," her husband protested, "what on
earth have they got to do with Lisa's death?"

Phoebe looked faintly bewildered. "I thought someone dropped one of those stone vases on her?"

"So they did."

"Then there you are, dear! If Lisa hadn't had them,
no one could have dropped one on her." She put the
dachshund gently on the floor. "I'll go and tell Francis that
the Inspector wants to see him. Come along, Battle, you
fat thing. A walk will do you good."

"If that dog doesn't get more exercise," her husband
remarked, "we shall have to have him fitted with casters to
get his stomach off the floor." He took a pipe from the
mantelpiece and lit it with a wax match. "Anything I can
tell you, Inspector?"

"I did wonder whether Mrs. Harcourt had any objection to her husband's coming here when he left Belguardo?"

"None at all. Naturally I consulted her when the idea
was first put forward and on all points subsequently. Lisa,
although difficult, was not a petty woman." Potter seated
himself on the arm of his chair. "I expect you've been told
of the breach between my mother and father?"

"A breach which you seem to have healed pretty
successfully."

"Well, it all seemed such a pity. Not at first, of
course. To begin with, I'm afraid I resented her. There she
was, I would tell myself, with everything she could possi-
bly want—a sort of fairy-tale existence. And here was I,

hard up, with a moribund business on my hands. Later, when I was more successful and had more leisure, I came to see that she was to be pitied—that I was the one who had everything; a happy home life, satisfactory children, a successful business, a circle of friends into which my half-sister might be drawn."

Finch nodded his understanding. Had there been a touch of complacency in John Potter's voice? He certainly seemed, for the moment, to have forgotten Lisa Harcourt's fate. But then, he was a comfortable man and perhaps it was more comfortable that way.

"So you became her friend?"

"Friend and adviser, yes."

"She took your advice?"

Potter shook his head. "You know what women are——" He winced suddenly. "I was forgetting. But as I said before, it doesn't seem possible. She had always been there, beautiful, extravagant, self-willed——" The broken, abrupt sentences ceased. John Potter shook his head in a bewildered fashion.

Phoebe came back, still followed by the dachshund. Mr. Harcourt, she said, would see the two detectives.

Finch and Slater followed her from the hall. Finch was conscious of a feeling of pleasurable anticipation. He was slightly ashamed to find that he was beginning to enjoy himself.

Francis Harcourt's rooms were in a separate wing of the house. Looking about him, Finch could see how inevitable it had been that he should take with him the furniture and fittings from his old home.

Ebony panelling, elaborately carved; delicate paintings on silk; a gold lacquer screen; curtains of salmon satin embroidered with threads of gold, turquoise, green, and purple; jade and porcelain, Tang horses, mythical figures, half animal, half bird, and intended originally to protect the graves of the dead; red lacquer furniture—wherever he looked, there was something of beauty and value.

A tall, distinguished, scholarly-looking man rose slowly from behind an ebony desk. He had melancholy dark eyes under bushy brows. "So this is the end of my wife's longed-for divorce," he said harshly. "She is dead and the boy a lost soul."

"Your wife wanted the divorce?"

"Indeed yes. Her first idea was that I should agree to pose as the guilty party." He waved to the two men to sit down. He sat down himself and picked up a smooth thin slip of white jade veined with brown. "She offered me quite a large sum of money in return."

"How large a sum?"

"Five thousand pounds."

Finch was surprised. "It was worth as much as that to her?"

"Yes. I had never seen her so much in love." The white jade slid through his fingers, backwards and forwards, as he spoke. "For all that, I refused to perjure myself. I doubted, too, whether the attempt would succeed."

"Owing to your wife's association with David Fray?"

"This was in late May or early June. At that time Mr. Fray's name had not come into it." Harcourt was courteous, urbane. But for the ceaseless handling of the piece of jade, Finch would have thought him unmoved.

"I see. Forgive me if I hurt you, but am I right in supposing that your wife had had other lovers?"

Harcourt nodded. "She was not a loving woman, but she was a very passionate one. And I, as you can see, am an elderly man and set in my ways. Yes," he added judiciously, fingering the pale jade as he spoke, "I suppose two people could scarcely have been more dissimilar. I am quiet, scholarly, and of regular habits. Lisa was gay, volatile, quite uninhibited, and practically illiterate. And yet an arranged marriage is often very successful."

Finch was surprised. "Arranged? By whom?"

"By Lisa. She led a very dull, restricted life. Great things had happened in the world, but not to her. She longed for the freedom marriage would give her, and I happened to be the only unattached man in her immediate circle. And the advantages to myself were obvious. A home I knew and loved. A standard of living I could never have afforded. The chance of a day's shooting—as a young man I was a crack shot. Oh, yes! The advantages to me were obvious." He sighed, leaning back in his chair. "All day I have been seeing her as I saw her that evening when she came to my rooms after the theatre, in a white frock against these curtains. Happy, laughing, the most beautiful living thing I have ever seen."

His voice ceased. The life and intelligence drained away, and he sat staring emptily at the richly embroidered draperies.

"You hadn't thought of divorcing your wife before?" Finch asked, thinking that the young Lisa had not been a person to reject. At thirty-seven she had been beautiful. At twenty she must have been breathtakingly lovely.

Harcourt looked at Finch, moving his head stiffly as if in pain. "From my point of view, she had given me no cause. She was discreet. An admirable manager. A charming hostess on the few occasions when I had some colleague to stay. She interfered neither with my comfort nor my sleep."

"When you refused to allow her to divorce you, how did she take it?"

"She asked *me* to divorce *her*. When I refused to consider that either, she flew into a temper and swore that she would force me to do so. A few weeks later she brought this young man, David Fray, into the house and there began the persecution that destroyed my peace of mind and my power to work. She gave noisy parties. She filled the house with a crew of young rowdies. There was dancing until all hours of the night. Cars leaving and arriving. I could do no work. Settle to nothing. I realised that Lisa could stand this sort of thing for a great deal longer than I could, and I told her that I would divorce her."

"And she?"

"She was all smiles. She said, rather like a child, 'There! I told you I'd make you give in, didn't I?' I remember that, for a moment, I thought that she was going to embrace me."

"And yet eleven months later she didn't even trouble to tell Mr. Fray that she intended marrying someone else."

Francis Harcourt smiled stiffly. "That I can quite

believe. There was a sadistic streak in Lisa. It was never so much in evidence as when she was happy."

"You think that she deliberately withheld the news?"

Harcourt nodded. "Inspector, I have seen my wife in the middle of a successful dinner party get hold of some unfortunate young man—particularly if he happened to be with a girl whom he admired—ask him his opinion on some topic of the day and then, in a couple of minutes, get him so tied up that he became an object of ridicule to the whole table. Yes," he added, still caressing the piece of jade, "I've seen many a grown man brought to the brink of tears as ignominiously as if he had been a seven-year-old."

"One might do that sort of thing once too often," Finch commented. The dead woman, he felt, was becoming as real to him, as familiar, as if he had known her for years. "When did you see Mrs. Harcourt last?"

"To talk to? Not since I left Belguardo. We met in the village occasionally, but we had nothing to say to each other."

"I see. And last night between half-past ten and eleven?"

Harcourt smiled thinly. "An alibi? I haven't one. I always take a stroll last thing at night. I may have been outdoors at the times you specify." He frowned to himself. "It is a little difficult for a practical person to credit, but I live largely in the past. At the moment I am at work on a book on China's two greatest poets, Li Po and Tu Fu. It gives me little interest in Paradon and the present."

"Then it won't be much good asking you if you can think of anyone other than Mr. Fray who might have had a motive for killing Mrs. Harcourt?"

For an instant Harcourt bent such a piercing gaze on Finch that the latter decided that, however far back he might go with Li Po and Tu Fu, where the murder of his wife was concerned, he was very much in the present. He thought too that Harriet had been right. Cups of cold poison would be right up Francis Harcourt's street.

"So there *is* some doubt as to David Fray's guilt?"

"A doubt, yes."

Harcourt said slowly, "I should feel less guilty myself if he were proved innocent."

"You feel guilty—of what?"

Harcourt was silent a moment. Still too, except for his moving fingers. Then he said, rather formally, "From the beginning I had the feeling that I was sacrificing David Fray, that he was too honest—too young for Lisa. That, by allowing myself to be manoeuvred into giving her a divorce, I had given her freedom to compass his ruin." Adding bitterly, "You see, Inspector, I knew in my heart that she would soon get bored with this overloving boy."

"I understand that Mr. Fray and his sister were brought up here. Did you know them before the divorce?"

"Oh, yes—but David hardly at all. Harriet—Mrs. Warry—was educated in Bramshot, but her brother was away at school. The holidays they spent with their uncle, Colonel Roper, wherever he happened to be stationed. Afterwards, for him, there was Oxford and his National Service."

"I see." Finch rose to his feet. "One more question. Who were your wife's solicitors?"

"Pierce and Pierce, 78 High Street, Bramshot. But if you're thinking that you may find the motive for the murder in Lisa's will, you will be disappointed. She was a very superstitious woman. She believed that to make a will was tantamount to signing her death warrant."

Said Finch slowly, "And the divorce had not been made absolute at the time of Mrs. Harcourt's murder."

Harcourt nodded. His expression was one of sardonic amusement. "And since Lisa, in law, was still my wife, I believe that I shall inherit the bulk, if not all, of her estate."

"I imagine so too," said Finch, looking at him mildly and thoughtfully.

The two detectives followed Harcourt back to the hall. As they approached they heard a tearful voice that they recognised as belonging to Amy Dimmick. There was also a queer rumbling sound. This proved to come from the elderly dachshund tucked under Phoebe Potter's arm. It was uttering low, menacing growls.

"And now the police are saying I never heard footsteps in the hall—but I did, sir, I did," Dimmick was protesting.

"Now, now, Dimmick, don't get so excited. I don't suppose the police said anything of the sort." Potter's voice was a nice blend of the soothing and the authoritative. "If what Best tells me is correct, they're merely saying that it could not have been Mr. Fray's footsteps you heard. Someone else's but not Mr. Fray's." He saw Harcourt and his companions. "Isn't that so, Inspector?"

"I certainly had no intention of upsetting Miss Dimmick," said Finch. He noticed that the licensee, Fred Best, was in the room as well, standing respectfully a little way from the main group. Noticed too that there was a decided change in the atmosphere, an uneasiness that had not been there before.

"*You* didn't upset her," said Potter rather shortly. "It was that surly fellow Gurney. Telling her that now she had neither home nor job."

"That was a terrible thing to be told," said Dimmick, mopping at her eyes with a small, lace-edged handkerchief. "Me, who's been at Belguardo for nearly twenty years, who had no life apart from the mistress—I couldn't rest for worrying about it. And when I saw Mr. Best and he told me he was on his way here, I asked him to give me a lift." She looked from Harcourt to Potter. "Oh, sir, what is to become of me?"

"I do call it a pity!" said Phoebe, ignoring Dimmick's lamentations. "Murder isn't too bad when you know who did it. Of course I was sorry for dear little Harriet, but really, David was *so* well placed for a murderer. He would have had everyone's sympathy, and would have got off with quite a light sentence. Now it will all be miserably uncomfortable. And in the end we'll probably find the real murderer had no better excuse than that Lisa provoked him."

"It was a wicked thing to do," Dimmick declared. "And to think I heard him. Why, he might have come upstairs and killed me too."

"I suppose he would have done, if he had known that

you were there," said Phoebe thoughtfully, giving the elderly dachshund a hitch up.

Dimmick gave a cry and shrank back in her chair. "Well, I'm not going to pretend I didn't hear him. I can recall those footsteps now, plain as plain. Heavy—and yet quick. The footsteps of someone in a hurry to get away— and no wonder, with the mistress lying there—like that." She wiped her eyes again.

"Heavy and yet quick," Harcourt echoed. He stepped forward until he was standing over her. "Can't you do better than that? For instance, was it Gurney's walk? That should be easy to identify."

Dimmick looked at him with a fearful eye. "Gurney?" she muttered, licking dry lips. "Was it Gurney's footsteps? I'd have to think, sir."

"Of course it wasn't Gurney," said Potter impatiently. "You couldn't mistake his walk for anyone else's." He turned to Finch. "Is Best right? Have you definite evidence that exonerates David from suspicion?"

"I couldn't go as far as that, but there are certainly some grounds for doubting his guilt," said Finch.

"Never in the house, he wasn't," said the innkeeper in an obstinate tone. "Cause why? He'd lost his keys down in the woods."

Harcourt smiled thinly. "The Inspector has been enquiring into my alibi," said he pleasantly. And at once the tension seemed to tighten.

Potter shot him a startled glance. "I was with my wife all the evening—for what that's worth," he said. And then: "Phoebe, can't you put that dog down?"

"Darling, you know Battle *always* bites Dimmick on sight," said Phoebe pleasantly.

The innkeeper gave a sudden chuckle which he tried politely to turn into a cough. The woman who had been Lisa Harcourt's personal maid did not seem a popular person.

"He's a nasty creature and I'll thank you to keep him away," said she spiritedly. Then her face twisted again with misery. "Everyone seems to have turned against me. It does seem hard after twenty years. And being the mistress's right hand, so to speak, all those years. In her confidence, knowing everything she did or thought. And her so gay and lively. And sharing everything. 'Look, Dimmick,' she'd say, 'look what I've had by post!' Or, 'What d'you think was said to me last night?' Little things, but they made up my life——" She dabbed her eyes again.

Finch wondered sceptically how many were tears of grief and how many those of bitter disappointment.

"Little things?" Harcourt echoed gloomily. "Aren't we all beleaguered by the memories of little things? Lisa and I were married for nearly seventeen years——"

"I think," Potter interrupted dryly, "that Dimmick is anxious about the future, not the past. And quite naturally. She can't live on air and she is no longer a young woman."

Harcourt drew his heavy brows together. "I see." He looked at the maid with distaste. "It rather depends on circumstances. Naturally I shall do what I can——"

"We'll both do what we can," said Potter good-naturedly. "So cheer up, Dimmick, and stop worrying. We'll see you through. Your mistress wouldn't have wanted you left unprovided for, and you shan't be. We'll talk of this again. Meanwhile I'll make myself responsible for your wages." He turned to the fat innkeeper. "Before you both go, Fred, give yourself a drink. You know your way about the kitchen."

"And close the door after you," said Phoebe, "so that I can put Battle down."

"Dimmick," said Harcourt when the pair had left the room, "was always a most avaricious woman. She *must* have saved a good bit."

"People who are good savers seldom want to touch their savings," said Potter dryly. "Hence her anxiety to be pensioned off."

"And the odd thing is that she must know that if Lisa had made a will she was just as likely as not to have left Dimmick out of it. I think her coming all this way so late at night——"

A sudden thought seemed to strike Phoebe. A most extraordinary change came over her face. It was as if a hand had passed over it, wiping all expression away. "So that's why Dimmick came!" she cried. "She realised that Francis would get the money. That Lisa had died just in time for her. That——"

"Phoebe!" Potter's furious voice cut her short.

Harcourt looked at her with astonishment for a moment. Then he smiled formally. "We can be certain that the point has not escaped the Inspecror," he said. "And, John, I won't have a word said against your wife. Except for her passion for dogs and horses, Phoebe is an admirable woman."

"But dogs and horses are so satisfactory!" Phoebe cried. As if to prove her words, she swept down on the stout dachshund, now nostalgically breathing in great gusts of Dimmick-tainted air from under the door, like a lion deprived of a particularly succulent Christian. She picked him up and buried her face in his silky coat.

Finch watched her curiously. For it seemed to him that she was using the dog to conceal the fact that, standing there in the warmth of the summer night, she had begun to shiver uncontrollably.

When the two dectives were back in their car Slater remarked, "Well, there's a jolly good motive for murder. Lisa Harcourt did die just in time as far as her husband was concerned. He admits that he was out at some time late yesterday evening, and we all know how unscrupulous collectors are. He'd probably murder his own mother for a nice bit of jade or porcelain."

"And, of course, there're more murders done for gain than for any other motive," Finch agreed.

The car turned out of the drive.

"Crumbs! This is a queer black-and-white world," Slater commented. "Always one half of the valley in shadow."

"I can't say that I thought that moonlight improved the Hall," said Finch. Adding, "What did you think of the Potters? They alibied each other, but with a devoted married couple, that means nothing."

Slater glanced at his superior quickly. "They had common sense on their side, I thought. John Potter *had* been away for several days. It *was* hellishly hot in London, so that he probably *was* tired. And we don't know of any reason for him to have murdered his half-sister."

Finch smiled faintly. "But I wasn't thinking of John Potter. It was his wife who interested me. Easygoing, comfort-loving, but strong, fit, and with the dangerous insensibility of the unimaginative. And why did she make that remark about Lisa's having died just in time?"

"You think that it might have been made to divert any possible suspicions on our part?"

"She certainly had some definite intention—if it were only to disconcert Francis Harcourt. And one does wonder what he had done to deserve it. It's a fascinating conjecture." There was a look of innocent pleasure on Finch's large bland face. "And all that talk of Amy Dimmick about knowing every thought in her late mistress's mind. What was she up to?"

"Probably expecting the murderer to take fright and hand out a nice large dollop of lolly."

Finch chuckled, a faintly sinister sound. "He's far more likely to reach for the second stone urn."

Chapter
9

If Peters' front garden was depressingly unimaginative and symmetrical, the back garden had the haphazard jelly-bag shape of so many country cottage gardens snatched from the land of reluctant farmers. In it were vegetables, a few old fruit trees, some long-established clumps of peonies, their heavy heads now bleached by the sun, and a patch of closely mown grass.

Here Finch was sitting in a deck chair, his long legs trailing in front of him, his cigarette end glowing red in the moonlight.

Slater lay on his back on the grass, his head cradled in his clasped hands. He had a diminishing pile of ripe plums beside him. Neither man was talking.

It was very quiet and still warm. There had been a light in one of the upstair windows, but now it had gone out. Peters was in bed. Slater imagined him asleep in an old-fashioned brass bedstead, its knobs glittering like eyes in the shadowy room, his mouth a little open and his red face and heavy moustache appearing very dark against the white bed linen.

Slater's mind occupied itself idly with the case, the various characters drifting in and out of his mind. John Potter parading his growing prosperity before his half-sister. His wife perhaps hunting Lisa with the same intrepid tenacity with which she hunted the fox. Harcourt, who had had so much to gain by Lisa's death. Harriet——Slater grinned to himself, seeing her in his mental vision, so cool, so brave, so undaunted, but with such an apprehensive eye for the approach of her old school chum, Detective Inspector Finch.

Peters had told them that Dimmick had just come out of the drive at Waltons when Fred Best had picked her up. What had she wanted with the Warrys? Or, for that matter, what had she really been after at the Hall? Recalling her conversation, it would be easy enough to read blackmail into her visit. Or, at least, kiteflying. And, no doubt about it, it was the realisation that the dead woman had left no will that had wrought the change in Dimmick. A change from grief to an iron determination.

Finch's voice reached him suddenly out of the darkness, a small, sad voice. "Archie, d'you remember Peters' saying that Lisa Harcourt was always going over to Paris to visit friends?"

Slater turned his head lazily. "Yes?"

"Well"—Finch's tone was even more lugubrious—"I know who those 'friends' were."

"Who were they?"

"Just our old pal and playmate George Gessington."

"But——Oh, Lor'!" Slater shot upright. "What makes you think that?"

"I don't *think* it. I know it. It was Gessington with whom Lisa was so much in love that she offered her husband five thousand pounds for a divorce."

"But how do you know?"

"Francis Harcourt said that his wife asked him for a divorce at the end of May or the beginning of June. He isn't sure which. Harriet told us that Lisa had met David at some school sports. But you don't have sports either in May or early June. They come at the end of the term."

"But if Gessington and Lisa were lovers, why should she have——"

Finch stirred impatiently. "Archie, wake up! Don't you remember? Gessington Senior was a pillar of the Non-Conformist Church, and an anti-man. And, if he were anti anything, it's pretty certain he'd have been anti-divorce."

"Of course he would. And they thought they might get away with it if someone else was the co-respondent."

"Exactly—only they were wrong."

"And then Gessington Senior died and Lisa—I say, that's a bit thick, isn't it? That poor clot!"

"Yes—and if he met Lisa last night and she told him the truth, as she may very well have done——"

"He'd have dropped that urn on her for certain."

There was silence for a moment, both men following their own train of thought.

"So that explains why the letters and any photographs had to disappear," said Slater slowly. "They'd have been dated prior to Lisa's visit to Italy."

"Given a woman of Lisa Harcourt's nature it explains practically everything that's happened in the last fifteen months. Look how it fits in. Lisa Harcourt met George Gessington and they fell passionately in love. He tells her that marriage is out of the question since his father holds the purse strings and would certainly cut him off if he got mixed up in a divorce, so they become lovers. But Lisa isn't satisfied. She wants to marry Gessington. So first she asks Francis Harcourt to let her divorce him. Then, when he refuses, she looks around for a suitable young man with whom to force his hand. And what better place to look than a boys' school—and here you'll recall Harriet saying that school sports weren't really in Lisa's line."

Finch's voice died away. When he spoke again it was to say, "D'you know, Archie, I can't help feeling that George Gessington would have known that his father's beliefs were of the 'till-death-do-us-part' variety. But perhaps George felt that it was worth trying." Again his voice trailed into silence. "No, the man who damned Lisa's murderer into hell wasn't the man to stand by and see her take another lover, whatever the reason. He *couldn't* have known what she was up to. Not at first, anyway."

"It looks as if he took her on again—if he ever gave her up," Slater commented cynically.

"Yes—whichever way you look at it, he's not a nice man, our Mr. Gessington. But he had to pretend to be one. Big-hearted George! That was his line. He couldn't afford to have David Fray brought to trial. Too many other facts would have come to light. The newspapers would have had a field day if they'd learned how he and Lisa had sacrificed the young man's career and happiness to further their own ends."

Again a silence fell. Again Finch broke it.

"I think it might explain Dr. Warry's behaviour too, but we'll see about that tomorrow." He spoke almost absently, his mind running on. He rose to his feet. "You can go to bed if you like, Archie. I'm going up to Belguardo. I want to get hold of Lisa's passport before that vanishes too. Once we have the dates on which Lisa visited Paris, it shouldn't take long for the Yard to find out whether Gessington was there at the same time."

"I'll come with you," said Slater. "I'd like to see Gessington doing a bit of sweating for a change."

Finch's car was still at the gate, since the police station had no garage. The two men got in and drove away through the sleeping village and up the hill.

They spoke only once.

"You were right about Dimmick," said Slater. "She's a menace."

"She likes money, and Gessington has plenty," Finch answered mildly. "We must hope her partiality doesn't lead her astray."

He left the car in the drive and they approached the house quietly, keeping to the grass verge. It lay in shadow, its outline cast, as if cut in thick black paper, on the gravel sweep before it. No light showed. Its windows were steel-dark, and not even the stealthiest sound came from within to greet them. Finch let himself in with the key which Bannerman had given him.

"I thought someone was to be left on guard," said Slater under his breath.

"So did I," Finch murmured back. "He's probably asleep in the kitchen. That's where he'd naturally gravitate. More homely than all this." He waved an explanatory hand which passed in and out of the light from his torch like a fish in a streak of moonlight.

"You're telling me," said Slater, hating the cold, fashionable black and white of the hall.

Finch was right. A middle-aged constable in uniform sat in one of the bucket chairs in the kitchen. His feet were in another chair, and his hands were clasped on his stomach. His lips moved in and out with a peaceful puffing sound as his chest rose and fell.

The two C.I.D. men tiptoed away and upstairs. They made certain that the curtains were drawn securely in Lisa's big bedroom; then they switched on the light. Finch remembered where the passport had been. He went straight to the drawer of the writing table and found it. He looked at it, then slipped it into his pocket.

He stiffened suddenly, turning towards the door. The next moment he had stepped swiftly across the floor and turned off the light. Silently, cautiously, he opened the door and stood peering through the crack.

He was rewarded by a rustle of sound as someone hurried past, silent on the thick carpet. Dimmick, he thought. Opening the door wider, he slipped out in pursuit, Slater at his heels—in and out of the faint reflection of moonlight through uncurtained windows, quiet as the woman herself.

She came to the head of the stairs and paused, tense, staring down into the dark and cavernous well of the staircase, while fear flowed out from her, filling the vacant spaces of the night.

A second passed—and another. Then, suddenly, as if history were repeating itself, the silence was broken.

Footsteps sounded on the marble floor.

Finch, stretching a hand past Dimmick's shoulder, felt for the electric switch. The hall blazed suddenly into light. Dimmick swung round with a scream of the utmost terror. And, from down below, Francis Harcourt raised his handsome head and looked up at them.

"So we meet again, Inspector," he said in his pleasant, urbane voice. "I seem to have done the one thing I wished to avoid—disturbed the household."

Dimmick let out a long, shuddering sigh. Her face was ghastly. "I'll not sleep another night in this house. No, not for a thousand pounds," she declared, clinging to the bannisters as if without their support she must fall. "I wouldn't have stayed this one if I'd known that people could come in and out as they pleased."

"I've had my key all the time," said Harcourt, "but I have never had the inclination to use it before."

"Perhaps you'll be kind enough to tell me why you're using it tonight," said Finch, going down the stairs. He was thinking several things about Dimmick. One of them was that perhaps she was right to be frightened, since, when the lights had been switched on, Harcourt had seemed to be heading straight for the stairs.

"When I left, there was an exceedingly valuable collection of Chinese jade and porcelain here, every one a museum piece," Harcourt responded. "It suddenly struck me that perhaps Lisa might have sold it. The idea prevented my sleeping. Finally I remembered my key and that there was nothing to stop me letting myself into the house."

"You might have known that you would find the police in charge."

Harcourt smiled. "You underrate me, Inspector. I thought that the police was represented by our friend whom I saw through the window, asleep in the kitchen."

Finch nodded. "And we may as well make use of him. Archie, see Miss Dimmick back to her room. Then rouse that fellow in the kitchen and tell him to stay outside her door. He can have a chair to sit on, but I'd prefer him to keep awake. Now, Mr. Harcourt."

Finch led the way towards the drawing room. Here, too, he drew the curtains before turning on the lights. When the long, lovely room sprang up around them, he heard Harcourt sigh as if, for him, the ghosts had not all fled.

Apart from this one involuntary sound, he behaved as if he had had no other thought in coming to Belguardo than to reassure himself as to the collection.

His eyes went to the tall, glass-fronted cabinet. "So Lisa did keep them," he muttered, as if to himself. "I thought she would—and yet I could not be sure."

Under Finch's fascinated gaze Harcourt produced a key ring from his pocket, chose a key, inserted it into the lock, and turned it. He seemed wholly immersed, taking out now a piece of jade, now a tall-necked vase or brilliantly decorated plate. His expression was intent, absorbed.

"I see there's something new here, bought, I imagine, by my wife on her recent travels."

He took from the cabinet a white porcelain figure of wonderful lustre and grace. "The Goddess of Compassion. Or, more properly, the Bodhisattva Kuan Yin. Bodhisattva meaning one who, having gone through the ten stages, was accounted worthy to become a Buddha but who preferred to work for the salvation of all beings. This figure was made in Tê-hua in the seventeenth or eighteenth century, by which time Kuan Yin was being represented as a charming and feminine figure, calculated to please the eye and the sentimental longings of her worshippers rather than to serve a purely moral purpose."

He replaced it in the cabinet, remarking regretfully, "What a tragedy that a bit has been chipped from its ear. It was not like my wife to have bought an imperfect piece, though I admit that the contemplative and somewhat enigmatic beauty of the figure is very pleasing."

He closed the door of the cabinet, locked it, and replaced the key in his pocket.

"You're not afraid of burglars with all these lovely things about?" Finch asked.

"I had Chubb locks put on all the downstairs windows, but Ambrose never so much as locked this cabinet until after Lisa, when a baby, managed in some way to crawl in and smash one of the pieces." He smiled at Finch. "A most lamentable affair, which I have never ceased to regret."

His dark melancholy gaze strayed over the once familiar room. It fell on the photograph standing on the piano. For a moment all expression went from his face. It had a strange set look, as though he had withdrawn into himself. Only in a backwash of feeling he exclaimed, "I told her—I warned her that someday something terrible would happen to her!"

Finch knew then that this elderly savant who had been Lisa's husband could not forgive her, even dead, her devastating gift of charm.

"In her photograph Mrs. Harcourt bears a striking resemblance to her mother," Finch commented.

"She had her mother's looks and her father's character. She was as self-willed and misguided as he was." Francis Harcourt walked over to the mantelpiece. He looked at the lovely empty face of the second Mrs. Potter. "Poor woman! It took Ambrose three years to discover that there was nothing behind that beautiful mask. In the end he came near to hating her, and she was afraid of him."

"I understand that his first marriage was unhappy too," said Finch dryly.

"Whoever told you that judged by externals only. Rachel Potter was the one woman in the world for Ambrose. They quarrelled—violently at times—but fundamentally they were deeply attached to each other. They were both hot-tempered and opinionated. An argument would blow up and in a minute they'd be shouting at each other. Throwing things perhaps. Or even—and this most people found shocking—resorting to blows."

Francis smiled faintly. "There was one classic occasion, I remember. The Potters were giving a dinner party, and a few minutes before the guests were due to arrive they had a disagreement about the seating arrangements. An argument ensued. Rachel declared that if the guests were not to sit at the table as she, the mistress of the house, wanted, then they should not sit at all. She began to clear the table. Ambrose tried to stop her. The damask tablecloth became entangled in their feet. By the time the first guests arrived the place was a shambles, and the Potters, their arms about each other, were roaring with laughter at the expressions on the faces of their visitors. We all ended by having a very lively and hilarious dinner at the Royal Hotel in Bramshot." He added, sighing for the happy past, "Rachel died within four years of the divorce."

"And the second Mrs. Potter?"

"She died in the early days of the war. Ambrose

survived both his wives to live on, a rather solitary and embittered man, until he broke his neck falling down the steps of the Swiss Cottage."

"You have known the Potters a long time?"

"I first met Ambrose in Peking when I was twenty-five. He was in the export trade. I was Commercial and Oriental Attaché to the British Legation. He was a much older man, but I was attracted by his great strength, his high spirits, and his knowledge of the Orient—and I adored his wife. Eventually they went back to England, but whenever I was home on leave I used to go and stay with them—first at the Hall, then here at Belguardo."

"Didn't that last affect your friendship with the first Mrs. Potter?"

"To begin with, she could not get over my not having broken with Ambrose. She wrote several times, upbraiding me and telling me that I must choose between them. Later she forgave me. Sometimes I felt that she had forgiven Ambrose too, but, right up to the time of her death, she refused to hear his name spoken. I think that she could not bear to do so."

"And Ambrose Potter? Was he similarly affected?"

"Indeed, no. He was a man of a singular lack of sensibility. Take this collection, for instance, formed whilst the Potters were in China. It was the fruit of many delightful hours spent together. One piece indeed, the one broken by Lisa, was of particular sentimental value, being a present from Rachel to her husband. When they parted she had them all packed up and sent after him. And he, quite cheerfully, arranged them in this cabinet to decorate the drawing room of the woman who had supplanted her. As for Rachel's gift, Ambrose bore its loss with the greatest equanimity, his little daughter's escapade becoming one of his favourite stories. Yes"—Harcourt sighed a little—"he was a strange, hard man."

There was silence for a moment. In it all sorts of dreams and shadows seemed to drift through the room, clear enough to Francis Harcourt, half perceived by Finch, with his Cornish ancestry. Phantoms, whose laughter and tears echoed faintly down the corridors of time. Finch wondered whether for Harcourt was included the last terrified cry of a murdered woman.

The clock on the mantelpiece suddenly struck three, giving point to the strangeness of Francis Harcourt's nocturnal visit.

Chapter
10

The next day was as cloudless as its predecessors. Already, by eight o'clock, the heat was beginning to collect in the valley. The dew had vanished and the treetops had a scorched and yellowing air.

To Finch, shaving by an open window, came the sound of voices. First the milkman, then the postman. Both had now accepted as a fact that David Fray had had nothing to do with the death of Lisa Harcourt. The postman went further. He remarked that in his view the London gentleman had done it. He based his belief on the grounds that Gessington's altruistic behaviour was against nature, and that he must be trying to cover up some dark deed of his own.

Finch smiled rather grimly to himself. Fred Best had certainly started something. As long as David Fray had been the only suspect, the murderer could afford to lie low. Now he would be alarmed, ready to strike out in any direction that seemed to threaten his safety. Finch felt his Cornish blood stir to this hint of danger.

He telephoned Sturgis at the White Hart. "D'you remember the date of Gessington Senior's death?"

"Yes, the first of May. Why, what's up?"

"I just wondered whether it was relevant," said Finch, and he rang off.

He had a mammoth breakfast, served, at his own insistence, to the three of them in the kitchen. Then he and Slater set off from Bramshot whilst Peters mounted his bicycle and rode away with a message for Miss Budgen.

At the police station Finch gave an account of his visit to the Hall and what had happened subsequently. He spoke too, of his strong suspicion that, from the beginning, it had been Gessington with whom Lisa had been in love.

Colonel Roper could not get over this duplicity. It seemed to fill his mind to the exclusion of all else. His reaction was old-fashioned and correct. "But the fella's a cad, a bounder, an outsider." He said a lot more, striding about the room, but that was the gist of it.

Bannerman was more interested in Harcourt's nocturnal visit to Belguardo. He spoke of it in tones of sinister enlightenment. "So he had a key," he remarked. "He'd had it all along. That's interesting. Very, very interesting."

Slater agreed with the Superintendent. His view, though no one asked for it, was that Harcourt had had the intention of killing the blackmailing Amy Dimmick and that the woman had recognised the fact and panicked.

Finch was inclined to take Harcourt's own explanation at its face value. "Of course, I may be wrong," he said. But he did not really believe this to be possible.

On the way back to Belguardo the two detectives called in at Waltons. The house seemed as much a home as the other one appeared a showplace. Its cool, airy hall. The mellow, shining pieces of antique walnut. The great bowl of scarlet snapdragons. Even the little maid, with her mass of freckles, eyes round as curtain rings and hands red from the washbowl, seemed to enhance the pleasant impression.

Dr. Warry had not yet gone on his rounds. He greeted his visitors genially, although Finch fancied that he detected a note of reserve in his manner.

"Too early for a drink, I suppose," he said, smiling and shaking hands, "but you won't refuse a cup of coffee, I hope? I always have one after my morning surgery. Yes, three cups please, Gladys."

Finch looked with interest at the man who had married Harriet Fray. He had, he decided, seen many such long, sardonic faces under the wigs of successful Q.C.s. Yet this one was marred by a look of petulance and nervous irritability. The mouth too set naturally in embittered lines. Not an easy man to live with, particularly for one as fiery, impulsive, and yet fundamentally candid and outspoken as Harriet.

Dr. Warry sank back in his chair. "I believe you know my wife."

"Yes, we met some years ago in Fowey."

Mark Warry smiled. "In those days Harriet was determined to be a painter. She'd have made a successful one too. Perhaps when the children are older she will take up her career again."

The little maid brought in a silver tray. On it were the coffee, biscuits, and the finest of china cups, all sparkling and gleaming. It seemed that Harriet, if she could not be an artist, had become a very competent housewife.

"And now to business." Dr. Warry put his own cup before him and lighted a cigarette. "I expected you yesterday."

"I had your report on the body. There seemed no reason to take up your time. Not, that is, until it was reported that you yourself visited Belguardo on the night that Mrs. Harcourt was murdered."

"That was what I was waiting to tell you. I called on Mrs. Harcourt to find out whether the announcement in the evening paper were true."

"You were angry about it?"

"On the contrary," said the doctor, "I was delighted. She and David were quite unsuited to each other. It was far better for him to recognise the fact than to have to face a lifetime of misery and disillusionment."

"I see." Finch's tone was dry. "And how was Mrs. Harcourt?"

"In excellent spirits, as one would have expected."

"What time did you get to the house?"

"I arrived about half-past nine. I really couldn't tell you how long I was there." The doctor ground out his cigarette. He raised his eyes for a moment to glance coolly at both men. "Half an hour? Three quarters? I really don't know."

"And when you left?"

"It was a wonderful night. I went for a motor ride before going home."

"You were alone with Mrs. Harcourt during your entire visit?"

"If you mean by that was my brother-in-law there, he was not. Nor did I see any sign of his having been there—nor of anyone else, for that matter."

"Since you were there for some time, how was it that Mrs. Harcourt did not offer you a drink?"

"I was driving. I refused one."

Finch raised an eyebrow. "And when you went to dinner at Belguardo, which I understand you did frequently, did you refuse a drink then?"

Dr. Warry shifted his ground with the ease of a fencer. "If you must know, it was a mistake, my walking round by the terrace. The front of the house was in darkness when I got there, and it seemed a good idea at the time. But Mrs. Harcourt was annoyed."

"You knew her well?"

"Very well indeed." His smile was crooked.

"Then perhaps you can help me. During the enquiry a curious discrepancy has become apparent. It appears that Mrs. Harcourt asked for a divorce two months before she met Mr. Fray." Finch paused deliberately, aware that the doctor was listening with an almost painful intensity and that he was a badly shaken man. "Naturally this has made me curious as to how long she had known Mr. Gessington and whether the two of them were in the habit of meeting as lovers in Paris last year."

Dr. Warry frowned, and his eyes were wary. "That is a very extraordinary suggestion of yours, Inspector," he said slowly, at last. "And if it *were* true, it changes nothing. David still was somewhere in the grounds, and I was in the house. My position, I recognise, was an equivocal one——"

"Dr. Warry, shall we stop this manoeuvring? I could make out a case against your brother-in-law. I could make one out against you, as you seem to wish. But I'm not interested in making out a case. Only in the truth. And the Yard should have no difficulty in proving or disproving this particular facet of it."

The doctor, conscious that the eyes of both men were on him, sat looking unhappily down at the desk top. Then he shrugged. "They'll prove it, all right," he said bitterly. "Lisa herself admitted it." Adding heavily, "That's the nightmare knowledge I've been taking round with me these last thirty-six hours."

"But you yourself suspected the truth before that," said Finch, pressing his advantage. "Your visit to Belguardo was to confirm your suspicions. Shall we go on from there?"

"As you wish." For Dr. Warry the effort at concealment was over. He looked now a desperately weary man—a sick one too. He began to speak. "When Lisa saw me first, she was angry. That was true enough. She hadn't wanted to be disturbed. But when she realised that I had come in no friendly spirit, she welcomed my visit——"

"Rather an unusual attitude, surely?"

"Not with Lisa Harcourt. Controversy, disagreement, and argument were the breath of life to her. Being ostracised when she was young had warped her character. At heart she was against all the world. She took great pleasure in inflicting pain. I believe she felt that in that way she was getting her own back. When I taxed her with my suspicions she readily admitted their truth. She appeared delighted at her own cleverness and forethought. She told me that Gessington Senior had been a man of seventy-six and that his son had not been averse to waiting until he could marry her in safety but that, right from the start, she had determined to get a divorce, only waiting until her lover was safely out of the way to set things in motion.

"Being entirely without principles herself, she found it impossible to believe that her husband would refuse to let her buy a divorce. And she was still honestly puzzled as to why he had refused. The necessity of finding a lover, she told me, had given her a great deal of thought, until suddenly she had remembered that I had a young brother-

in-law." The doctor's face was grim. "Yes, she deliberately
sought him out. The fact that she disliked his sister, my
wife, gave an added fillip to the idea of making use of him.

"I had expected Lisa to deny the truth of my allega-
tion. Her candour filled me with a priggish anger and
disgust. When I upbraided her she turned on me and told
me exactly how my conduct had appeared to her since I
came here." He added with a wry, sardonic smile, "It was,
no doubt, salutary but not palatable. It also—and you may
have difficulty in believing this—took me completely by
surprise. I had been certain that right was on my side,
that my ill health and my wife's insensitiveness to my
needs justified my behaviour.

"I had never been Lisa Harcourt's lover. No, nothing
as healthy. I had done far worse. When I came down here
I was desperately sorry for both Harriet and for myself.
When I realised that she was delighted at the change I felt
outraged, defrauded. I told myself that if she were so fond
of the country she must have disliked our life together in
London. Our happiness then had all been a fraud, a sham.
I turned against one who you must know is the most open,
the frankest, of feminine creatures. And then, when I met
Mrs. Harcourt, I persuaded myself that she, and she only,
could restore my lost way of life.

"I never saw my behaviour through any eyes but my
own until Lisa stripped me of my pitiful pretensions. I had
the bad manners to accept invitations that did not include
my wife. I was conceited, self-centred, a poseur—— Oh, I
don't deny that she made me furious, but I was flabbergasted too. Anxious to get away and examine this monstrous accusation of hers. I rushed out of the house, threw
myself into my car, and drove here, there, and everywhere. When I returned home and opened the front door
I heard the telephone ringing. It was Dimmick to say that
Lisa was dead."

"You say you spent some time driving around. Can
you prove it?"

"I didn't see anyone about. In these parts most people go to bed early. But I can map out my route and
someone might have noticed my car. It's a white saloon."

Dr. Warry smiled faintly. "I have often found that the colour helped identification."

"I expect we'll find someone who saw it," Finch responded. "But to get back to the murder—when you returned to Belguardo, did everything, apart from the dead body and the overturned urn, appear the same as it had earlier?"

"Exactly the same. So much so that the whole thing seemed, for a moment, like a ghastly joke prepared against my return by Lisa herself."

As, in a sense, it had been, Finch thought. He said in his soft voice. "And now perhaps we'd better speak off the record. I suppose you rubbed the urn clear of possible fingerprints?"

The doctor nodded. "I apologise."

Finch wagged his head. "More people have remained under suspicion because well-meaning—er——"

"Fools, Inspector. Go on, say it."

"Well-meaning fools, then, withhold or destroy vital evidence. Did you do anything else?"

"No. There simply wasn't anything else to be done. I admit I looked round to see whether David had left any incriminating evidence, but there was nothing. Nothing at all."

"In fact everything pointed to a visitor who came in, murdered Mrs. Harcourt, and went straight out again."

Dr. Warry's face stiffened. "I suppose so, yes."

"Yet one thing struck me as unusual. The lights."

Dr. Warry caught his breath. "Didn't Dimmick switch them on? I took it for granted she had done so. A sort of instinctive reaction to fear."

"She says they were like that when she came down and discovered the dead body. And, talking of Dimmick, I believe she came to see you last night?"

"Yes. She wanted something to make her sleep. I could see that she was in a highly excitable state and I gave her a couple of pills."

"Which she either omitted to take—or which had no effect."

"They'd have acted, all right, if she'd taken them. That's why I only gave her the two."

"You say she was excitable. In what way?"

"Her pulse was rapid and she had a high colour. Then she talked a lot about the unfairness of losing her home and how she and her late mistress had been all in all to each other. I must confess I wasn't very sympathetic. The surest way to Dimmick's good graces was liberality—in her direction. She must have put by quite a comfortable amount."

"That seems to be the general impression," said Finch slowly. "But to get back to Mrs. Harcourt. Did she give you the impression that she had anything on her mind?"

"Anything unpleasant? Quite the contrary. When I first saw her she was lying on that long chair of hers, smiling dreamily to herself and looking, for all the world, like a cream-fed cat." He hesitated. "One thing did strike me as strange. I had come near to taking her by the shoulders and shaking her. My intention must have been obvious, for she stepped back. Not frightened. No, certainly not that. It was rather as if, by my action, I had roused some doubt or anxiety in her mind."

"She didn't seem in a hurry to get rid of you?"

The doctor laughed shortly. "On the contrary, I think she had more to say if I had stayed to listen!"

"Then I think that's all." Finch rose to his feet. "May I suggest that you tell your wife what you have told me about Mrs. Harcourt's affair with Mr. Gessington?"

Dr. Warry smiled thinly. His eyes were shadowed. "The time to tell my wife anything seems to have passed."

"I think you underestimate Harriet."

"And I think you underestimate the unhappiness I have caused her," Dr. Warry answered with finality.

Finch did not press the point. It was enough for him to know that Mark Warry still loved his wife. That being so, it would be a strange thing if they did not come together again.

Dr. Warry went with them to their car. "Ironical to

recall the number of times on which I have given advice on how to patch up a broken marriage," he remarked.

"A clear case of 'Physician, heal thyself,'" said Finch smiling. "I'm sure you'll do it."

"I wish I could be as certain." The words were accompanied by a smile of great charm. It quite altered his face. Finch could see then the man with whom Harriet had fallen in love.

Chapter
11

Reeves came hurrying from Belguardo to meet the car. His pink and white face was flushed with the telltale colour of excitement.

"Mr. Harcourt's here, sir. He's waiting in the drawing room to see you."

"Alone?"

"No, sir. Constable Hillier's with him."

"Good. Anything else happen?"

"A Mr. Sturgis was here earlier. He said it'd be all right for him to take photographs."

"And Peters?"

"Haven't seen him this morning, sir."

"Right! I'll come in." But Finch did not move. Instead he sat staring down the wide straight drive as if half expecting to see the tall thin figure in black standing in the bright sunshine beyond the gateway. The space remained obstinately, tantalisingly empty.

Francis Harcourt was wearing a light tropical suit. He stood looking out of one of the windows at the garden. His fine hands were clasped behind his back. Standing at the end of the room was a thin, sharp-faced young man with red hair.

Harcourt turned as the door opened. "Ah, Inspector! Any developments?" His voice was as pleasant, as urbane as ever, but the perspiration glistened on his forehead and his face had a curious pallor.

"Developments that might lead to an arrest? I'm afraid not."

Harcourt passed a hand wearily over his face. "I'm sorry to hear that. It seems I'm not going to sleep until the mystery of my wife's death is solved."

And last night, Finch thought, you were only interested in the safety of the collection—or weren't you? He said aloud, "Did you want to see me about anything in particular?"

Slater, a slightly smug look on his lantern-jawed face, took out his notebook and pen.

"I've been wondering whether perhaps robbery might not have been the motive for Lisa's murder," Harcourt replied. "My wife had some very valuable jewellery, which, I imagine from past experience, she would have taken abroad with her. Could she not have been followed here and murdered by a jewel thief?"

A jewel thief who had not even bothered to remove that engagement ring with its great flawless diamond? Finch thought it highly improbable. Indeed, if David Fray had been eliminated, the suspects had narrowed to a very small circle indeed.

"We haven't had time to check the contents of the safe officially. Would you know if anything were missing?"

"Certainly. The more important pieces, at all events. That was why I came to see you."

The three men went up the handsome staircase and along the passage to the dead woman's bedroom. The safe, a small modern affair, was hidden behind a picture. As if it were the most natural proceeding in the world, Harcourt opened it. Inside it was piled high with blue leather cases engraved with the gilt monogram "L.H." He took out several and opened them. A diamond and sapphire bracelet, a magnificent diamond necklace, two diamond and emerald clips, a diamond brooch . . .

Harcourt returned them to the safe. "My wife seems to have added considerably to her collection since I left her. Quite natural, I suppose, but somehow I had not thought of it. You'll have to forgive my stupidity. I'm afraid anno Domini will take its toll."

Finch's mind, like that of an actor, could operate at several levels. He had been listening to what Harcourt was saying. Below this he had been listening to something quite different. Communication was faint between them, but it existed.

The man beside him was afraid.

Finch thanked him for coming. He saw him off. As soon as his tall, stooping figure had been swallowed up by the rhododendrons, he made for the drawing room.

Hillier was still there, staring about him, a puzzled frown on his sharp-featured face.

"Any idea what that was in aid of?"

"No, sir. I don't get it at all. Mr. Harcourt didn't do anything. Just strolled round, looking at the pictures. He glanced into the cabinet, but only as he passed. Then he came to the window and stood looking out. That's when I saw his face. It was ghastly."

Finch's eyes narrowed. "D'you mean that he didn't look like that when he arrived?"

"No, sir. He looked a bit worn and grey, but not all that bad."

"Whose idea was it that he should come in here?"

"His, sir—before he knew that I was coming with him. 'I want to see the Inspector,' he said. 'If he's not here I'll wait.' And off he set, as if he'd known all the time that you weren't in."

"I suppose he could have been upset by the sight of someone seen from the window." Finch was thinking again of Miss Budgen. She seemed to be becoming a mild obsession with him. He answered his own question. "No, it's more likely that he came up to look for something in this room, something that Hillier's presence prevented him from recovering——"

Finch hesitated. He was not really satisfied with this explanation. "We'll have to test it," he said at length. "We can't afford to miss a chance."

The three men set to work. Outside, the garden lay silent in the heat of the August sun. Its dreaming beauty made the quiet house with its unsolved murder seem even more sinister and mystifying.

They heard the village bus approach, grind to a halt, and go on again.

"Enter the fair maid, Dimmick," Slater muttered, grinning.

Finch glanced through the window. "No, there's only Peters, and he's on a bicycle." He went into the hall to speak to him.

The stout constable was hot. He wiped his forehead with a large and spotless white handkerchief, and his air was desolate.

"You've been a long time. Couldn't you find Miss Budgen?"

"No, sir. She wasn't at home. She'd been there, and recently. The fowls were still eating some scraps she'd thrown out for them." He added in a burst of bewildered candour, "I don't think she was far away at any time, but she wouldn't come forward. I kept calling, and I looked about too, but it wasn't no use. She didn't mean me to find her."

"Did she avoid you as a rule?"

"Me, sir?" Peters seemed astounded at the thought. "Lor', no, sir. She usually passes the day. 'Morning, Constable,' she'll say. 'What a nice day.' Or, 'Evening, Constable. It looks like rain.' You know, sir. She was gentry, for all her queer ways. But avoid me? Oh no, sir. She——"

Two figures appeared in the road beyond the gate, Amy Dimmick and the mourning figure of the elusive Miss Budgen. They were deep in conversation.

A roar came out of Peters. "Miss Budgen, miss! Excuse me, sir." He plunged for his bicycle.

Miss Budgen looked up, startled. Then she vanished with the same celerity as on the previous day. Dimmick turned in between the drive gates.

"Zeal!" Finch groaned. "All zeal. Now we've lost her again."

Dimmick paused as Peters flew past her. She stared after him, then came slowly towards the house.

She saw Finch. "Poor Miss Budgen," she said primly. "Frightening her like that." Dimmick was carrying a string bag. In it was a bag of eggs, some butter, and a screw-top bottle of cream. "She was asking me when the funeral was to be, but of course I couldn't tell her. I did say it wouldn't be just yet."

"That's quite right. There'll have to be an inquest first." Dimmick had now, Finch noted, a way of glancing at him out of the corners of her eyes. It gave her a sly and slightly sinister air that did not fit in with her neat respectability. "Have you managed to find a room in the village?"

"Yes, sir—with some people called Pigott, who have a farm on the Bramshot road. We've dealt with them for a long time." Again she gave them that oblique look. He thought for a moment that she was going to say something further. If so, the impulse passed. "I'll take these along to the kitchen," she remarked, alluding to the string bag.

Peters returned with the same energy, if not the same speed, with which he had gone down the drive. He was hotter still, and his face was an alarming shade of red.

Finch went to meet him. "Better come inside and take off that coat. I can't afford to have you getting a heat stroke. I gather you didn't have any success with Miss Budgen."

"No, sir. Not much doubt of it now. She doesn't mean to be found."

"I think we shall have to——" Finch broke off.

From the drawing room behind him the telephone had given a sudden ting. Someone in Mrs. Harcourt's bedroom had just replaced the receiver. In his mind's eye there arose a picture of Dimmick and Miss Budgen in earnest conversation. He felt again that curious stir of uneasiness.

"Archie, nip upstairs quick as you can. Find out who was telephoning and to whom. Then lock up that room."

Slater was soon back. "Miss Dimmick, it was, sir. I ran into her coming out of the bedroom. She said she'd been ringing Short and Sons, drapers, of Bramshot, about some black material for a dress. When I said I'd have to check up on it she said she'd only tried to get them. The number had been engaged."

"A bit of quick thinking on her part?"

"Yes, sir. She's a smooth liar, all right." Slater added significantly, "She still had the string bag."

"I see. Instead of going to the kitchen she went straight up the back stairs to the telephone. And that means that, if she didn't know it before, she now knows the identity of the killer." He wondered what else she knew.

Frustration settled on him like a clamp. He was bitterly aware that if only he had, by some freak of chance or his own prescience, been listening in, he might have heard the voice of Dimmick talking with the murderer.

"Miss Budgen knows."

"Knows what?"

"That you murdered Mrs. Harcourt."

Yes, it could have been like that. Amy Dimmick preserving her own vested interests, closing her mind to the possible consequences of what she was doing. And Miss Budgen——

Superintendent Bannerman telephoned. Scotland Yard had just rung through. George Gessington's alibi was cast-iron. And they had confirmed Finch's suspicions. The dates on which Lisa Harcourt had visited Paris corresponded with those on which Gessington had been there.

"No less than nine visits by the pair of 'em," Bannerman rumbled. "Too many for it to be coincidence." Adding bitterly, "The C.C.'s all steamed up to arrest David. Got it all worked out that Mrs. Harcourt told him how she'd fooled him. Told him—and laughed. He's sitting in his office now just waiting for the signal from you to go ahead. All hunched up like a—a praying mantis. First he wouldn't consider how the news might affect the boy. Now he can think of nothing else. He makes me *sick*!"

Bannerman's voice had risen to a roar. It echoed through the hall, causing Peters to grin widely and the telltale colour of excitement to creep up Reeves' neck.

Finch sighed as he replaced the receiver. The Superintendent's telephonic habits were a great trial to him. So bad for discipline. He was troubled too by a feeling of indecision foreign to him. He went outside and stood staring out over the dark blue-green trees as if the sight of them might resolve his difficulty.

"Whose idea was it to plant all those fir trees?" he asked Peters.

"It was Mr. Potter did it, sir. The idea was to get rid of the rhododendrons. And they were planted by Major Fray's grandfather as cover for pheasants. But he hadn't reckoned on their habits. They spread and kill everything in their path. And you can't get rid of the pesky things. Pretty nigh indestructible, they are. They won't burn. Rabbits won't eat them. Bulldoze them up and you split them into cuttings which root themselves. So when Mr. Potter bought the land from the Frays he planted the firs, the idea being that they'd shut out so much light that even the rhododendrons would die. That was over thirty years ago and they haven't died yet."

"And the whole hillside is like that? Fir trees above and the rhododendrons low down."

"Well, sir, I don't know about low down," said Peters, the literal-minded. "Most of 'em have grown pretty well as high as trees. Looking for the light, I reckon." He added, "But round the Swiss Cottage Mr. Potter did get rid of them. He planted all sorts of fancy trees instead. Cypress, silver firs, pines, cedars, and the like."

"An arboretum of dark trees, bosky from the roots up," Finch groaned. "Heaven forgive him. I suppose he couldn't be expected to foresee that one day we'd be chasing a missing witness through them." He added, glancing at Peters, "What chance d'you think we have of finding her?"

"Not much of one, I'd say, sir. Miss Budgen, poor soul, is like a wild creature. She knows every twist and track—pretty near every tree and bush. You see, she lives off the land, as you might say. Mangels and greens out of the fields. Rabbit snares and the odd pheasant." Peters added, in response to a quick glance from Finch, "Shines a torch on them after dark, sir, then brings them down with a stone. A real poacher's trick. Ah, she's an artful one, is Miss Budgen. You'll have a job catching up with her." He added respectfully, "D'you reckon she knows something about the murder? She and that Miss Dimmick are two of a kind, right enough."

The words started another line of thought in Finch's mind, one that might prove profitable. They *were* two of a kind. Both were preoccupied with thoughts of money, although with Miss Budgen it was more of a necessity. Both women, after comparing notes, now had something to sell. Dimmick, he suspected, had first tried to locate the murderer in a general way, and then, having learned his identity beyond doubt, had found herself in a position to telephone him. But Miss Budgen——

Yes, he thought he knew where she would try to peddle her knowledge.

He sent Peters off to the White Hart. "Ask Mr. Gessington to come and see me at his convenience. Then tell Fred Best that I'm anxious to interview Miss Budgen. Find out if he's seen her. Or if she's seen Gessington. Then telephone me here."

Slater came out of the house. "No clues, sir," he said. "There's nothing hidden in the drawing room." Finch did not answer. Slater glanced at him curiously. "What's the trouble, sir?"

"I've been wondering if I'd be justified in organizing a search for Miss Budgen."

"Since you want to see her, what's the objection?"

"Just that I'll be betraying the fact that I *do* want to see her. Still, I'm trying the White Hart first. If that fails, I'll have to get some men out and trust to luck that we'll find her before the murderer."

Slater's glance sharpened. "Why shouldn't we find her first?"

Said Finch slowly, "Peters compared Miss Budgen to a wild animal. And while it's comparatively simple for a wild animal to avoid a group of amateurs, it's not so easy for it to escape a trained hunter."

"If the murderer is Harcourt, he's no hunter."

"You forget. Harcourt himself told us that he was a crack shot. One doesn't learn that sitting at a desk."

Ten minutes after Finch's message Gessington's car

came streaking up the drive. Arrived at the front door, he sprang out and strode into the house, well dressed and cool-looking in a pale grey suit. He found Finch in the drawing room. "You have some news for me?"

"I hoped you had some for me. Have you been approached for money by a Miss Budgen?"

"Who in heaven's name is she?"

"She was very friendly with Mrs. Harcourt and was by way of being a pensioner of hers. She's going out of her way to avoid us and I was hoping it was because she has some information she hopes to sell you."

"She hasn't contacted me yet. What d'you want me to do?"

"Go on talking money," said Finch dryly. "It's a language both she and Miss Dimmick understand."

"Dimmick!" Gessington laughed shortly. "The daughter of a horse leech. What else?"

"By ways of news? What there is concerns you."

"I don't think I understand." He was watching Finch with cold grey eyes, devoid now of expression.

"I think you will. The police have discovered that every time the late Mrs. Harcourt went to Paris, you went too. This happened not once, nor twice, but no less than nine times."

Gessington dropped his lids. Even so, the handsome face could not hide its own ruthlessness. "Coincidence, Inspector."

"Was it a coincidence that these visits ceased for both of you when David Fray came on the scene?"

Gessington's face coloured slowly, more with fury than embarrassment. "Damnation!" he exclaimed violently.

"Then you admit that your liaison began long before Mrs. Harcourt met Mr. Fray?"

Gessington put a foot in a chair seat. He leaned his arm on his knee in a negligent attitude, his hand dangling. "Would it serve any purpose if I denied it?" he asked insolently. "No. So let me make a virtue of necessity. And in return tell *me* who gave it away?"

"You gave it away yourself," Finch answered with

equal coolness, "by having Dimmick remove your letters and photograph. I couldn't help noticing their absence."

Gessington shrugged. "I don't see what else I could have done," he said in a reasonable tone of voice. "Their presence would have betrayed me even more surely than their absence."

Said Finch politely, "Would you like to tell me about your association with Mrs. Harcourt?"

Gessington seemed to consider this. " 'Like' is hardly the word," he said at last. He looked beyond Finch, around the room. He began abruptly, "I first saw Lisa Harcourt in a restaurant in Piccadilly in January of last year. She was with another man. I don't know who he was, for, to the best of my knowledge, neither of us ever saw him again. She was wearing a black suit, I remember, and a little hat covered all over with scarlet cherries. I couldn't take my eyes off her and she knew it. The waiter told me her name, but he knew nothing more.

"When they looked like coming to the end of their meal I paid my bill and went outside. A minute or two later Lisa came out, looking more wonderful than ever in a mink coat. She had the wild sort of beauty that was set off by furs. She was alone and looking for a taxi. I offered her a lift in my car and the thing was done."

At first Gessington had spoken slowly. Now his words came out in a flood. For him Lisa had been recreated—to move and smile before his enchanted gaze.

"If ever a couple were made for each other it was Lisa and myself. There was nothing ethereal, nothing poetical about either of us. We both knew what we wanted. We both liked the same things—plays, dances, food, fast cars. We were—hedonists, if you like. For three magical months we saw as much of each other as we could. Then I had to go to South America on business for the firm. Our principal representative out there, the silly fool, had got himself mixed up in politics. He was in jail and the firm was in trouble with the regime then in power. It meant my being away for some months, but Lisa was wonderful about it. She had accepted the fact that there could be no talk of marriage as long as my father was alive, but, to my surprise, I hadn't been gone long before she began to write to me as if we were—or would soon be—free to marry. I thought that it was just her way of consoling herself for my absence. Then one day I had a letter to say that her husband had divorced her—and not to worry because my name hadn't come into it.

"For a time I was stunned, incredulous. Then I felt so angry, so—so outraged that I could willingly have strangled her myself. I knew Lisa, I told myself. I hadn't been the first. Besides, she'd got used to having a man and couldn't get along without one. The divorce was six for me and half a dozen for herself."

As he had been speaking, a remarkable change had come over Gessington. His face was suffused with colour; the veins stood out at his temples. His lips were distorted and writhed with remembered fury. His voice was low, and it shook.

"I wrote and told her that I'd done with her. And, perhaps fortunately for myself, just after, I was caught up in a revolution. It took me all my time to stay alive—to keep the business alive. And all the time Lisa was writing to me. She didn't seem able to appreciate what she'd done to me. Then she began to write as if I were in the wrong. She even accused me of having found another mistress." Gessington laughed a short, barking laugh. "Then I heard that my father was very ill. I flew back, and six days after my return he died. I suppose that, without realising it, I'd been softening towards Lisa. Anyway, I wrote to her, telling her to ditch young Fray——"

"You did what?" Finch asked, startled.

"Told her to——" Gessington smiled. It was not a pleasant smile. "You don't think I had any kindly feelings towards that young man, do you?"

"And Mrs. Harcourt? How did she take the news of your father's death?"

"My letter crossed with one from her telling me that she had thought Paris was too near home and that she was on her way to Rome and asking how soon could I join her there. Well, what with one thing and another, I couldn't make it for three weeks, but when we met it was as if we'd never been parted. I stayed on and on, letting everything slide, but at last I had to come back. I parted from her at Victoria and two days later I opened my morning newspaper to see that she was dead—murdered."

"And then?"

"I never doubted but that young Fray had done it. I cursed his name and the government which had done away with the death penalty. I thought of coming down here and beating him up. Forcing a confession out of him. Dropping a great pot on his face—only I'd have ensured that he saw it coming. And then, suddenly, I realised that my fate was bound up in his. That he wouldn't be the only one on trial. That no one would believe that I hadn't known that Lisa was getting a divorce: There would even be people who would think that I was the instigator of the idea."

"A bit hard to make the change, eh?" said Finch mildly.

Gessington fell silent. His eyes stared. "It was hell," he said in a soft purring voice that was infinitely dangerous.

Finch looked at him. "It seems that you have wasted a great deal of emotion on the wrong man," he said equally softly.

Gessington's head jerked up. His eyes were startled. "But the case seemed——"

"Mr. Gessington, things in this world are frequently not what they seem—particularly in murder cases."

Said Gessington slowly, "Then my affair with Lisa may never be brought up?"

"By us? No. But there are always the newspapers." Gessington's face darkened. He frowned, then the frown smoothed itself out. "And I shouldn't try that either," said Finch softly.

"Why not——" Gessington broke off. "Try what?" he asked sharply.

"Try to buy Sturgis of the *Daily Record*. I know him well. He'd crucify you for it."

Gessington's face coloured. He stared frowningly. Then he strode out of the room.

Dimmick was in the hall. "Out of my way, woman." He brushed her aside, sprang into his car, drove away.

"If Mr. Gessington paid you by cheque," Finch told Dimmick, "I should get it cashed before he has time to stop it."

Dimmick was too sharp to pretend to misunderstand him. "I did what I did for the mistress's good name," she said with a self-righteous air. "And not for money." She walked away up the stairs.

Finch was still staring after her when Sturgis came into the house. The reporter was dressed as on the previous day, except that now a handkerchief, knotted at the corners, took the place of a hat. "Gentleman just passed me like a streak of lightning. It may have been imagination, but I fancied he left behind him a distinct smell of fire and brimstone."

He lit a cigarette, spun a chair round, and straddled it, his arm resting along the back. "I got a good picture of Gessington outside the White Hart," he remarked. "Pity he'd never been to this house. It may not be to everyone's taste but, by God, it's photogenic. I could really have made something of this. Scene of a passionate and ill-starred romance. All that sort of thing." He added with a sly glance, "A Paris hotel won't be nearly as romantic."

Finch grinned. So Sturgis knew. "I have a feeling that Gessington's on his way to see his solicitors about being protected from people like you."

"Let him try." Sturgis went through the motions of rubbing his hands with ghoulish glee. "All we want now to make my day is a body." He put some ash into a vase of white roses. "I hear you're looking for a Miss Budgen."

"I'm hoping she'll turn up at the White Hart. If she doesn't, I'm having some men out from Bramshot to search the woods."

Sturgis nodded. He stared down at what remained of his cigarette. "I guess I'll join the searchers."

Finch looked at him quickly, aware of a sudden cold twist of fear in his stomach. "Why d'you say that?"

Sturgis shrugged. "Me, I'm easy to entertain. Besides, Francis Harcourt has left the Hall. He just walked out—into the woods."

Chapter
12

The two detectives had a cold meal laid for them by Gurney in the dining room. There was cold chicken, ham, and salad drenched in oil. There was a Cheddar cheese, biscuits, and an elaborate chocolate cake. Slater looked at it appreciatively, but Finch was too disgruntled to care.

"What's that woman Dimmick doing in the hall every five minutes?" he grumbled, taking his place at the table. "It begins to look as if Miss Budgen told her more than the name of the murderer."

I hadn't noticed that she was hanging about the hall, sir," Slater answered.

Finch stared. "Your lack of perception doesn't alter the fact." His face was troubled.

They ate for a while in silence. Then Slater remarked, "It was John Potter who agreed to take care of Dimmick's future."

"Perhaps because, at the moment, he is the only one with the financial resources to do it." Finch added more amiably, "If Harcourt murdered his wife the motive was probably her fortune. If it were one of the Potters—or anyone else—we're back at our original question. What did Lisa do to get herself done in? Coupled with which we now have another query. What was it that Dr. Warry's violence suggested to her? Was it that some course of action on which she had decided was dangerous?"

"If so," said Slater, "she seems to have done damn all about it."

141

Gurney came in with coffee. Finch asked him to describe in detail the events of the Monday evening.

Gurney paused, the tray in his hands. He did not speak for a minute. Finch was startled at his expression of hostility.

"I don't know what you want," he burst out, "nor what good it'll be. Talk, talk, and nothing decided." He fell silent, waiting on them sullenly, walking with his odd, crablike movements.

"As far as I know," he said at last, intimidated by the weight of deliberately attentive silence, "she didn't do anything special." He hesitated, then began again. "She arrived in a car she'd hired in London. She didn't drive through the village but made a big detour to come in Durrington way. That's how no one knew she was back. She brought a hamper of food with her from Fortnum's. What you've been eating came from them. She was happy. Quiet, but sort of—glowing."

"That is not the impression you gave me first. I understood that she was wildly happy."

"That was later. She sort of worked up to it."

"D'you mean that you watched her getting happier and happier?" Finch sounded faintly incredulous.

Gurney considered. "No, sir. It was when I was going to fetch the tea things. She'd had it in the drawing room. As I crossed the hall, she came out. 'Gurney,' she said, 'it seems as if, all of a sudden, I have everything I want in the world.' She went into the garden room and the next time I saw her she had a great armful of flowers and she set to work to fill the house with them, singing to herself." He added dully, "She had a voice like a bird, soft and clear and sweet."

"All of a sudden I have everything I want," Finch echoed. "But Gessington's love—even the fact that they could marry—wasn't 'all of a sudden.' Quite the contrary. Gurney!" His voice sharpened. "Wake up! Think, man. What happened to Mrs. Harcourt 'all of a sudden'?"

Gurney looked at him with dislike. He preferred his dreams. "I don't know."

"Did she have any visitors? Miss Budgen, perhaps?"

"I didn't see Miss Budgen."

"How about the post?"

"There was a pile of letters and parcels. There might have been something there. I hadn't sent anything on for the last ten days. She'd written and told me not to, as she might be back any day."

"When and where did she open her post?"

"In the drawing room, sir, whilst she had tea." Gurney's voice was more alive. "Very untidy she was always. When I went in to get the tray there were letters, envelopes, brown paper, and string lying everywhere."

"Doesn't sound as if there were anything interesting there."

"It doesn't follow, sir. Mrs. Harcourt would leave the most private letters about. I used to read them sometimes. I reckoned if she didn't care, neither would I."

"Did you read any of them that day?"

"Only one, sir. It sickened me. It was from some lady saying she'd heard that the mistress was going about Rome with a perfectly fascinating man." Gurney's lips curled with disgust. " 'A big blond beast,' she called him."

Finch nodded. "Yes, I found that one too. And several other recent ones. But there wasn't one that remotely concerned Mrs. Harcourt's death. How about the parcels?"

"There was one from the cleaner's. That had been here some weeks. There was a smallish box from the firm which did up the Swiss Cottage. That arrived a couple of days ago and had the Meerschaum pipe in it. Then there was a dress box from a London dressmaker and a great sheaf of white roses from Mr. Gessington."

Finch nodded. "Did you ever read any letters from Mr. Gessington?"

Gurney smiled sourly. "I didn't have much time, did I—with him only just back?"

Finch eyed him with a slow, benign smile. "It seems that Mrs. Harcourt had been in love with Mr. Gessington for some fifteen months."

Gurney stared. He didn't say anything for a moment. They could feel his stretched nerves tingling in the hot silence. "That's what I mean," he said heavily at last. "You could tear your heart out for her and she wouldn't care. She..."

Finch let him run on. He stayed for a time, listening, feeling the quality and depth of the man's grief and bewilderment.

He did not think that Gurney had killed Lisa Harcourt.

The telephone rang in the hall. Finch left the dining room to see who it was.

Peters' voice came on the wire. "There's been no sign of Miss Budgen, sir. And I've looked round Mr. Gessington's room, in case she'd been in and left a letter, but there was nothing. Fred Best has put a chair in the room opposite for me. He'll keep watch downstairs and I'll watch through a crack——"

The voice broke off. A confused muttering succeeded. Someone else had joined in. Peters had his hand only half over the receiver.

Fred Best's voice came suddenly, an excited whisper wheezing through layers of fat. "That you, Mr. Finch? He's got away, sir. The gentleman from London. He says he'll be back tonight, but it's my belief he's flying the country."

"Thanks, Best. I'll see he doesn't do that. We'll pick him up on the road. And keep an eye out for Miss Budgen, will you?"

"That I will, sir," said Best heartily. "If she knows something, you shall have it. Get her in the cellar, I will, and drop the trap on her."

"Fred Best, you surprise me," said Finch austerely. He hung up.

He walked into the hall, staring down the drive. "I wish those Bramshot men would make haste. Now we've drawn a blank at the White Hart, the sooner we begin the search for Miss Budgen, the better. And, Archie, ring up the Yard, give them the make and number of Gessington's car. I want it picked up and followed."

The Army hut which was Miss Budgen's home had fulfilled some secret and obscure function during the last war, and now was come upon only by those who knew the woods well, or by chance.

It was dilapidated, ugly, and discoloured by the raindrops of past seasons. A small brook, its water reduced to a trickle, ran into a basin scooped out by Miss Budgen. It was her only water supply.

At the back of the hut was a tumbledown shed and a wire run. Here lived four scrawny, aging hens, as eccentric as their owner. For one thing, they still laid eggs with surprising regularity. For another, they were given to motiveless fits of terror, when all four ran blindly about their pen, cackling and flapping their wings.

Miss Budgen approached her home circumspectly, a tall, gawky figure wearing a miscellaneous collection of black garments. A veil floated down her back. It was attached to a high, once glittering, turban-like hat, from which most of the jet bugles had gone. Under it was a lined and sallow face with a pinched mouth and eyes so faded as to appear almost colourless.

It had been easy enough for her to avoid Peters, but his persistence had annoyed her. It would have annoyed her father, the Admiral. Impertinence, he would have called it—and so did she. She was not in the habit of talking to policemen, and the sooner they realised it, the better.

Once assured that the village constable was not in the hut awaiting her return, she set about getting herself a meal of sorts, darting about with swift but clumsy movements. She was in a hurry. Peters, she knew, would be back. He had, she thought disdainfully, the persistence of the mentally slow.

She was really quite pleased with the way things were going. "I do believe you'd try and make money out of my dead body." Lisa had said that the last time they'd met. It had been a very rude, unladylike thing to say, and certainly not paid for by the ten-shilling note she had tossed to her. But, in a way, it had turned out to be the truth. And how Lisa would have relished the joke—if it had concerned someone else. Miss Budgen gave a cackle of spiteful laughter, peering into the battered tin where an egg was poaching.

The laughter sounded high and wild in the hollow curves of the hut. It seemed to go on—and on, echoing in the silence that would have been so much safer. She frowned, turning this last word over in her mind. Had she meant wiser? She decided, that for some reason not yet examined, safer was the more appropriate word. It followed then that she, Maud Budgen, daughter of Admiral Budgen, was afraid.

She tried to think of the future—so much brighter than it might have been. So much more worth thinking about. But nothing came. Perhaps because her mind was filled suddenly by a great wave of blind, shrieking terror. It went on and on like a machine, ceaselessly fed from some agency outside her control.

She sat very still, her mouth distorted, her work-grimed hands trembling. The water boiled up in the tin. The egg flew to the top, solidifying as it did so, casting off pieces of rubbery white which in their turn flew round like satellites.

With a great effort she got up, forcing her shaking knees to support her. She went to the open door. She stood there listening. There was nothing to hear. A vast silence had fallen on the woods. Nothing stirred or cried out. Only suddenly, at the back of the hut, the ancient fowls began their senseless running and cackling.

"Shut up!" Miss Budgen shouted, clenching her fists. And the dark trees politely blanketed the unseemly words.

She went back to the table and slid the discoloured, leathery egg onto a thick piece of bread and butter. She began to eat hurriedly, cramming her mouth. The need to be gone was strong in her, yet she could not bring herself to waste the food she had prepared.

And then it happened. In the distance a pheasant shot up with a harsh cry of alarm. Nearer, some small birds chattered the same warning. Someone was coming.

Peters! Miss Budgen plunged awkwardly to the door. But it was not Peters. Between the rhododendrons, walking carefully, came a well-known figure. And suddenly she knew that, all along, the day had been moving towards this moment. Towards an appointment made and now, perhaps, to be kept.

She went inside and closed the door. It was a ritual gesture. It didn't alter anything, only confined her rising panic to the small circumference of the hut.

A knock sounded on the door.

Slowly Miss Budgen backed away, aware suddenly of her own mortality, aware that she had only to open that door, put out her hand—and find death.

The knock was repeated, but not urgently. A voice, a pleasant voice, called her name. A more urban creature might have been reassured. Miss Budgen knew better. Softly, silently, she withdrew into the farther room, closing the door.

There was a small window at the end of the hut, the only one out of sight of her caller. It was too high up, too small, one would have thought, for anyone to get through. Miss Budgen, thin, wiry as a length of old ivy, and driven by the fear of death, managed it with the aid of the rickety chest of drawers which stood beneath it. She wriggled through and clawed her way to the ground.

It was several seconds later that her visitor, becoming impatient, opened the door of the hut to find it empty.

Sergeant Pickering came into the hall, brisk and smiling. He saw Slater. "Here we are, back again at the same old job. But at least Miss Budgen ought to be easier to find than a whisky bottle."

"Except that Miss Budgen can move about." Slater thought him aggravatingly optimistic.

"An elderly lady like that?" Pickering smiled, brushing up his stiff crumb-brush moustache. He went into the drawing room to speak to Finch.

Finch put down the pile of letters he had been going through for the second time. He told Pickering the position. "So it's not only a question of finding Miss Budgen. It's a question of finding her before the murderer does so."

Sergeant Pickering went out to organise the search. He was just as brisk but not quite as self-assured.

Slater came in to answer the telephone. It was the Yard, to say that George Gessington's car had been picked up on the London road.

"Good!" Finch threw down the letters. "Not that I expect——" He broke off. His eyes had been caught by a glimpse of the roof of the Swiss Cottage.

He stood for a moment, staring. Miss Budgen, he thought. Is that where she is? Has she been using it to supplement the meagre comfort of an old Army hut?

"Archie, go and ask Gurney for the key of the Swiss Cottage. There must be one about—with all those men working there."

Slater hurried from the room. Finch followed him into the hall to speak to Hillier.

"I'm leaving you in charge here. Don't let anyone else use the telephone. If it rings, you're to take the call. I'm going to visit the Swiss Cottage now. When I come back we'll begin a thorough search of this house. Later on I'll get enough men up here to take it to pieces——"

He broke off. He had a sudden strong feeling that he was being silently watched. He swung round. Amy Dimmick stood at the head of the stairs.

She came hurrying down. "I've been thinking, sir, that I made a fuss about nothing last night. If it's all the same to you, I'll sleep here as usual."

"You feel like that because it's still daylight," Finch told her. "It'll be very different when it's dark." He had an impression that the sallow-faced woman was indulging in a species of swift and unpleasant calculation. "No, you must keep to your original arrangement."

"Very good, sir," Dimmick answered quietly, but her eyes glinting at him gave her away. She was angry and dismayed.

When she had gone, Finch asked Reeves how many times she had been through the hall.

"A good many, sir," he answered readily. "She gave the flowers fresh water. Then she answered the door—only there wasn't anyone there. And once she asked me if I'd like a drink of lemonade."

"Why did she do that?"

"I suppose because it's a hot day, sir."

Finch looked at him with patient wonder. He spoke to Hillier. "Keep an eye on Miss Dimmick. If she wants to do anything, don't let her. And, more important still"—he looked at Reeves—"if she wants you to do anything, don't do it."

Hillier grinned widely, but his companion only looked puzzled.

Slater came back with the key. "Gurney says it's the only one."

"The Swiss Cottage has been untenanted for five years. If Miss Budgen had wanted to use it she could easily have laid her hands on a key in all that time."

They set out. They kept moving in an upward direction, knowing that it must bring them eventually to their destination. It was rough going. Even under the trees it was close and humid. There was no single path. It was simply a matter of circumventing the bushes and of making up the ground lost in so doing.

"Appropriate in one way to think that a life-and-death struggle was already taking place here before we came," Finch remarked. He explained the idea of planting the Douglas firs.

"Who was this chap Douglas, anyway?"

"He named and introduced the firs into Europe. I seem to remember he came to a bad end. Fell into a pit dug by the natives of Hawaii to catch wild animals. Unfortunately it was already inhabited by an infuriated bull."

"Good—— Oh!" said Slater with some satisfaction. He had just tripped for the third time over a straggling root.

They passed the grassy space where the whisky bottle had been found. The sunlight there seemed dazzling in comparison with the mournful, shadowy landscape in which they moved.

They found themselves facing a wall of gently swaying green, soft to the touch, baffling, and faintly aromatic.

"The building must be in the centre of this little lot," Finch remarked. "There'll be a clearly defined path somewhere. Must be, after all the work that's been done there."

They found it, a wide, flagged, serpentine path. It wound in and out of the silver-green trees, never giving a clear view of more than a few yards. It seemed very quiet now, so that their footsteps sounded louder than they should have.

"It's like getting to the palace of the Sleeping Beauty," Slater muttered. He brushed some twigs from his shoulder.

"Don't say that." Finch was thinking of Miss Budgen. No princess and, if she were there asleep, unlikely to be awakened by a kiss or anything else.

The path emerged into the open. The Swiss Cottage was before them. Built entirely of wood, it stood on an outcropping of rock which extended some eight feet above the clearing.

It consisted of a single room upstairs and down. The lower one had two small, dusty-looking windows and, presumably, a door at the rear. The upper was reached by an outside staircase leading to a wide verandah. The roof was of split logs, and elaborate woodwork decorated the eaves. A red rose grew up one of the supports. The trees hung heavily about it, and the silence and loneliness of the ornate little building struck them with uneasiness.

They climbed the rough steps. They walked to the back of the building and found an unlocked door. They went inside, blinded for a moment by the contrast with the sun. After a moment they began to make out a solid shape in the centre of the room. It grew into a great pile of neatly stacked logs. There was a partition at one end. Finch walked over and opened the door. Beyond was a water closet and a wash basin.

"Must have septic drainage out here," he murmured, "and no expense spared." He walked round the logs, half expecting to come across the body of Miss Budgen.

"She's not here." Slater had climbed to the top of the pile, sending some of the logs rolling and raising a cloud of dust. He did not know whether he was disappointed or not. "Maybe she's underneath."

Finch played his torch over the wood. "From the dust, I'd say they haven't been touched since Ambrose Potter died."

They went out, up the stairs, and onto the verandah. They looked across the clearing, but, as they had half expected, there was no view. Only the sight of leaves and more leaves in infinite shades of green.

"Old man Potter must have grown to hate life," said Finch slowly, "to have spent his days immured up here."

He turned and unlocked the door. As it swung open he followed, listening. There was nothing to be heard. He waited, to be certain of the silence, his eyes taking in the room beyond. It had painted walls and a painted ceiling. It was overfull of furniture—fat club chairs, their once green leather faded to an apricot-yellow, a Turkey carpet, a great leather settee. A fireplace—"Deep enough," Slater muttered, "to roast the proverbial ox."

The walls had been covered with the spines from leather-bound books. They were stuck on in rows, resting on simulated shelves in white paint. The ceiling was painted to resemble a silken tent top, trailing its fringed ends to shape the corners of the bookcases, then falling in stiff, painted folds, separating one mock bookcase from the next.

Finch pressed the electric-light switch experimentally. Nothing happened. It seemed that the chalet had been wired but not yet connected.

"Rummy idea," grumbled Slater, staring at the walls.

"A Victorian conceit. I've seen it before." Finch was prowling round the furniture, peering behind the couch, under the centre table. He paused to look at a pipe rack in which were five meerschaum pipes similar to the one he had examined in the garden room.

It was a sad room. Everything in it seemed remote and a little unreal. The silence was heavy. Shadows filled in the corners, and the painted curtains had a listless air, as if weighted with old dust—or dreams.

"I suppose Lisa Harcourt planned to use it for herself and Gessington," Slater remarked. "It'd make a nice private love nest for them, entirely unconnected with David Fray."

"I suppose that was her intention." Some idea had half formed in Finch's mind, but Slater's words had distracted him so that he had lost it. He had a feeling that it had been important. The place depressed him. He was glad to walk out of the room and into the fresh air.

At the first turn of the path he looked back, searching the windows. And, patterned over with the reflection of leaf and branch, they seemed to gaze back with an air of mute hostility.

At Belguardo, Hillier had a bit of news for them.

"Dimmick's like a cat on hot bricks, sir. She'd been hanging round on one excuse or another ever since you left the house. Gurney says he caught her trying the glass door into the garden room."

Finch's eyes narrowed. "So she wants to get in there, does she? We must see if we can't oblige her by clearing the coast." He thought a minute. "Hillier, go up and ask her if there is a second key to the Swiss Cottage. Let her know I'm taking you down there. Archie, you go in and unlock the glass doors so that we can get in from outside."

Archie was first back. Then Hillier appeared. "There's no key, sir, other than the one Gurney had. Mr. Potter wouldn't have but the one."

"A nuisance, that. You'll have to use my key."

Finch was careful not to look up at the house as the four of them crossed the gravel. For all that, he would not have minded taking a bet that Dimmick was watching them go.

When they were in the woods he halted. "I and my sergeant are going back to the terrace. You keep out of sight for fifteen minutes, then you can come back. I suggest you sit down and have a smoke to pass the time."

Finch and Slater made a wide detour. They emerged onto the terrace as they had done on the previous evening, close to Gurney's bungalow. Silently, cautiously, they crept along the terrace, keeping close to the wall of the house. They were scarcely aware of the glare of the sun and the heat striking up at them from the burning stones underfoot.

Very quickly and cautiously, his body flattened to the house, Finch leaned forward and stared into the garden room through the glass panels.

Amy Dimmick was there. Feverishly, swiftly, she was lifting one ornamental flowerpot holder after the other. Now she stood on tiptoe to peer into the ivy-covered wall trellis. Now she stooped to push aside some hanging creeper.

Finch opened the glass door. "Lost something?"

Dimmick gave a cry of dismay. She whirled to face him. "Oh, it's you," she gasped. Then: "You shouldn't have done that. Not come in so silently."

"Shouldn't I?" His voice was pleasant. He perched himself on one of the iron tables. "But then, I was curious. I wondered what you were looking for."

Dimmick was silent. She hung her head, less from embarrassment, Finch thought, than from a desire to give herself time to think.

"Well?"

Dimmick raised her head. "I know I shouldn't have done it, sir," she began in faltering tones, "but left as I've been—— Besides, someone will find it—and who's got a better right than me, now the mistress is dead and can't use it?" Her eyes looked past Finch as she spoke.

So that's it, he reflected. She's lying. Every time she looks past my shoulder she's lying. He thought back to his first interview with Dimmick. What a lot of trouble he would have saved himself if he had recognised the signs then. He said aloud, "But what exactly is it you're looking for?"

"Mrs. Harcourt was careless about money. She'd find she'd run out and had none. So she made a habit of hiding small sums about the house." Dimmick was growing more fluent as she progressed. "Often I've seen her go round, picking up the pots here. Laughing and saying, 'Now I know quite well I hid some money, but where did I put it?'"

"Yes?"

"Well, sir. I thought I'd as much right as anyone. More right than some——" Dimmick's voice faltered to a halt.

It was a nice performance and an interesting explanation. Only Finch didn't believe a word of it.

"I can't imagine that anyone would object to your having any small sums like that," he agreed. He seemed struck by a sudden idea. "I tell you what. Sergeant Slater shall look for you. He's an expert at that sort of thing. If anything is hidden here, he'll find it."

Dimmick shook her head. "It's not worth wasting your time, sir." She kept smiling, but it was an effort.

"On the contrary. We've nothing to do at the moment. It'll be a pleasure to help you." He slid into one of the shell chairs, one long leg crossed over the other. A lighted cigarette dangled from his fingers.

Dimmick stood just where she was. At first she managed to remain calm. Gradually, as the extent of the search became obvious, she began to show signs of uneasiness. A spot of colour burned on each of the sallow cheeks. Her body was tense. Her eyes followed Slater's every move with painful intensity.

"That's the lot, sir," said Slater at last. "I've looked everywhere, short of turning out the plants. And I can see they haven't been disturbed for months."

They both looked at Dimmick, but she, with the failure of the search, had regained her composure. She was her usual self—quiet, respectful, attentive to what they had to say. Only the shortness of her breath betrayed her.

"It seems that there's nothing hidden here after all. From my point of view, it's a pity. You may have another point of view—and the murderer a third. And it's his that gives me most concern."

"In what way, sir?" Her tone was one of mocking respect.

"Since I've been here, I've been told over and over again that Mrs. Harcourt had two confidantes, yourself and Miss Budgen. You have been boasting openly that you knew Mrs. Harcourt's every thought—emphasising the fact that you heard and remember the murderer's foot-steps. Miss Budgen is going to great pains to avoid the police. Do you think the behaviour of either of you has escaped the murderer?"

"I can only speak the truth, sir." Dimmick's face was as empty of expression as an egg.

"But not the whole truth, I fancy. A murderer is notoriously an ill person to deal with. You may think you have him at your mercy. You can ring him up, threaten him, and, in the end, find yourself sleeping snugly enough along with your late mistress on a mortuary slab."

A flicker of something that was like fear passed over the thin face. "I'm sure I don't know what you mean. If I knew the identity of the murderer d'you think I'd keep it to myself?"

"Since you ask me—yes, I do."

Amy Dimmick had the last word. "I suppose it's your calling makes you like that—suspicious of everyone." Her small, respectful smile was pinned to her lips like a shield. "I'll collect my bag from the hall and be off, sir. The bus passes in five minutes' time. I can stop it at the end of the drive."

Finch saw her go. Her bag, he noted with a certain grim amusement, had been hidden from sight behind the window curtains. Dimmick retrieved it with complete self-possession.

He watched her walk away, tall, neatly dressed. A very ordinary sight. Just a woman walking down a drive, carrying a suitcase.

"Either of you men know these Pigotts? They have a farm on the Bramshot road."

"I know them, sir." It was Reeves who spoke. "They have what's known as the Home Farm. It's their land at the top of the hill. They serve most people round here with chickens, guinea fowl, and the like. They're a respected, well-to-do family. Dependable, I'd say, sir."

"In that case I'll ring them up. Ask if they'd mind having a policeman about the place to keep an eye on Miss Dimmick. Hillier, you'd be a good man to go. Can you drive a car?"

"Yes, sir. When shall I start?"

"As soon as I've telephoned." Finch turned to go into the drawing room. He was aware of the sound of the approaching bus. He glanced back, through the open doorway. Dimmick was already out of sight.

In a minute, he thought, she'll be on the bus. Hillier should overtake it before it's out of the village. He'll be waiting for her at the other end. She'll be quite safe then. In spite of this, he was conscous of a curious uneasiness, almost of fear.

It possessed him like a premonition of disaster, and yet nothing had changed. Then he had it. Nothing had changed, but something was wrong—very wrong.

The bus had gone right on into the village without stopping.

Chapter
13

The sky was a wide floor of blue. The air was still and golden. Birds piped cheerfully overhead, and everywhere was the sight and sound of high summer. In such a setting violence seemed incredible. Yet it had taken place.

The murderer had moved quickly—appallingly quickly—and his second victim lay dead. Amy Dimmick had been stunned by a blow from behind, dragged behind the bushes, and there strangled. A piece of thin cord had bitten deeply into her scraggy neck.

She lay on her back in a tangle of old deadwood, some of it newly broken. A few green leaves adhered to her frock like an appliquéd pattern. One shoe was off, and her face was black and horribly swollen.

"Killed almost under our eyes," Slater muttered, half under his breath. "It doesn't seem possible."

"It was easy enough." Finch's voice had grown bleak. He had underestimated his opponent, and this was the result. "The murderer hid in the bushes. Dimmick's attention was fixed on the approaching bus. He—or she—took a single step forwards and struck. I don't suppose Dimmick ever saw her assailant."

"But then she must have been strangled whilst the bus was actually passing" Slater sounded incredulous. Shaken too.

Finch shrugged slightly. "Work it out for yourself. The murderer hadn't much time." Uneasiness had sprung up in his mind and ran, a cold current, in his thoughts.

157

With Amy Dimmick dead, the murderer must move quickly if he were to remain safe—and now only one person lived who knew his identity.

The two men had been searching about as they spoke. But again, as in the first crime, the murderer had come and gone, leaving no trace.

"Archie, have a look in Dimmick's suitcase. I'm going back to the house to see how many of our suspects I can place. I wish I had someone to work with less boneheaded than Reeves. Still, I can get Peters back to relieve you. He'll be no more use at the White Hart. As soon as the news of this fresh murder gets out and the village realises the killer can't be Gessington, I fancy they'll clam up on us. We'll find we might as well be operating in the Gobi Desert for all the help we'll get."

Finch had come down in his car. Now he swung it round and sped back to Belguardo. He sent Hillier to find out if Gurney were in the house. Then he telephoned Waltons. The little maid servant answered the call.

"Is Dr. Warry there?"

"No, sir. He's still on his rounds."

"D'you know where I can get hold of him?"

To Finch it seemed that his voice was falling into a vacuum of silence. That he spoke into a deadly hush. It was cold too at Belguardo, for the atmosphere of death was all about him. He hunched his broad shoulders against it.

"The mistress might know where the doctor's gone."

"Perhaps I could speak to Mr. Fray?"

"He's in the orchard. He'll be a minute or two, if you'd hold on, please."

"No, never mind. I'll send someone down. It's Inspector Finch speaking."

He was frowning thoughtfully as he replaced the receiver. He was not really worried about David. Mark Warry, too, might well prove to be more fortunate this time than on the night of Lisa Harcourt's murder.

He dialled the Potters' number. At first the telephone returned only the empty sound of its own ringing. Finch was just going to hang up when someone lifted the receiver. Phoebe Potter's voice came rather breathlessly. She had, she explained, been coming in from the garden when she had heard the telephone.

Her husband, she told Finch, had gone over to Durrington on foot to see the vicar about Lisa Harcourt's funeral. Such a complicated business to get hold of him, since the two livings have been amalgamated. Her husband had left the Hall about half-past two. She did not know when he would be back. He and the vicar were old friends. He might stay to tea—or even supper.

Finch enquired for Francis Harcourt. There was the slightest of pauses before Phoebe's lazy voice came down the line. No, he couldn't speak to him as he was out. She did not know where he had gone, or when. The first she had heard of his departure was when, at about twelve o'clock, her husband had found a note from him lying on the hall table.

At Finch's request she found and read it to him. It said simply, "I can't settle to anything. I feel I must get away for a bit." It was signed "Francis."

"What d'you think Mr. Harcourt means by 'get away'?" Finch asked.

"I don't know. It isn't like him to behave like this." Phoebe sounded genuinely puzzled. "I can only suppose that he was more upset by his wife's death than one would have imagined. He's so reserved. One never really knows what he's thinking or feeling."

Finch thanked her for her help and patience. He asked her to get her husband and Francis Harcourt to ring up as soon as they came in.

For the first time it seemed to strike Mrs. Potter that there might be some special reason for his questions—or had she been unable to trust the steadiness of her voice until now?

"Why d'you want to speak to them?" she asked. "Has anything new happened?"

"Yes, I'm sorry to say it has. Amy Dimmick has been murdered."

"Oh dear!" said Phoebe—inadequately, he felt. Without speaking again she replaced the receiver, severing the connection.

Finch rang up the police station at Bramshot. He told Bannerman of the lady maid's death. He asked for the police surgeon and some more men.

Bannerman was startled. "The murderer *has* put himself out on a limb now. It strikes me that Mrs. Harcourt must have found out something pretty discreditable about him." Adding with some satisfaction, "And that doesn't sound like David."

Finch noticed that Hillier had returned. He nodded to him as a sign that he should remain where he was for the moment. "I'll send one of your men down to Waltons to enquire into the household's whereabouts at the time of the murder," he told Bannerman. "But David Fray is out of it. From the direction of the blow that stunned Dimmick, it's obvious that the murderer is above the average height." He hung up and turned to the redheaded constable. "Did you find Gurney?"

"Yes, sir. In his bath, trying to get cool—or so he said. I could hear water splashing, but whether Gurney was actually in the bath I don't know. When I tried to look through the keyhole there was something hanging over it."

Finch sent him to Waltons.

Hillier took one of the police cars and drove away in it, down the drive and out into the white dusty road. Slater was there, searching for clues along the grass verge. He saw Hillier and raised a hand in salutation. Except for him, the road was empty.

It all looked so normal, so peaceful, that Hillier was seized with the same feeling of astonishment and disbelief that had affected the Scotland Yard sergeant.

The green, too, was quiet. A shepherd's dog was lying in the shade and two small children were playing at houses. Incredible!

He turned in at the drive of Waltons.

Harriet Warry opened the door. She had been expecting, if not Hillier, then someone from the police. David was with her. They were both pale and anxious.

"Hullo, Hillier!" David came forward. "What's the trouble?"

Hillier grinned. "Afternoon, sir. Afternoon, ma'am." His face sobered. "Miss Dimmick's got herself murdered."

Harriet turned her head, closing her eyes. "Dimmick? Oh, no! That's horrible."

"Yes, it's a bad business." Hillier described how it had happened. He ended by enquiring as to Dr. Warry's whereabouts.

Harriet's heart missed a beat. "I don't know where my husband is at the moment." Her voice fluttered a little. "I expect he's with some patient."

"Out on his rounds, is he? You've no idea where I could get hold of him?"

"You might try Winfold's at Lake Farm," David said. "I heard him tell Gladys he'd got to go there and might be a bit late for his surgery at six."

"Six?" Hillier looked at his watch. "It's eleven minutes to six now. I might just catch him on the telephone."

"Of course. Use the one in the surgery." Harriet showed him where it was and gave him Winfold's number. She closed the door on him and hurried back to the hall. "David, you'll want an alibi. Shall I say I was with you in the fowl house?"

"Not on your life. It might come unstuck, and then where would I be?" He added thoughtfully, "Wonder why Dimmick was killed? Knew too much for the murderer's peace of mind, I suppose."

Hillier came back, grinning all over his foxy face.

Harriet stepped forward. "He was there?"

"No—but he had been. I missed him by two minutes. And he'd been there for the best part of an hour."

"An hour? Mrs. Winfold must be pretty bad."

Hillier's grin broadened. "It wasn't her, sir. It was Paradon Belle."

Harriet stared. "D'you mean old Winfold's prize Friesian?"

"That's it. She was having trouble with her first calf, and the vet's away for the day."

David grinned. "Mark must have been pleased."

"Oh no, David!" Without thinking, Harriet flew to her husband's defence. "I remember when Battle was ill and the Potters couldn't get hold of the vet, Mark sat up half the night with him."

"So he did, sis." David's gaze was quizzical. Was the stage all set for a grand reconciliation scene?

"And your own alibi, sir?"

"I haven't much of one—I was in the orchard, mending the fowl house."

"Alone?" Hillier was writing in his notebook.

"Yes. The henhouse isn't the most salubrious spot on a hot day."

Hillier put away his notebook. "I daresay it's not of much consequence. I heard the Inspector say that, from the direction of the blow, the murderer must have been above the average height."

"Oh, Hillier! Then that means that they're both out of it—my brother and my husband." Harriet's voice was husky. It broke on the last syllable.

"That's right, ma'am."

"I go out and someone else comes in." David spoke airily, although he felt almost sick with relief. He wondered whether now, with the pressure lifted, he would remember just what it was he had done on the night of the first murder.

"The baker told us that you're searching the woods for Miss Budgen?" said Harriet.

"Yes. There's some idea that she knows the identity of the murderer and is keeping out of our way, hoping to sell the information to this Mr. Gessington. But, since he's left the village, I reckon we shall find her before she finds him." He saluted, stepped into the police car, and drove away, leaving behind him a pool of silence and a strange sense of unreality.

"Oh, David!" Harriet clung to him for a moment. Then she drew away, her face radiant. "What shall we do to celebrate?"

"For one thing, I won't go back to the fowl house. For another, I'll have a stiff whisky and soda. Being Murder Suspect Number One is a bit harrowing to the nerves."

"All right. You take two deck chairs into the orchard and I'll get some drinks. I must tell Gladys too."

"Don't worry. I bet she was listening."

"Of course she was—but she'll still like to be told."

Harriet went back into the house. David collected the chairs and set them up under a cherry tree. He went back to meet his sister and take the tray from her.

The sunlight slanted through the trees and patterned the grass. Birds bustled in and out of the branches, searching for the last of the cherries. Life seemed very peaceful all of a sudden, and a little unreal. It was as if, Harriet thought, they had just landed after a rough sea crossing.

David felt in his pocket. "Have a smoke?" He produced a packet of cigarettes and his lighter.

"I smoke far too much," said Harriet, taking one. She stretched lazily, falling into what began as a happy silence but soon changed into one full of dismay.

Now that Lisa had gone, the gulf that had yawned between David and his twin sister had gone too. The old silent communion had been re-established so that, sitting close to him, she had become aware that Hillier's news that he was no longer under suspicion had made no real difference to him. He was still desperately unhappy.

In the midst of her dismay he sighed sharply and ground out his cigarette, as if he had just determined to hurry away, but he made no move and his face was expressionless.

"What are you thinking of doing? Going back to the motor showrooms?" she ventured.

He frowned, pressing his lips together for a moment before he spoke. "I don't think so. I've had rather a sickener of that sort of smart-aleck existence. I did think of emigrating, but I don't think I'll do that either."

Harriet stuck out her lower lip and blew the soft damp hair from her forehead. "Too hot," she murmured. And then: "I shouldn't like you to emigrate." She turned her head to smile at him. The smile stiffened on her lips as she met the weight of his misery moving towards her like a desolate cloud. "What is it, David?" she asked. "What's wrong?"

He looked away across the peaceful orchard. "It's

Lisa. I believe she always meant to marry Gessington—only he didn't want to be involved in a divorce case."

Harriet's eyes widened. "I don't believe it." And then she remembered when Lisa had first told her of the divorce, the underlying falseness of which account she had been conscious. She stared at her brother whilst all the blood drained slowly from her face.

David smiled at her. "I only told you so that you'd understand why Mark didn't want Scotland Yard called in. After all, it's a bit thick when a chap's driven to spend his time with a cow."

At Belguardo, Finch had telephoned to the White Hart for Peters. Then he had gone upstairs and begun a search of Amy Dimmick's bedroom. He had not been there more than a few minutes when Reeves came up to find him: John Potter was on the telephone.

He had, Potter said, not long been home. He had been horrified to learn from his wife of Dimmick's demise. Yes, he quite understood that he must give an account of his movements. He did so, backing it up with the names of people he had spoken to—or seen—whilst out.

He admitted that he had known that Dimmick was going to stay at the Home Farm. He had met one of the Pigott boys whilst on his way to Durrington. Where had he been at the time of the murder? Probably sitting in a cornfield, smoking his pipe. He hadn't been in a hurry to get back to Paradon—and how right he had been.

Finch thanked him for answering so many questions so patiently, enquired whether there was any news of Harcourt, and rang off.

He and Slater walked down the drive to speak to Peters, now on guard in place of his sergeant. The news of the murder had spread through the village, and most of its inhabitants were gathered a little way off, silently staring, although there was nothing to see but the familiar figure of their own constable.

Finch called Peters, who stepped forward to meet him. The villagers kept their distance.

"Mr. Potter says he walked into Durrington," said Finch in a low voice. "Which way would he have gone?"

"Out the side gate at the Hall and up the road there." Peters turned, pointing. "He'd have skirted the quarry and walked along the sunken lane which runs above the woods. After that . . ."

"Thanks! That's all I wanted to know." Finch added to Slater, "So if John Potter set out with the idea of catching up with Miss Budgen he was very well placed to cut down through the woods to find her."

"And when he failed with her, decided to try for Amy Dimmick on the way back," Slater agreed.

"Trouble is," Finch pointed out, "we don't know that he did fail."

A police car came up the hill, scattering the villagers. It was followed by a second, smaller car. From the first car stepped Superintendent Bannerman and three uniformed men, one of whom carried a camera. From the second came the police surgeon, who, directed by Peters, disappeared into the bushes to examine the corpse.

Bannerman was still wearing the crumpled tussore suit, and his collar was wilting. He suffered from the same feeling of incredulity as had Slater and Hillier. "Murdered whilst the bus was passing? It's not possible."

"It's quite possible," said Finch in his soft voice. "No paraphernalia needed. Just a knowledge of the times the local bus ran, good nerves, and a strong pair of hands."

Bannerman stared. "You're a cool one."

Finch shook his head. "Not me," he murmured. "The murderer. That's why we still don't know who he is—although this murder, unlike the first, was pretty carefully planned."

The police surgeon had little to add to Finch's own deductions. He got in his car and drove off. An ambulance arrived, scattering the silent onlookers. Amy Dimmick's body was carried out on a stretcher and taken away. As if this had been the lowering of the curtain at a theatre, the crowd began to disappear in twos and threes, silent as they had come. In a couple of minutes the road was empty but for the police.

Chapter
14

The police went from door to door in the village. They were met with lowered eyes and reluctant voices. No one had seen anything. No one had heard anything. They had been busy indoors at the time. They had had their curtains drawn against the heat.

"We're not getting much co-operation," Bannerman remarked, striding impatiently up and down the black and white hall. "The murderer might well have been seen by half a dozen people, but they're not saying."

"They don't see why the murderer should hang just to please a bunch of foreigners," said Finch.

"I'm not a foreigner!" cried the Superintendent, stung. "There're dozens of us Bannermans round about these parts."

"I know. All wonderful big and strong," Finch agreed. "Still, you're a policeman. That's enough for them."

The driver and conductor of the bus in which Amy Dimmick had planned to ride to the Home Farm had been questioned. So had the passengers. No one had seen or heard anything suspicious. They were all a little sceptical of the police theory.

It was Pickering who came on the Army hut, battered, forlorn, its walls slimy with damp and its door gaping wide. He went in, followed by the constable whom he had with him. It was hot and close inside. The windows crawled with flies, and a sour smell rose from a rubbish bucket standing near the oil stove.

"For heaven's sake!" Pickering muttered. "An admiral's daughter, isn't she? How did she come down to this?"

"The Council ought to be told. They'd put her in a home quick enough."

"You're young," said Pickering, "and that makes you hard. Old people have a right to live as they like—even when its like this." His wandering gaze fell on the battered table which stood pushed against the wall to steady it. His heart fell. "She's been back for a meal. *And* she didn't finish it."

He felt the water in which the egg had been cooked. It was no more than the temperature of the hut. The stove was cold. He walked into the farther room and stood just within, staring around.

The gray, trailing bedclothes, a black coat turning green with age, the wrecked remains of a once elaborate summer hat hanging from the looking-glass, a rickety chest of drawers . . .

He saw that the miscellaneous articles on the top had been pushed roughly aside, leaving a clear space. And that above it was an open window. Could she have—— He did not think it possible.

He walked round outside the hut. The four scrawny hens, dozing in the heat, opened rheumy, disinterested eyes to watch him as he passed. At the back he found the marks left on the wall and the rain-water pipe by Miss Budgen's departure.

He sent the constable for some more men. Whilst he waited for their arrival he fed the hens. He was a kindly man. He felt certain that their owner would not be returning to do so.

Slater had taken over the search of Amy Dimmick's bedroom. He was fascinated to find that she had nearly two thousand pounds skilfully invested. He wondered which of her mistress's admirers had been her financial adviser.

He found a letter from a married sister, too. It was dated the day before and begged Dimmick to leave Belguardo, since "it is not nice to be mixed up with the police." It was a pity, Slater reflected, that Dimmick had disregarded the advice. Her sister would be upset. Or perhaps she would rather have the two thousand pounds, he reflected cynically. He made a note of her name and address and went downstairs to report the failure of his search.

The evening seemed settling in for one of negative results and frustration.

For a time it was punctuated by reports of people who had either seen or spoken to John Potter. "And their name was legion," Finch murmured, cracking the joints of his long fingers in an absent-minded manner.

"Damn it!" Bannerman burst out. "Mr. Potter can't have gone looking for Miss Budgen. He's covered for practically every moment bar the ten minutes it would have taken him to walk up the road and along the lane." He threw down the list Finch had compiled. "I suppose that proves he's no murderer."

Finch lit a cigarette. He looked at the Superintendent through the smoke. "It proves nothing but that he's no fool. Find someone who saw him on that bit of road between the Hall and the sunken lane and you may get a very different picture."

Bannerman thought it out. "You mean we've no proof that Mr. Potter left the Hall at the time his wife says he did?"

"Exactly. Make it even fifteen minutes earlier and it leaves Potter with enough time to drop down the hill to Miss Budgen's hut and back again."

Bannerman grunted. "I suppose there's no one in the village who'd take her in and say nothing?"

"No. She's too much of a mischief-maker to have endeared herself to anyone."

"Then perhaps Pickering is right and she is dead."

"I don't think so. A dead body is a dead weight. Murder her in those woods and you wouldn't get her far," Finch answered almost absently. All his thoughts were concentrated on that dead, scrub-infested darkness beneath the fir trees.

What *had* happened to Miss Budgen? She had not

returned to her hut. Nor had she been to the Swiss Cottage, for a police constable was watching for her there. And if she were dead, why hadn't Pickering been able to find her body?"

"Well, if she's not dead yet she ought to be all right," said Bannerman. He spoke truculently, as if to convince himself as much as anyone else. "And we've got a couple of men watching the Hall through field glasses. The Potters can't leave without being seen."

Finch raised a satirical eyebrow. "And after dark?"

Bannerman brought his hand crashing down on a small table, narrowly escaping splitting it in two. "We've got to find her before dark," he said. "We've got to." He went out of the house and down into the woods to spur on his men.

Finch remained where he was, conscious of his own tiredness, letting his thoughts drift with the smoke from his cigarette, waiting for some fact to come along. But none did. Only the long line of protagonists, alive and dead, passed before his mental vision.

Once he murmured, "Jolly unhealthy, that. John Potter should have kept up the feud. Or, if they had to meet, given Lisa a good poke on the jaw to remind her to keep a civil tongue in her head . . ."

And again: "Ghosts aren't the only type of haunting. There's something there, in the Swiss Cottage . . ."

The clock on the drawing-room mantelpiece struck eight. Outside, Bannerman passed the windows on his way back.

The sun went down behind the hill, but the heat did not ease up. Under the trees it was stifling. The light began to fail everywhere. The sky hung low, a dirty grey tinged with sulphur. The air too was yellowish and unreal. The garden seemed transfixed in sharp-cut symmetrical patterns.

Bannerman came into the drawing room. Sweat was shining on his forehead, and his tie was like a piece of chewed string. There was a storm coming, he said. He hoped that it wouldn't break before dark. After that it might help to drive Miss Budgen into the open. Finch remarked that, according to Pickering, it looked as if what was wanted to find her was a spade.

And the waiting, the heat, and the deathly silence went on.

At a quarter to nine Pickering had to give up.

Bannerman kept back some of the men to search those rooms that had not already been searched by the Scotland Yard men. This was more to keep himself occupied than from the hope of finding anything helpful.

Finch sent Slater up to the Hall. Ostensibly he was to enquire if there had been any message from Francis Harcourt, who seemed to have disappeared as completely as Miss Budgen. Actually he was to make certain that the Potters were still at home.

He came back with disquieting news.

The Potters had both been in. They had heard nothing, so they said, of their paying guest. Then the telephone had rung and Phoebe Potter had snatched the receiver up, only to cast it down on the table beside the main body of the instrument, declaring hysterically that if she heard that sound just once more she would go mad. Her husband had fetched her a drink and suggested that, early as it was, they should both go upstairs to bed with a book and forget the whole damned business.

"And the telephone receiver remained off?" Finch asked.

"Yes, sir."

"I see. So now we can't telephone to them."

"You think the call was deliberately contrived?" Bannerman had come downstairs to hear Slater's report.

"Not the call. That just furnished the excuse to cut us off from the Hall. The Potters aren't to be disturbed. They've gone to bed. For the sake of Mrs. Potter's health, they're taking no more calls, answering no more enquiries."

"Perhaps they mean no more than they said," Bannerman remarked doggedly.

"Oh, my sainted aunt!" said Finch wearily. "Of course, they may be as innocent as a couple of baa-lambs—as home-loving as their dog, Battle. All I'm saying is that they've deliberately put it out of our power to prove it."

Owen Sturgis came up from the village. He looked hot, untidy, and cheerful. He went straight through to the kitchen. He returned carrying a screw-top bottle of beer, a glass, and a plate of ham sandwiches.

"More food in the house than that fellow Gurney will be able to eat." He added virtuously, "In fact, if anything happens to him it'd be a kindness to move in here."

Bannerman eyed him sourly. "You seemed pleased with yourself."

"Why not? I've had a good day."

"A woman has been murdered."

"What of it? She wasn't my type." Sturgis took a bite from a sandwich, ate it, then remarked conversationally, "So your men didn't manage to find Miss B.?"

Bannerman's small eyes gleamed red. "They did not."

"A pity." Sturgis began to whistle "The Teddy Bear's Picnic."

Bannerman glared at the reporter. Then, turning abruptly on his heel, he walked from the room and stumped away upstairs.

Sturgis chuckled. He finished his sandwich. "What are you waiting for?" he asked Finch.

"For something to happen."

The front doorbell rang.

"Perhaps this is it."

They went into the hall. Slater had just opened the door. Beyond it, in the fading light, stood David Fray and an old M.G. sports car. He was looking away across the garden. He turned at the sound of the door opening.

"Hullo!" said Finch. "Remembered something more? Come on in." He was startled by the change in the young man. He looked very different from the shivering, haggard boy whom he had interviewed the previous day. He seemed to have grown much older, to have matured during the last twenty-four hours.

David smiled faintly. "Yes—for what it's worth. It's still all pretty shadowy and insubstantial—rather like the worst sort of nightmare. But I know now I never entered this house. I can remember threshing about in those damn shrubs and then bursting out of them. I remember reeling across the gravel, to be brought up short by the wall of the house."

Finch nodded encouragement. It was not quite as he had visualised it—but it was near enough.

David's eyes met his levelly. "I remember looking in at the window and seeing someone over by the garden-room door." He added quietly, "The murderer, I suppose."

A tense little silence followed. So they had got round to him at last, Finch thought. This person whose footfalls Dimmick had heard on the night of her mistress's death.

"Who was it?"

"I'm sorry. I don't know. It was just a dark outline. If it hadn't moved I probably wouldn't have noticed it was there."

"Think back. It didn't remind you of anyone you knew?"

Was David speaking the truth? Or didn't he want to identify the murderer?

"Heavens, no!"

"Was it a man or a woman?"

"I thought a man. But then, I never imagined that the murderer might be a woman."

"Had it a lot of hair? No hair? Or a hat?"

"I tell you I don't know." David hesitated. "As a matter of fact, it seemed to contract and expand before my eyes. I suppose because I was drunk."

"What way did it go?"

"I didn't wait to see. I was so startled I sprang away from the window and damn near fell flat on my face."

Finch nodded. That last bit was true, anyway. Perhaps the rest had been. "Dimmick says the footsteps went towards the front door. So if you wouldn't mind repeating your performance of last night? Just the bit where you looked in through the window? It's not as late as it was then, but with these clouds hanging about, it's probably almost as dark inside." He was hoping that the exercise would suggest something further to the young man. "Archie, we're going outside. You put out the lights and then act the part of the murderer." He added, as he led the way from the house, "I take it that the door of the garden room was already closed when you saw this figure?"

"Yes, it must have been. The figure was just a darker patch against a dark background."

The front door shut behind Slater. The lights in the hall went out. David felt a chill close about his heart. It was like—so terribly like that other evening.

"Get on, laddie," urged Sturgis impatiently. "Get on."

Obediently David turned and peered in at the window. And in the near darkness inside, Slater's footfalls rang out on the marble floor.

David moved away with a gesture of repugnance. "I remember now," he said wearily. "Dimmick was wrong. When I saw that figure it was going towards the drawing room."

Finch caught his breath. As Francis Harcourt had been doing on the following night. As he had done that morning. Had it been he on the night of the murder too, frustrated then in his design by hearing Dimmick moving about upstairs? And, if so, what had he been after?

Sturgis's loud, cheerful voice broke in. "You're no actor, laddie. If you'd looked in as openly as that, the murderer would have seen you. In which case it's unlikely that you'd still be with us. Here, let me have a go, and Archie Slater can cross the hall again."

The next minute he was giving a realistic impersonation of a drunken man. His head lolled. His eyes rolled in the direction of the hall window. Suddenly he burst out laughing. "If that isn't the damnedest thing! Take a look through this first pane. Blow me if Slater too isn't expanding and contracting!"

Finch peered through. "So he is. Must be a flawed bit of glass put in during the war. I suppose as it was a small side pane, it wasn't worth replacing."

He led the way into the house and across the hall. He was conscious of a great feeling of expectancy. He paused on the threshold of the drawing room, staring, alert, half expecting the long, lovely room to have changed in some significant particular so that the truth would leap at him.

There was no change. Everything was as it had been.

The valuable furnishings, the pictures and porcelain. The scent of flowers. The photograph which recorded Lisa's dark, passionate beauty. The faint shadows and echoes of past days, apparent to those susceptible to such things.

"There's nothing different," David declared. He looked about him coolly, but his detachment was a pretence. His face wore a look of bewilderment and desolation that was touching.

Finch, catching his eye, looked hastily away. So he knows, he thought. His brother-in-law must have told him. Or perhaps he worked it out for himself.

Sturgis was poking about, spectacles crooked on his broad nose. Slater watched him with an ironical look.

"I know! I know!" said Sturgis, stopping in front of the sergeant. "I'm just wasting my time, since you've already searched the room. But the murderer must have been after something. What was it?"

"The only thing that's new is this," said Finch. He took the figure of the Goddess Kuan Yin from the cabinet and set it carefully down on a low table. "Harcourt says his wife must have picked it up on her travels."

"She probably did," David agreed. "It wasn't here—when she went away."

"It's got something," Sturgis declared. "Pity it's chipped."

"Just what Harcourt——" Finch broke off, staring. Then he said slowly, "He told me that Lisa managed to get into the cabinet when she was eighteen months old and break one of the pieces."

"So what? Babies are just as destructive as puppies. I've got five children, so I ought to know."

"Yes—but suppose it wasn't true? Suppose Ambrose for some purpose of his own took the piece and hid it away in the Swiss Cottage? And that the men working there found it at the same time as they found the meerschaum pipe?"

"Wait a minute," said Sturgis, wagging a stubby finger. "I'm not with you. What meerschaum pipe?"

Finch explained, arranging his own thoughts as he did

so—arranging them as far as possible; for the sequence of events still didn't make sense.

"But even if what you say is right—and Harcourt did look ghastly after glancing into the cabinet—where is it leading us?"

"It must lead somewhere," said Finch, frowning down at the serene Kuan Yin. The mystery as he saw it was not so much why Ambrose had taken the porcelain figure down to the Swiss Cottage, but rather why he had lied about it.

"Suppose Harcourt came here last night simply to make certain that the collection hadn't been dispersed? Suppose that in the telling of that story of the breaking of one of the pieces in the cabinet the whole incident returned vividly to mind? Suppose that on his return to the Hall he . . ." Finch's voice trailed away as his thoughts flew forwards.

"He what?" Sturgis demanded.

Finch had it now. "Suppose he had remembered that it was a porcelain figure of Kuan Yin that Lisa was said to have destroyed, and that that too had had a bit chipped out of one ear?"

"Harcourt remember a thing like that for— what? Thirty-five—thirty-six years? Oh, come off it!"

"You forget that Chinese porcelain is his passion and that we're talking of museum pieces—rare—unforgettable. Besides, that bit had a special connection in his mind with Rachel Potter—and he had been in love with her."

"But if you're right, what has it got to do with Lisa Harcourt's death?" Sturgis straddled one of the chairs and hitched it nearer to the detective. "Seeing that the dame in question was cruel, crooked, and capricious, maybe the solution is the same. Something so outrageous that we haven't come round to it yet, eh?" He looked hopefully over the top of his spectacles at David, who was standing in front of the fireplace, nervously running a finger along the cool surface of the chimneypiece.

David swung round. "To be candid, I don't care what the solution is," he said quietly. "I've had enough of this house and its problems. I only wish I might never see it or hear of them again."

He did not say good night. He simply walked unhurriedly down the long lovely room towards the door—and, without turning for as much as a single backward glance, closed it with finality behind him.

Finch thought it closed on many things—young love, trust, youth itself.

Sturgis stared at the closed door. "A chap with such self-control as that ought to go far," he remarked.

Finch did not answer. He had gone back to his contemplation of Kuan Yin. He picked it up. There was nothing written on it, nothing concealed inside it. What was the secret of this small, exquisite figure with its inscrutable Eastern face and gently contemplative air? Had the murderer's interest lain there, along with Harcourt's? Were they perhaps one and the same person?

The clock on the mantelpiece struck eleven, and overhead Bannerman's footsteps sounded as he walked restlessly up and down.

A car came up the drive. Finch recognised the note of its powerful engine. So Gessington is back, he thought. He heard the front doorbell ring and Slater run down from upstairs to answer it. A moment later the industrialist came into the drawing room.

He looked tired, but his brief return to the world he knew, where money was power and strings could be pulled, had restored his shattered ego. Against his unconcern, his granite face, fate itself seemed to have no weapon.

"Good evening, Inspector. I saw the lights in here and thought I might find you."

"You have some information for me?"

"Yes—from Miss Budgen."

"You've seen her?"

"No, she wrote to me." There was a sort of cold amusement in his clear blue eyes. "I found the letter in my bed at the White Hart when I got back. Between the sheets. Most indelicate." Languidly he held out a single piece of cheap writing paper, folded in half. "I haven't had a chance of following it up yet."

"And it remains highly unlikely that you will."
Bannerman had come in with Hillier. He stared at Gessington
with fury, and his face turned an alarming shade of red.

"You think not?" Gessington lowered himself into one
of the comfortable chairs and lit a cigarette with care and
deliberation. He was not to be overawed by any provincial
policeman, however large and disapproving. Finch noticed
that he took care to choose a chair from which he could
not, by any chance, meet the eyes of the photograph.

" 'Dear Sir,' " Finch read aloud, murmuring, " 'I understand that you are anxious for information that will lead
to the arrest of the murderer. I can give you that information . . .' " Finch paused. No one spoke. Bannerman was
breathing heavily, and Gessington's face was a mask of
enforced indifference.

" 'I had been expecting Lisa's return, and seeing the
light shining from the garden room, I went in to welcome
her home. She told me of her engagement and I know that
you will not misunderstand me when I say that it was not
only this that had caused her happiness. She had with her
a packet of yellowing letters tied up with a ribbon. She
wouldn't tell me who had written them, but went dancing
about the room and out round the fountain, holding them
above her head. All in good time, was what she said.
Someone was due to have a great big surprise. . . .' "

Again Finch's voice died away. Outside, the dusk
pressed against the windows. Inside, there was only the
picture evoked by the letter, a picture of the graceful
figure of Lisa Harcourt dancing among the strange green
plants and around the flashing fountain, holding high a
pile of ancient letters.

Finch took up his reading. " 'Since her sad death I
have had an opportunity to examine these letters. They
are not actually in my possession but I know where they
are. If you are interested, no doubt we can come to some
arrangement mutually satisfactory . . .' " His voice trailed
away once more.

"But what was in the letters?" Bannerman asked,
bewildered.

"I don't know—yet." Stray thoughts were scurrying

through Finch's mind without sequence or meaning. Like the room—the night—they had about them a touch of phantasy, as if strangeness begat strangeness. "Now we have three things suddenly appearing in the house: the pipe, the Goddess Kuan Yin, and these letters. And the letters—obviously the most important—have vanished again."

"But what letters were they?" Bannerman persisted. "And who wrote them?"

"They were love letters, surely—since they were tied up with a ribbon," Finch answered. "As to who wrote them, one of the parties concerned must have been Rachel Potter. As to the other—— Ambrose Potter? Francis Harcourt? Both men were in love with her."

Sturgis gave his sudden ribald laugh. "And lovely Lisa laid her sacrilegious little paws on them, eh?" He gave a half ironical bow in Gessington's direction. "If you'll pardon the hard words?"

Gessington said nothing, just gave him stare for stare; but the barriers he had so recently erected were crumbling. Unwelcome reality was creeping in again.

"I begin to see some sense in this affair," said Sturgis.

"Me too," murmured Slater.

"But what concern was this to Lisa?" Gessington demanded. "What did she do with the letters?" Perhaps he hoped to be spared some pain by a last-minute illumination. If so, he was to be disappointed.

Said Finch slowly, "She used her knowledge of their contents to destroy a dream image round which her murderer had built his whole existence, and was herself, in turn, destroyed." His voice grew even slower. "Yes," he said softly. "Yes, it was as simple as that. I feel certain of it. So the next thing obviously is to get the letters and . . ."

"*Get* them?" Bannerman broke in. "You know where they are?" His brow lightened a little. Action was always agreeable to him.

"Lisa returned them to the Swiss Cottage for safety. You see, Dr. Warry's anger earlier that evening must have suggested to her that her second visitor might be even angrier, that he might try and take them from her by force. So she put them back—all but one, maybe—in

whatever hiding place was contrived by Ambrose Potter."
Finch's voice died away. He looked startled and oddly
disquieted.

"You're thinking the murderer too may have worked
out where the letters are hidden?" Bannerman asked.

"I'm not worrying about his finding the letters,"
Finch retorted, making for the door. "I'm worrying about
his finding Miss Budgen. I've just realised where she's
been hiding all this time—in the Swiss Cottage, along with
the letters."

A feeling of acute dismay fell on them—all except the
reporter, Sturgis. He was pleasantly excited. They took
Hillier with them and a couple more of the Bramshot men
and hurried out into the night.

To Gessington, left behind, the house seemed very
quiet and empty. After a moment he rose to his feet. He
walked slowly and deliberately across the floor to stand in
sombre contemplation of his lost love. His face twisted
suddenly. He who had cut across honour and decency to
get what he wanted now found himself inescapably trapped
in the torture of his own desires.

One of the men upstairs heard the sound of a crash
from inside the drawing room. When he came down, the
room was empty. The photograph had gone from the
pinao. It lay in utter ruin in the grate.

"Looks as if someone ground their heel on it," he
muttered, puzzled. "Now who'd want to do a thing like
that?"

Outside, Finch led the way at a fast pace, seeing not
the ground on which he walked but the small ornate
building in which an obstinate and half-crazed woman,
defenceless and in utter solitude, awaited the coming of a
murderer.

Bannerman tripped over a sprawling root and swore
under his breath. "How d'you know the letters are in the
Swiss Cottage and that we're not on a wild-goose chase?"
he asked irritably.

"Because when Peters saw Mrs. Harcourt's dead body,
she had a red rose tucked into the bodice of her frock.

And, although Belguardo is surrounded by roses, the only red ones grow by the Swiss Cottage."

"And this hiding place——" Sturgis took up the questioning. "No one's found it, yet you say it's big enough to hold a woman."

"Only because no one has had any reason to look for it," Finch answered. "The walls are covered with mock books in painted bookcases, and I believe one of those bookcases to be a door. It's a Victorian idea and was sometimes used in libraries to hide the entrance into a cloakroom."

"I get it," said Sturgis. "The Age of Delicacy. Everything hidden, from table legs to gents' lavatories."

"That's it—although in this case I don't suppose the hidden space held anything more than a washstand with a jug and basin—and perhaps a looking-glass on the wall."

"Miss Budgen's been a bit cramped, hasn't she?"

"I imagine she stayed in the room most of the time. After all, the Swiss Cottage isn't a place you can come on without warning."

Bannerman, thinking of the many visits his men had paid through the day, grunted in disgust.

They fell silent, hurrying on. The light from their torches bobbed up and down in a sea of darkness. Occasionally a breath of wind rustled through the branches overhead or stirred the leathery leaves of the rhododendrons so that they rubbed together with a dry, papery sound as if they were dying at last. But for the most part it was close and still. Long before they reached their destination the little group were hot and sweating.

They came to the arboretum, the cypress, silver firs, pines, and cedars planted by Ambrose Potter. They went up the serpentine path and so out into the little clearing.

The trees stood round in a flurry of movement, their soft branches undulating with an odd and rather uncomfortable suggestion of some sort of subhuman life. The sky was dark and overcast but, for all that, after the blackness of the woods, they could see the Swiss Cottage well enough.

Its sturdy roof. Its two lower windows, empty and

blank, like the pale stare of an idiot. And in between, door and windows lost in the shadow of the overhanging eaves.

No light showed anywhere. Not a sound came from within. The red-rose tree shot up, tall and straggling, and they could smell the scent of its flowers in the warm air.

Sturgis looked round him. "It's like being surrounded by a surging sea," he remarked to Slater.

"Or being a very small Christian in a very large amphitheatre," said Slater.

"Oh, come on!" said Bannerman impatiently.

Finch sent two of the Bramshot men to search the downstairs floor and then to stand on guard.

"Shall I come up with you, sir?" Hillier asked hopefully.

"Not," said Finch firmly, "unless you hear me scream." And he posted him to stand guard under the verandah.

The four remaining men ascended the stairs, their footfalls echoing confusedly on the hollow treads. They walked along the verandah and saw that the lock of the door into the painted room had been forced.

And, as they stared, a breath of wind, stealing out from the trees, swung the door a little on its hinges with a horrid suggestion that someone had but lately passed—whether in or out, they could not tell.

For a moment they all stood listening, but silence covered the room like a blanket. It was dark as a cavern and seemed to breathe an uneasy sense of hostility and danger.

Finch shone his torch round about so that the room sprang fleetingly to view: fanciful, unreal as the books which were not meant to be read, the draperies that could not be drawn, the chairs and couches standing round with an uncomfortable suggestion of waiting for a company of ghosts.

Finch found their air of silent expectancy unnerving. "Miss Budgen!" he called, stepping inside. His heart fell. A question needs an answer. When there is none, the silence becomes not silence at all but a waiting vacuum into which something else must drop. Disappointment, perhaps, anxiety—or fear. Fear of an answer that does not depend on speech.

Whilst Bannerman filled the door with his mighty hulk, Slater and Sturgis began a search of the room. Finch crossed to the great open fireplace. "Might be to the right. Or to the left," he murmured. "Or both, perhaps." He paused suddenly, listening, looking back towards the outer door. "Did you hear anything, Archie?"

"No, sir—but I'm not feeling too happy."

"Nor I." Finch's voice was troubled. He was uneasy, although the reason for his uneasiness escaped him. He turned back, running his fingers along a row of books. They caught in a depression at the foot of a brown calf spine. He pressed—pulled. The whole bookcase swung towards him and the light from his torch slid through the opening.

A packet of letters lay on the floor, close to the right-hand wall. A fat packet, creased by much reading and tied with a faded blue ribbon. But that was not all. Two shabby black lace-up shoes stuck out, close to the letters. They were still on their owner's feet.

Miss Budgen was there. She was sitting propped up against the wall in a windowless space like a cupboard— and she was dead. Horribly dead.

"Like a wild beast," Bannerman muttered, his ruddy colour fading. "What's come over him?"

"His mind's going," Finch murmured. "He's getting farther and farther from the normal world." And then: "I don't like this. I don't like it at all." He shivered suddenly.

Sturgis joined him, stepping out of the gloom. "You mean because the letters *are* there?" he asked. Adding with a wry grimace, "Yes, I see what you mean."

An uncomfortable silence fell. In it there was the soft note of leaves rustling, the creak of wood, a gentle sighing of wind—but not the sound for which they listened.

"A few minutes earlier and we might have caught him red-handed," said Bannerman, not understanding what troubled the others.

Finch nodded. "He's not far," he agreed. "She's been dead—what? Ten minutes? fifteen?" And again that odd little silence fell. "Still, we could try and lure him out. What d'you say, Archie?"

"I'm all for it, sir," said Slater with feeling.

"Then nip down and tell those fellows. Whisper it into their ears. No action unless the murderer comes out shooting. Hurry, or the storm may break and spoil everything."

"Right, sir." Slater sped away. Sturgis looked quickly at Finch, then away again, whistling almost inaudibly with affected unconcern.

"But what are you going to do?" Bannerman asked. It was plain to him that the other three men were disturbed beyond his comprehension.

"I'm going to read to him."

"Read——" The Superintendent peered at Finch as if he were out of his mind. "What good will that do?"

"Well, he's a consistent fellow," Finch said in his soft drawl. "He's already strangled three women rather than have the contents of these letters known. It's not likely that he'll stand by without a protest and hear a flatfooted policeman proclaiming their contents to the heavens. Only question is, will his protest take the form I hope?"

Bannerman grunted. "Then get on with it." He stepped into the background and put out his torch as if metaphorically cutting himself off from the whole proceeding.

Slater came hurrying back, to shine his torch on the letter in Finch's hand.

Finch began to read, standing just inside the open outer door. " 'My darling,' " he read and Hillier, outside, raised his head sharply in surprise. " 'It's no good. I asked John—I almost went on my knees—to get him to join this party of school friends going to Greece, but he refused. Obstinate, tiresome creature, he refused . . .' "

Finch paused. The silence seemed to have intensified, as it does before the breaking of a storm. From inside the room there came not a sound. The gloom of the little building, the proximity of the woman so recently dead, Finch's own conviction that the murderer was not far away—all combined to oppress them with a sense of gravity. They were, all but Bannerman, anxious too.

Outside, Hillier leaned forward suddenly, peering in front of him. The profound silence following on Finch's voice had been broken by a single sound, a sound so small and stealthy as scarcely to be audible.

Finch took up the reading again. This is a mad business, he thought. To whom was his voice addressed? To the red-haired constable in the shadows beneath the verandah? To the silent trees? To the night wind ruffling their topmost branches? Or did they indeed reach the ears of the man who had loved Rachel Potter beyond reason?

" 'He said that I could not afford the expense—which is quite true, if it had been my money I was going to spend—and that he could not leave me in any case. So there it is. I can't move him. That means that we must not meet whilst he is at home . . .' "

In the room, the tension was growing. A large moth flew in, attracted by the light. It whirled madly round the torch until Slater struck it down and trod on it. Bannerman, watching glumly from the darkness, thought that it must be his imagination that both men were a little pale.

" 'No, we mustn't meet. *We must not.* Suppose he found out? Sometimes I dream that he has found out and I wake up wringing wet with sweat. Oh, darling, darling, what have we done? Our lovely, lovely life together and now it must stop . . .' "

Finch's voice ceased abruptly, for beyond the quiet, clear voice another sound had intruded. And, even before they understood what the sound was, they were aware that it was there.

To Hillier's strained gaze it seemed as if a ripple ran softly through the trees in front of him, as if someone—or something—were approaching, as if the words of love floating out on the warm air had evoked some monstrous response from the deep and listening trees.

The atmosphere of nightmare lay upon his quick and sceptical mind, making him a prey to fears he would instantly have repudiated among other surroundings. He's coming, he thought, half expecting to see a creature, part man, part beast.

"The letter is signed Rachel," said Finch's voice, suddenly recalling Hillier to himself. "Rachel Potter. And the date? Roughly two years after she divorced her husband." He raised his voice a little. "Who was she writing to, I wonder—this lady with the inflammable pen? This respectable woman who was so anxious to get her son out of the way so that she could take some lover? Archie, give me another letter."

The trees parted suddenly. A man stepped into the open. He walked slowly and stiffly forward, his face raised in an attentive attitude, a grey face of desolation which yet had a certain grandeur about it. It was as if its possessor, hopelessly and irretievably lost, was buoyed up by the feeling that he had been engaged on a crusade that to him, at least, had been just, even noble.

Now the four men upstairs heard it: the sound of footsteps approaching through the darkness—on the sun-baked ground, the open stairway, on the verandah it-self——

And suddenly the tension had eased. The light flickered in Slater's grasp, then grew still. Sturgis relaxed his taut attitude, and Finch gave a sudden quick sigh.

Bannerman, turning to look at him, perceived that not only had some hope been fulfilled, but that some dread had passed away.

The clouds parted a little, so that a little light filtered through. And, against this pale gleam, the squire of Paradon, John Potter, stood outlined, motionless, in the doorway.

" 'My darling——' " said Finch, as if he were beginning another letter, though indeed he did no more than hold it in his hand.

Potter took a step forward. "Keep your filthy tongue still," he said savagely. "And your filthy mouth closed. My mother never took a lover. She simply, God help me, went back to my father. They were lovers. Here, in this building. That's why he bought it. So that they could make love to each other." His voice rose. His shoulders rocked against the near darkness—and sanity seemed to rock with him. "They didn't mind about me—except that I was in the way. They didn't mind that he had another wife—except that she was in the way. They cared only about each other."

"And Lisa Harcourt told you this?"

"Yes. She telephoned and said that she must see me. I thought that it must be about her marriage. That perhaps she was going to ask me to give her away. Instead she told me that the figure of Kuan Yin had been found. I was going to get it when I heard Dimmick walking about upstairs." His voice had grown flat, dulled with weariness and grief.

"But the letters?" Finch prompted him.

"Lisa only gave me one to read, although she told me that there were others. She said we must have all the lights on because the ink was faded. But it wasn't that. She wanted to see my expression when I realized the letter's contents." The voice ceased its nightmare monotone. John Potter put his hand up to his head as if it hurt him.

"And then what happened? When you'd read the letter, I mean."

"Lisa laughed. I think she'd been laughing for some time but I hadn't heard her. A thick red mist seemed to have come up from somewhere." His arms swung out awkwardly as if measuring its immensity. "And through the mist I saw her face. Saw it change to sudden fear. I think I must have struck it, for suddenly it wasn't there any longer—only the mist." His hands tore suddenly at his collar. "The red mist."

The breath gurgled in his throat. He staggered, spun half round, and fell onto the floor.

Finch dropped to one knee beside him. "Looks like haemorrhage of the brain. I suppose the excitement was too much for him."

"What degree of excitement is too much?" Sturgis wanted to know feelingly. "Waiting to see what would happen nearly killed me." He added, "Mind if I get back to Belguardo? I can just about get my story through before the deadline for printing the first London edition."

"Will Mr. Potter survive?" Bannerman asked.

"He might—if he gets through the next twenty-four hours," Finch answered. "We'd better look round for some sort of stretcher to move him."

"He won't get better. Why should he?" The reporter

made a gruesome gesture of putting a noose about his own neck.

"You reporters are nothing but a lot of ghouls," Bannerman declared sourly. He put out an arm like the trunk of a tree, took hold of the solid outer door and with a single savage wrench, tore it from its socket. "There's your stretcher for you."

While they carried John Potter down the stairs Slater scouted around in the trees. He emerged close to where the squire had appeared. He carried a two-gallon tin in his hand, and there was a startled look on his face. "It *was* petrol," he told Finch.

Finch looked at it solemnly. "I'm glad I didn't know. It would have quite spoilt my diction. When Potter didn't throw anything I felt certain it was paraffin he'd brought with him."

Bannerman had been carrying one end of the improvised stretcher. Now he paused. "D'you mean Mr. Potter was going to fire the Swiss Cottage?"

Finch nodded. "Yes, the first move on our part and we'd have been for it. Why else had he left the letters there but to destroy them?"

There was a sudden vivid streak of lightning. The thunder muttered in the distance.

Finch looked at Bannerman in his tussore suit. "You're liable to get wet in that outfit."

Bannerman glared. "So what? D'you think I'm soluble?"

"No, sir," said Finch meekly. "Inflammable."

Slater gave an involuntary chuckle of amusement, but Superintendent Bannerman was not amused.

Chapter
15

With the thunderstorm of the previous night, the weather had broken. It was grey and cheerless. The temperature had dropped sharply. It was very different from the day on which the two Scotland Yard men had arrived. The atmosphere inside the police station had changed too.

The Chief Constable stood, military-looking and competent. It was a bad business about John Potter, but it would have been much worse if he had not died. Bannerman in a dark suit looked less truculent and therefore less like a bull. The junior members of the constabulary were conscious of a feeling of pleasurable importance, as if they had, for a little while, been caught up in something exciting and of national interest.

The murderer had been caught and he had had the decency to die on them. The case was over and could soon be, if not forgotten, then ignored. It was this last reason that made Colonel Roper so anxious to tie up the few remaining loose ends.

He stopped his restless pacing to say for the third time, "The fella's not turned up. Oughtn't we to do something about it?"

Finch, large, bland, and imperturbable, shook his head, also for the third time. "Harcourt realised that his friend and host was the murderer. He didn't know what to do about it, so he simply walked off—right into the next county, I expect. He'll come back as soon as he sees the morning's newspaper."

"The morning's newspapers?" The Colonel broke off his pacing. "Have you seen the *Record*? One thing, it has so much to say that the way Mrs. Harcourt made use of David gets rather pushed into the background."

Finch nodded. "The world is so full of a number of things I'm sure we should all be as happy as kings," he said politely. He wished Harcourt would hurry up. He was getting bored with this single-minded Army man.

"The boy's come out of it very well, really," Colonel Roper went on. "No doubt he'll be ready to settle down now. Fooling about selling cars never was a suitable occupation for him, but, of course, it gave him plenty of time off, which was what he wanted."

"Lucky there're several Frays in a position to help him," said Bannerman. He added emphatically, "In a position *and* willing." He glowered at Finch, whom he still did not like.

A car drew up outside the police station. From it Francis Harcourt descended. He disappeared into the building and a minute later a police constable showed him into Colonel Roper's office. The time was half-past ten.

He looked worn and grey and years older. He apologised for his tardy arrival. "I walked and took an occasional bus," he explained. "I spent the latter part of the day on the Sussex Downs and the night at an hotel in Lewes."

Colonel Roper shook hands with him heartily. "Awkward place to get out of—Lewes. Station at the foot of the hill and all that," he said, shocked at his visitor's appearance. "Now, what'll you have? Sherry? Whisky and soda?"

"You're very kind." Harcourt sank rather heavily into the chair the Colonel offered him. "Under the circumstances, I think—a sherry."

For a moment there was a pleasant and hospitable bustle. It was early for spirits, but the Chief Constable was a kindly man. Bannerman would have drunk anything to get things going. Finch and Slater could drink beer at any hour. They accepted sherry with resignation.

"You realised, then, that Potter had killed your wife?" Colonel Roper remarked, making it sound quite a natural proceeding. Adding, "Cheers!" before he drank from his glass.

"I *suspected* it," Harcourt corrected. Adding with a wintry smile, "It is surely almost impossible to accept the idea that one's friend is a murderer. Of course, if I had had any idea that those two other poor women were to die, I would have brought my suspicions to you at once. As it was, I'm afraid I simply took the easiest way out."

"It was the Kuan Yin that told you that John Potter was the murderer, wasn't it?" Finch asked.

Harcourt looked at Finch. "So you worked that out, did you?" Adding, "Yes, although I might never have suspected that the one at Belguardo and the one given by Rachel to her husband were one and the same, had it not been for something John told me a few months ago."

He fell silent a moment, his fine, austere-looking profile outlined against the window. He seemed not so much collecting his thoughts as mentally exploring the past.

"When I went to live at the Hall I had no idea that the anniversary of Rachel's death was kept as—as almost a holy day." Again that wintry smile touched his lips but not his eyes. "A form of ancestor worship brought back from the East, perhaps. On that day the Potters took flowers to the grave. Flowers were put in Rachel's bedroom. And most of the day was spent in talking about her. It must have been a sad trial to Phoebe Potter, but she bore it well."

He shifted his position, crossing one long, lean leg over the other. The untouched glass was still in his hand. "It was during this anniversary that John told me of what might be called the flight of the Bodhisattva Kuan Yin. I had known, of course, that the figure held a very special place in the household. The Goddess of Compassion, given as a love token by Rachel Potter to her husband— how could it be otherwise? I had known too that Rachel had packed it up and returned it to Ambrose, but the exact details I was to learn then from her son.

"It appears that after Ambrose left her, Rachel was like someone demented. She would neither sleep nor eat.

She spent the time roaming the house, sometimes even calling aloud her husband's name. This, as you can imagine, was a sore trial to John, then a boy of fourteen. And when, one day, he heard her weeping bitterly in the library, he went in to see if he could assuage her grief. He found her, her head lowered on her arms on the table in an attitude of utter despair and all about her the paraphernalia necessary for the doing up of parcels. He put his hand on her shoulder and spoke to her. She raised her head, exposing to view a face so thin and wearied that it tore his heart, and said, 'I was going to send the Kuan Yin to Ambrose, but my hands shook so much that it slipped out of my grasp and broke. Now I know that the gods have decided against me and that Ambrose will never come back.' And from that attitude he failed to move her."

"The breakage being a bit chipped out of one ear?"

"Exactly. It was that that I remembered. Not, of course, when I went to Belguardo. Then I wanted only to satisfy myself that the collection was still there." Harcourt sipped from his glass, loath, perhaps, to go on. "As was only natural, the sight of the collection set my mind dwelling on the old happy days in China. What a pity, I reflected, that that one figure, so beautiful, so perfect, so rare, had been broken. But at least, I told myself, the fact that Lisa had smashed it beyond repair no longer seemed the tragedy that it had done. A bit chipped from the ear? No, every time one looked at it, it would have been a fresh aggravation."

Harcourt broke off to look attentively from one face to another. "It was then," he said solemnly, "that the improbability of two similar figures, both chipped in the same manner, turning up in the same place, struck me. I realised for the first time how unlikely it was that a baby of eighteen months could have climbed onto an upper shelf in the china cabinet. And if she had not done so—— If Ambrose had lied—and I knew he was capable of lying—— If the figure that had belonged to Rachel and the one now at Belguardo were one and the same, what then? Knowing Ambrose and Rachel as I did, it was not difficult for me to find the answer. The Goddess of Compassion had been reinstated. Rachel and Ambrose had, as far as it were possible, resumed their life together."

During this story the Chief Constable had agitatedly turned his lean figure into the semblance of a corkscrew. Now he sighed heavily. "Better have another sherry, my dear fella," he said, untwining himself and taking the other's glass. "Anyone else have one? I'm going to."

"I take it that when Mr. Potter deserted his first wife, and for some time afterwards, you were abroad?" said Finch.

"Yes, I kept in touch with both of them by letter, but I didn't come home until Lisa was nearly a year old."

"I see. Rather an uncomfortable position for you, wasn't it?"

Harcourt was silent a moment, sipping his sherry. "D'you know," he said thoughtfully, "I do believe that my insistence on going to see Rachel whilst staying at Belguardo was what gave Ambrose the idea of doing the same. Yes, the more I think of it, the more certain I become. I can see him now, glowering at me when I told him that I was going over to the Hall. I thought for a moment that he was going to fly into one of his famous passions, but his face cleared. 'You do as you like, my boy,' he said, and he grinned. Yes—he grinned and went abruptly out of the room."

"Then he already regretted his second marriage?" Finch asked, fascinated by Harcourt's story.

"He was wretchedly unhappy. I could see that. He could scarcely restrain his impatience in the face of Diane's prattling stupidity. He adored Lisa, but she was a baby— and Rachel was only half a mile away across the valley."

"But to return to the moment when you realised that the two figures of Kuan Yin were one——"

"I tried to argue myself out of my conviction. I told myself that it was impossible, that I must have made a mistake and that the Bodhisattva Kuan Yin at Belguardo had lost a finger or her nose. I made up some cock-and-bull story that probably deceived no one so as to get into the drawing room. I knew then, without any shadow of doubt, that before me stood Rachel's present to Ambrose.

That it had reappeared after more than thirty-five years, and I could guess how and from where it had come." He paused, sighed deeply, then continued, "Of course, at that time I had no idea of the existence of the letters. But I did know how sharp Lisa had been in putting two and two together. I knew, too, how much suppressed hatred for each other there was in that pair, who shared the same father but different mothers. I realised that if Lisa had convinced John that his whole life had been based on a lie—that, in the last year of his mother's life, he had again played second fiddle to the father he hated—yes, then he would have killed her and in just such conditions of blind fury and horror."

Colonel Roper shook his head sadly. "If you'll forgive my saying so, your wife must have been mad to tell him."

"If egotism were madness," Harcourt responded, "then Lisa *was* mad."

The conversation continued a little longer. Then Harcourt rose to go. "And Mrs. Potter?" he said hesitantly. "How is she taking this?"

"Too much shocked to be questioned," said Colonel Roper, sighing.

Finch looked at him wonderingly. Recalling Phoebe's tight-lipped and frozen fury, he thought the Chief Constable's reply slightly misleading. But Bannerman, nodding ponderously, seemed to concur—and he had been there at the time.

"With Mr. Potter dead," said Finch dryly, "I don't suppose that we shall trouble his widow much."

"I'm glad to hear it." Harcourt looked considerably relieved. "I'll tell her what you say." He shook hands, and a constable was summoned to show him out.

When Finch turned he saw that both the Chief Constable and Bannerman were looking pleased.

"Murder's a nasty business, not fit for a woman," said the Colonel. "I was glad to hear what you said about Mrs. Potter."

Finch gave the slightest of shrugs. "In law a wife is always supposed to have acted under her husband's influence. Besides, we'd never prove anything."

Colonel Roper's face fell. "You mean you *do* think Phoebe Potter knew what was going on?"

"When you have a devoted couple, and a telephone call for the husband from a woman they neither liked nor trusted, what would the wife do? Go to bed and to sleep? Or stay awake to know what it had all been about?"

"Stay awake, I suppose," said the Colonel reluctantly.

"Exactly—to see a man reeling under the shock of the discovery of his mother's treachery, and the horror of having killed the woman who proved it to him."

"Y-es—But that doesn't exactly implicate Phoebe Potter."

"What implicates her, to my mind, is her character. Slow to action or to anger, but, when once roused, implacable. It wouldn't surprise me a bit to learn—which we never shall, if the villagers can help it—that she signalled to her husband from the high ground when Dimmick left Belguardo so that he could be sure of intercepting her beyond the lodge gates."

Colonel Roper was tugging at his small moustache. "I've always thought of her as lethargic and rather silly."

"A lethargic woman who's a noted rider to hounds? A silly woman who was quick enough to bamboozle me by an attack on Francis Harcourt, simply because she realised her own behaviour had struck me as strange?"

"Why was it strange?" the Colonel asked.

"She became momentarily dumb on realising that Dimmick had come to the Hall as a blackmailer. No, in defence of things she believes to be worth while, Phoebe's not silly at all, but capable, even formidable."

"But where's all this leading us?" Bannerman wanted to know.

"Nowhere—that's what I was telling Harcourt. We don't *know* that Phoebe Potter helped her husband murder Dimmick. We don't know that it was she who suggested where the letters might be hidden—Miss Budgen too, for all we know. We don't know that the idea of arson wasn't born in her brain—but we do know that John Potter was the poorest fire-raiser I've ever seen. His mind simply wasn't on it.

"And finally there's the psychological aspect of the